CHILD OF EVIL

The Senator, clearing his throat, folded the newspaper. Carefully, stalling, he tucked in the edges and slowly slipped it back into his pocket. "Let me make sure I understand you. Are you saying that . . ."

That I eliminated the librarian. Killed her. The slightest flicker of long, lovely lashes and a brief, uncouth scratch. Full lips, smiling. *Her functioning is ceased.* The tone was obliging yet taunting. *She is no longer a problem.*

Now the old man considered, cautiously veiling his thoughts. "We only began to discuss what to do about her. We saw her as a *potential* problem, nothing more." He shrugged. "I hadn't decided what we should do."

I decided.

"Yes," Baldwin replied carefully, forcing a smile, "you certainly did. And I would not be so foolish as to question the accuracy of your judgment, of course not!" The old man arose, struggling for self-control, and a control well beyond that. "The point is, you had no authority to arrive at such a conclusion alone. Taking human life needlessly is impudent, an impulsive act which, however logical or even correct the decision may prove to be, denotes the essential immaturity of the person reaching the decision."

A mischievous smirk. *I am a child.*

THE
OFFSPRING

J. N. Williamson

LEISURE BOOKS ∞ NEW YORK CITY

A LEISURE BOOK

Published by

Dorchester Publishing Co., Inc.
6 East 39th Street
New York, NY 10016

Printed in the United States of America

The central belief of ancient . . . religion was that attainment of an afterlife depended on the corpse remaining undisturbed . . . One trouble with interpreting pyramids in this straightforward way is that not a single body has ever been discovered in any of them . . . Invariably, the sarcophagi are empty. In some cases, they were even found closed and sealed, apparently untouched since the time they were first put there—and still empty. So what happened to the bodies?

—Francis Hitching
*The Mysterious World:
An Atlas of the Unexplained*

DEDICATION

To Mary, my wife, with whom I have learned or experienced everything worthwhile, and much more we could just as easily have skipped. Whatever this woman of love, courage, beauty and decency deserves, I, as well, seek. And for Maryesther Williamson, my mother, who should perhaps have had as much confidence in her extraordinary talents as she did in my own. For each of them, for quite different reasons, I wish things had been different.

ACKNOWLEDGMENT

An article by Patrick Huyghe entitled "The Star of Enlightenment" (Science Digest, March 1981) gave credit to George Michanowsky as the first to see a connection between ancient Sumer and Vela X. It also alludes to Michanowsky's book, The Once and Future Star (1977). Other valuable sources in making this novel include The 12th Planet (1976) by Zecharia Sitchen and, as almost always, various facts, insights, notes and reports from the body of work of the irreplaceable Colin Wilson.

THE OFFSPRING

"And The Last Shall Be First . . ."

Supposing that somewhere in the Universe there is an intelligence or force . . . that's beaming projections of various kinds . . . It may be extraterrestrial or inter-dimensional . . . Whatever its nature, it has some deep sense of what human beings are thinking and it provides us with visions that reflect the concerns of the human mind.

—D. Scott Rogo and Jerome Clark
Earth's Secret Inhabitants

Goety, *or black magic, was concerned with the evocation of . . . spirits supposed to be superior to man in certain powers, but utterly depraved . . . supposed to have made a pact with the Evil One.*

—H. Stanley Redgrove, B.Sc.
Magic and Mysticism

The thing that impresses me most about America is the way parents obey their children.

—The Duke of Windsor

Some reincarnationists believe that before it is invested with a body, the soul of man is free and fully alive . . . and when he is conceived in his mother's interior, his death begins. The womb is thus the symbol of the tomb.

—Benjamin Walker
Man and the Beasts Within

Prologue

An archeological dig in Iraq. Late spring, some 16 years ago.

"Very well, Spandorff, you got me here but why I came halfway around the world on the word of a former student that I shall see something wonderful, I'll never know." The distinguished man of many talents frowned, fretting, and peered down at the other. "What is this nonsense of yours about 'the very birth of civilization?'"

Spandorff did not seem to hear the question. "Oh, I know why you came, Senator Baldwin. There are precisely three reasons, and each is overshadowed by the eternal conflict between your colossal ego—and mine."

Tiny, bronzed and homely as a capuchin monkey, the archeologist fairly tap danced his excitement in the cool, mountain tunnel, trying not to laugh at the expression of detestation of his prominent guest's long face. Clouds of ancient dust mushroomed beneath Spandorff's nimble, nervous feet like so many miniature nuclear explosions. Gleaming motes from several strands of light filtering through space in the eternal stone were granted a brief, microscopic life of their own.

The fellow was mad, of course. Baldwin, informed in every scientific discipline before pursuing a political career, saw how his former student's smile glittered beneath his oversized skull, as he briskly rubbed his hands together. The gesture suggested some kind of religious ecstasy, and Baldwin looked away, mildly shocked.

"Very well, Spandorff, I'll play your game. Why did I come here?"

"First," came the instant, highpitched reply, "there is your insatiable hunger to get to the very root of humankind's reason for existence—not because you're awed by creation but because you think there is a Rosetta stone to make all knowledge accessible to you. Second, Senator, you're cursed by a sound memory and remembered what I outrageously promised you, twenty-four years ago. And third, you hope I am wrong so that you may make a fool of me again—but you *do* believe me!"

"You and your psychotic ideas belong to another day in another life," replied the middle aged giant, following Spandorf into the freshly excavated chamber. He longed to sit but was loathe to sully his splendid white shirt or shorts. In his first personal visit to a dig after years of studying prehistory, Baldwin was aware that he looked better equipped for tennis. "Both of us were younger, Spandorff. Convinced still that life contains more fine, mysterious questions than pointless answers."

"And we were correct, dear Senator—right all along!" The little man detected his guest's weariness after the long climb and whipped out a voluminous, multicolored scarf. Energetically, he brushed at the campchair from which he'd directed the last phase of the excavation before sending the workers away. "Best of all, there are both profound riddles to ask—and profound answers to them! Do sit, sir, and recollect the way we sensed—instructor and pupil—the marvels that lesser men did not dare to conjure."

"I wonder, Spandorff," Adam Baldwin said, lowering his bulk into the campchair but still filling the space with his height, bulk, and supreme assurance. "It is precisely the imaginative lack of those practical, lesser men which provided them with a head start I could never quite overtake."

Sweating from the climb, but strangely chilled now that they'd reached their destination, high in the ancient cliff, the Senator crossed his long, bare legs and allowed a leather case he carried to slip to the dusty ground. Here, at the opening of the shaft, he and Spandorff faced a boom-and-winch arrangement as well as buckets of finely bedded sand and silt. Such a clay-like deposit would never have been expected here, by most men; but that was like Spandorff, who was made up of perversity and the ghost of Louis Leakey. Leakey it was who had proved, at the Oldivai Gorge in Africa, that men walked the earth a full million years earlier than any other expert believed.

What, then, was it that Verblin Spandorff had come to believe? Baldwin squinted into the shadows of the chamber, saw clearly a be-jeweled, probably ancient table or stand, upon which something lay in crumbling linen. Feeling suddenly restive, even nervous, he made out a cookpot, several strange utensils—and an orderly, almost shining cleanliness to the dig which suggested how important the little man considered his find.

Recalling Spandorff, the most brilliant student he'd ever had, hadn't posed a problem. Everyone who met the clever imp remembered him, even a middle aged ex-professor who'd nearly become President of the United States. Spandorff possessed an inordinate facility for belief, even at twenty; he'd projected a faith in rare possibilities, all around them, simply awaiting discovery. He only grew tiresome when others saw that he could believe anything, anything at all.

Yet he'd used a first-rate intelligence to earn top marks at Northgate, even from a then youthful professor of ancient history named Adam Baldwin. While fellow students hit their books hard to allow time for social pleasures, Verblin Spandorff dogged Baldwin in the corridors, in the cafeteria, and finally followed him home. He'd appeared starved for information of all kinds, almost as if he'd been a bright youth from a less progressive planet who craved knowledge with which to save his untutored people. Once Adam Baldwin had assumed the boy would become an author, a fantasist; instead, he'd concentrated upon archeology, used his capacity for believing in his notions with a startling intuition to locate several marvels of the past, and rubbed the noses of his skeptical and scornful peers in the dirt of forgotten burial mounds.

It was getting late now and the faint sunlight, shifting, played upon the cloth covered object in the ancient chamber. *Is that a mummy?* Baldwin asked himself. *But this is Iraq, not Egypt.*

What in hell has the little madman found?

The promise to which Spandorff alluded had been given in anger, on a night in the former professor's apartment. Verblin had materialized with a bottle of inexpensive port and a new vineyard of sprouting questions and opinions. He'd told his mentor that evolution seemed, at best, a partial answer; that if those who opposed it knew more about the theory, they'd attack it as a quaint explanation which weakly covered most of the facts—but not all. "With old-fashioned scientific detachment," the student had insisted, "it would be easier and also allowable to believe that Man was actually created."

Perturbed by the youth's temerity, the twenty-seven year old Adam Baldwin had shifted the conversation to the topic of the earth's age. As the wine went down, he found himself agreeing with Spandorff that each anthropological discovery shoved the origin of mankind back another incredible number of years. And that led, quite naturally, to the question of exactly when Man ceased being a knuckle-dragging cretin and embarked upon that which came to be called Civilization.

"Oh, there's an exact moment," Verblin had retorted, "when we sought a civilized existence." The youth had grown more expansive and annoyingly brash as the wine level fell. "It's not a question of centuries, or even decades, Professor."

That had been a moment. Baldwin, by wondering "when" it had begun, had meant some reasonably specific but certainly vast period of time. No one thought civilization had done anything but develop, and that, gradually. "What are you saying, man?" he'd demanded. "Come, the wine makes you a fool!"

"Nothing of the sort. It definitely was not a procedure or a prolonged sequence of events." He'd been insolent, that second; unforgiveably condescending. "The inception of civilization," Spandorff declared, "was . . . an *event!*"

Well, they'd quarreled after that, bitterly; the budding relationship was smashed. Asked to identify the event which could conceivably be so awesomely progenitory, the boy had taken refuge in the mists of mystical belief. He simply *knew* he was right. And confronted by derision from a professor who'd studied not only ancient history but physics, molecular biology, computer technology, anthropology, and psychology, young Verblin Spandorff's swarthy little face had writhed with anger. He'd said he felt challenged by a sanctimonious intellectual club as barren of demonstrable evidence as he; but that the club was claimed by an Establishment, a creature anathema to the students of Spandorff's time.

"I promise you, Professor Baldwin," he'd shouted, standing, "I shall prove my hypothesis to you one day! I shall acquire credentials similar to your own, so that you shall come when I call. And call, sir, I shall—from the farthest corners of the globe! Then—we'll see who has the last laugh!"

Very well, the lunatic has his chance, thought Senator Adam Baldwin, watching the older Spandorff scuttle to the threshold of the excavated chamber. Idly, the towering genius reached out a huge hand to destroy a fly whose entire evolutionary history he could have delineated, and wondered if the little monkey's luck had held and he actually had the goods.

It was conceivable, since Verblin had held adamantly to his early goals while Adam Baldwin had continued to acquire facts, knowledge, and prestige from a variety of sources. He had been elected United States Senator from Indiana because he'd learned how to project pleasingly his scientific contributions while bypassing questions about his work on the hydrogen and neutron bombs. He'd learned enough about the techniques of blackmail to work as a covert representative of a government agency the government said did not exist, and then used all that as a foundation from which to seek the highest possible American office.

And he had learned enough more about science to possess a secret that was surely as valuable, as powerful, as anything the tiny archeologist had discovered . . .

"No doubt," began Spandorff, rousing Baldwin from his recollections, "you imagine that you are inside a mountain in contemporary Iraq."

"This is to be a lecture, eh?" asked the Senator, irritably nudging his leather case with his toe.

A smile, but the mad monkey again avoided his question. "From a ledge beyond this cooling chamber, dear former Professor, it happens that I can see traces of the prosperous city-states which dotted this region many thousands of years ago: Sippar, Umma, Legash, Endo. City-states which did business with Assyria, Elam, Egypt." Bright eyes glittered. "This mountain rises up from the oldest city in ancient Sumer, once called Enki or Ea—translated frequently as Oannes, god of wisdom and patron of mankind. And it was here, Sumerians claimed, that kingship descended first from Heaven. Later, the city was named Eridu."

"From which the word 'erudite' is derived," interrupted Baldwin. "Must you add obviousness to your other liabilities of character?"

"Perhaps the people themselves descended from this very mountain," Spandorff said dreamily, as if he had not heard, "to find that swampy plain which became Man's first real home. Or perhaps they originated further east." He blinked his eyes at Baldwin. "Yes, I rather think that's true. I shall discover the facts soon."

"I am entirely aware that the Mediterranean basin seems to have been the birthplace of humanity." The Senator's craggy face complemented the interior of the mountain wall. "But that does not alter the fact that civilization developed over a period of innumerable centuries, even tens of thousands of years."

Verblin Spandorff spun, facing him directly. "You don't mean to tell me you remain a gradualist? Surely you know the problem, Senator Baldwin!" The little man ticked facts off on his fingers. "There were three distinct species in our development from the primate: *Australopithecus*, a miniature hominid roughly 1.75 to 4 million years ago, upright with a brain one-third your size."

"Yours, I suspect," Baldwin snapped, crossing his arms. Why did he feel abruptly that

Spandorff was onto something? "He sounds more your type."

"Secondly, *Homo erectus,*" Verblin continued, "who appeared somewhat more than 1.8 million years ago, with a brain three-quarters in size of the present, noble, human brain belonging to *Homo sapients.*" His small eyes flashed. "But the difficulty refuses to go away, sir—the problem that each of our ancestral species remained fundamentally unchanged throughout their million year stopovers on this planet! The problem that Homo erectus is very, very different from modern man."

"I know the unanswered questions," Baldwin growled. "If it all happened gradually, where is there any indication of a gradual change? Where are the missing links?"

"They never existed!" Spandorff exclaimed. "Forever there will be links missing from our lovely, little chain of life—because it all happened virtually . . . overnight! Just as I said!" Suddenly he leaped forward and pressed his dark, ugly face within inches of his former mentor's famous features. "You—all of you— were wrong while I was right. Civilization's birth was an *event!*"

"Prove it," Baldwin said, eyes narrowing.

"I shall. Oh, I shall!" Now Spandorff hooked his right foot round a half emptied crate of explosive caps and tugged it over for a perch. "The beauty of it is that all of you, with a head start on me and with your closed, confiding club in full operation, should have been the ones to make my astonishing discovery. You had access to the same fundamental facts: That

17

the Sumerians developed writing approximately five and a half thousand years ago, despite early credit being given to the Egyptians. That people of Sumer invented movable types, ages before Johann Gutenberg, rubber stamps used in wet clay—printing! And an advanced mathematical system based on a sexagesimal or mundane 10 with a 'celestial' six, for the base figure of 60—and with it, they developed the 360 degree circle! Oh, yes, Professor;" Spandorff smiled, his breath very foul, "I see you haven't kept up. Within only a few miles of this mountain the first brain surgery was accomplished, the wheel was used for overland transportation, and petroleum products for fuel, painting, cementing and caulking were developed."

"I keep up," the Senator snapped, "on everything. In 1956, Professor Samuel N. Kramer suggested that Sumer also produced the first law codes, medicine, schools; the first library catalogue, pharmacopoeia, agriculture; even the first system of cosmogony and cosmology."

"Excellent!" The little man slapped his thighs. Their positions as student and mentor, Baldwin saw, had been neatly reversed. "My compliments!" Spandorff pointed abruptly. "I daresay you don't know that modern Iraq has extracted artifacts from the Parthian period, between 248 B.C. and 226 A.D., including a copper cylinder and an iron rod—identified by the archeologist Konig as . . . an electric cell; A functioning battery!"

"I heard something of it," the Senator said softly with a gesture of one huge hand. "There's so much to read."

18

"And you, sir, concentrated upon reading about the Egyptians," Verblin replied in a conspiratorial whisper. There was no one in the mountain with them but he said it as if saving his professor from shame. "Who were taught how to build pyramids by Sumerians they regarded as gods, and gave them something neatly useful for working within the darkness of such structures. Know about that, do you? Eh? Ever hear of Sir Norman Lockyer who saw, on Egyptian tomb walls at Dendera, engravings which unmistakably indicate the use of insulators and . . . electric lights!"

"Get to the point, man!" Baldwin demanded. "It's getting dark and we'll have the devil's own time in descending."

"One final, ancient discovery," said Spandorff, "and the lecture becomes show-and-tell time." He laughed, clapped his small hands together. "I'm certain you do recall the miniature clay tablet dug from the ruins in 1912? Written in cuneiform, thousands of years old, it contained an exact star catalogue."

Baldwin frowned. "Priceless thing," he agreed. "Amazing. Small enough to hold in your palm. And it mentioned an immense, exploding star, or starburst. What of it?"

Spandorff slowly arose, backing toward his mysterious excavation. Narrowed beams of light from the ceiling enhanced the brightness of his eyes, hollowed his cheeks. "Over the past few months, dear former Professor, I have been in communication with certain Australian astronomers. It seems that in the area precisely shown by the clay tablet, a quickly spinning neutron star—a pulsar—exists to this day.

Labeled PSR 0833-45, my profound mentor, it appears to be the remarkable remnant of an ancient supernova of the constellation Vela. It is called Vela X."

Baldwin was pale. "Explain. Don't keep it to yourself, man! What does all this mean?"

"It means," said Spandorff, "that at a certain point in time—which I have identified with the aid of my computers—the most brilliant thing ever witnessed by the eyes of man became visible from this area, six thousand years ago!" He did his mad jig, applauding himself as he bobbed in and out of the shadows. "A supernova now some thirteen hundred light-years from this solar system, it virtually exploded with stunning intensity—and *civilization began at that moment!*"

The Senator stared, expressionlessly. Then, relaxing, he rocked back in the campchair and clapped wide, laced palms round a bare knee. "You're preposterous."

"Want to see the Australian preliminary findings?" Verblin seized his chance for the last laugh, employed it heartily, thunderbursts of hilarity exploding from his thin lips. "Why, Vela X was four times closer to earth than the Crab nebula which, as you know, is cited in all records of the ancient Chinese—because it re-structured Oriental thinking!" He doubled over with delight, gasping out the words. "So you can just imagine what good old Vela X did to the friendly folk of Sumer!"

Baldwin shot to his feet, furious. "That's not conclusive proof, damn you! It's impressive, I'll grant you, but . . ."

"Ah, but what other explanation fits so well?"

Verblin tried to stop spluttering as he looked up into the older man's crimson face but went on chuckling. "It was after Vela X that the complex legal code was written which is much older than old King Hammurabi's, who was supposed to have devised the first one! What else could explain such lightning-like cultural development, Professor—UFOs?" He reached up to clap Baldwin's broad shoulders, further ruffling his dignity. "Don't you see it? They had to record such a fabulous sight, they were driven to invent writing! And its religious implications are profound!" Thunder, as if endorsing his views, sounded over the ancient mountain.

"And so, Spandorff," Baldwin said tightly between his teeth, "is the extent of your madness. If you have no more than that for me, I have wasted my time." He turned, reaching for his leather container.

"Oh, there is more." Something in the little man's tone of voice froze the Senator and, when he turned back to Spandorff, the archeologist was gesturing for him to enter the excavation site. "More, perhaps, than you really want to know."

Adam Baldwin stared. Spandorff had stopped beside the jewel laden stand of antiquity. Delicately, but with a flare of the proprietorial, he was resting his hand on a draped object. It was startlingly chilly, nearly cold, in the chamber, and the Senator shuddered. Heretofore he had made such inquiries through correspondence, journals and books. Something about the atmosphere of this alcove, exposed after thousands of years, or something in Spandorff's manner, was oddly daunting.

"Behold, Baldwin," whispered Verblin Spandorff, stepping back. "Behold the mother of civilization . . ."

Lightning glimmered against the spaces of the stone. The middle-aged man of renown took a single glance, then retreated a step. "What rubbish are you attempting to sell me, Spandorff?" he cried, dusting his palms. "I see that you have found a mummy—of sorts. What of it? I'll grant you there's been talk that the Sumerians failed to receive the credit given ancient Egypt. But—but she isn't even in a sarcophagus! Who is she?"

"I told you," the archeologist replied softly. "And that is all I intend to tell you—about her." Fawningly, he caressed a forehead still swaddled in cloth; tiny flecks of powder adhered to his fingertips. "In Egypt the central religious belief was that attaining an afterlife depended upon regal corpses remaining undisturbed. But my dear Professor, there has never been a single body found in the pyramids—because they were decoys."

"Decoys?" Baldwin gaped at him.

"Egyptian priests were worried about grave robbers. That is why they elected to remove the bodies of prominent people, and re-bury them where they would be safe." Spandorff smiled. "Few people even know these facts, but facts they are. And not long after writing and legal codes were developed, the government of Egypt, taught how to navigate great rivers by their unpretentious Sumerian cousins, ordered that the sacred bodies of the pregnant queens of Egypt—whose wombs contained princes, and the future of the nation—be removed. To Sumer."

"But the mummies that have been found," Baldwin protested, "were treated with spices and resin, their vitals excised and kept in canopic jars!"

"*Those* mummies," Verblin smiled, "did not include the little mother whom you see before you. Think it through, Professor: a supernova like Vela X that close to earth might have bombarded everyone with cosmic rays—the effect of which we may only surmise. There may even have been physical mutations in addition to the favorable influence upon Sumerian minds. In point of fact, there were. Because before Vela X began civilization, we were a different species altogether." There was a clap of thunder and the little man had to shout over it. "This pregnant woman is the last of the old kind of human being. She and the child she carries received a total exposure to—*bioflux*."

"Bioflux?" repeated Baldwin, again reddening. "The energy form that occultists have discussed for decades? My dear Spandorff!"

But Spandorff was nodding. "It had been believed for hundreds of years that an energy is diffused uninterruptedly throughout the universe. Particles, atoms, molecules and electrons are only the more visible units of such cosmic energy. And when it permeates living things on this planet, it emanates from their tissues, organs, and cells. With properties of magnetism, and electricity, including polarity."

"You're mad!"

"If so, so was Hippocrates. Both he and the Bible refer to *dunamis*, as 'power' and 'virtue.'

The ancient Chinese called it *ch'l*, the Moslems named it *baraka*. The Iroquois Indians referred to it as *orenda*, the Polynesians as *mana*." Verblin smiled confidently. "And Paracelsus called it *mumia*," he finished, "describing the powerful impulses which arose from mummies, and speaking of the 'vital essence of man.' "

"I'm leaving now." Baldwin, trembling, tucked his leather container under one arm. The flesh on his bare legs and arms was crawling. "I doubt that an autopsy of that— that 'mother of civilization' would support an iota of your absurd claims."

Spandorff reached up to touch his cheek. "Dear Professor," he said, "what about an examination—of the living child dwelling in the mother's womb?"

"Living child . . . ?" Slowly, Baldwin stepped closer to the still form of the jewel encrusted platform.

"I mentioned certain other discoveries of mine." Spandorff's fingertips prodded the abdomen of the ancient body. "More precisely, I've learned other secrets of Sumer. How this place is kept cold and humid, for example, to sustain the mummy. How the mother, herself, is dead but the being within her womb is— viable." His dark eyes raised to Baldwin; now, even Spandorff was filled with wonderment. "Professor, the child was ready to be born approximately six thousand years ago, this month. It would enter our world with the genetic make-up of humankind as it existed before Vela X, but under the cosmic influence of the late Twentieth Century."

"In God's name, man," Baldwin asked

huskily, "what are you saying?"

"That the child in this ancient mother's belly is *still ready to be born.*" He glanced away. "I doubt that it would be, however, in God's name."

"It would require . . ."

"The information contained in this document," replied Spandorff, drawing a packet of papers from his pocket. "To ensure its safe delivery." He shrugged. "I'm a thorough fellow, Professor; give me that much. I discovered a second Sumerian tablet here and translated it."

"May I see it?" asked Baldwin, extending his hand.

"No!" Spandorff replied. He began replacing the documents in his pocket. "First, you see, I want you by my side when I announce the discovery—a tribute to our old friendship, perhaps, and I've had my laugh at your expense." He smiled and his teeth were yellow from lack of attention. "But with your reputation, there'll be fewer questions, an elimination of skepticism and doubt. And my laughter will ring out in every scientific establishment on the planet earth."

"That cannot be permitted to happen," Baldwin snapped.

From his leather container he drew a small, automatic pistol he'd brought to Iraq with him. In case Verblin Spandorff's luck held one, last time.

The bullet from the small pistol pierced his former student between the eyes, and a scarlet shower added another evidence of death to the writings on the stone wall behind the still form.

It took time to get his own men up to the digs but finally they'd clambered to his aid, loyal workers who believed in the same unsavory aspirations Adam Baldwin held dear. When once they were started back down the mountain with their precious burden, the faint aroma of long-gone herbs and spices wafting eerily from the ruffled mummy wrappings, Baldwin, who'd remained behind, dragged a sizeable box into the chamber. He took things out of it, then paused, breathing hard above the body of his former student. Most of the blood was on the other side of the head and Spandorff still seemed pleased with his work.

"Your very stupidity may preclude the possibility of meaningful, gradual evolution, I'll give you that," Baldwin conceded tersely, placing the dynamite about the stiffening corpse and wiring it to the wooden beams supporting the chamber. "Unless all evolution is literally descent."

He was safely on Iraqi soil when the mountain itself seemed to explode. Dealings with minor fuctionaries in that part of the world were always irksome and the mammoth noise provided a convenient diversion. Without incident, the Senator, his associates, and their precious cargo entered Baldwin's private Lear jet to take their leave.

Safely airborne, Adam Baldwin patted the documents for delivery of the child and locked them in his leather container with his pistol. Swiveling to see it, he gazed almost tenderly upon the well concealed mummy. He already had a daughter. He rather hoped this one would be a son.

Of course, it wouldn't be the way it was with sweet Elizabeth. Indeed, he'd probably have to enlist his scientist daughter's aid as a surrogate mother. But that was all right; he wouldn't think of this child as a son, daughter, or even grandchild.

He'd think of it as . . . *the Offspring.*

> *The notion that such a force (as* Bioflux*) exists is at least four thousand years old . . . It can be projected and transmitted outside the body, to influence the mind and body of animate objects. It can be transmitted from a distance by concentration.*
>
> —Benjamin Walker
> *Man & The Beasts Within*

* * *

A Page from the Private Journal of the Late Verblin Spandorff

Baldwin is due here soon. He sends my mind reeling back in time. I find that I feel rather the way I did when a final exam was coming up: sure that I have given all that I have, certain I'm knowledgeable as hell, yet desperately afraid that the professor will somehow pose the one question for which I have no answer.

My mind has even begun pulling the kind of tricks on me it used to pull, before I reinvented self-discipline and followed a straight line approach to success as an archeologist. I'd completely forgotten what it—my mind—used to do, and is doing again, and it's hard to put into words. Baldwin, I know, believed I should be a writer because of it.

What I'm trying to write down is that, under conditions of great tension, my imagination be-

27

comes so preternaturally alert that it makes all manner of unasked-for connections. Example: I wrote the words "knowledgeable as hell," in the preceding paragraph, and my mind takes off on a tangent. People are "crazy as hell," "talented as hell," "smart as hell." Is it possible that the God I have always seen in the shadows at the back of my mind had been shaking His head, tsk-tsking over my pursuit of the truth about Creation? Does He resent the fact that I call myself a scientist, just as Baldwin did before his God complex overcame him, and believe I should be as honest about it as the old professor? Because, if it comes down to that, is my unconscious mind trying to tell me something? Is it Hell that contains all the smarts, all the craziness, all the talent? Is "knowledgeable as hell" something more than an expression?

And for that matter, is the fact that I fully intend to have revenge upon Adam Baldwin and all the smug little agnostics of the spirit as wrong as religious teachings suggest? Does vengeance always have to be His?

Another example of the way my mind has begun producing tangential imaginings, presumably because it fears to hone in upon the professorial confrontation scheduled for it, is tied to the expression, "reeling back in time." Time travel is supposed to be a disreputable topic for a scientist; according to all we know about the laws of physics, it's impossible. Yet here I am, twenty years later, grudgingly accepted by my peers and famous enough as a searcher for the buried truths to have my digs financed by half the universities in the world—and the motions filling my frightened heart look exactly like the ones I experienced as a brilliant, erratic student with unpopular ideas. I mean, I feel sophomoric, young, vibrant with excitement! Haven't I gone back in time, then? And how can I be sure all my strong, intuitive leaps to judgment about things like civilization beginning with an event are not accurate recollections from another life I lived, myself, in ancient Sumer?

Here's an example of my refurbished, sophomoric thinking: Once upon a time, there was an aged prospector who had never amounted to a damn. He wandered into a ghost town one day, hoping to spend the night.

Well, he nearly expired on the spot. Because, down in the center of the old ghost town, he saw two extraordinary things: A huge, shining contrivance rising from the ground—shaped like a lever. And an enormous, slimy, curled up snake.

But the snake didn't strike. Instead, it reared up on its tail and said, "Good morning, old fellow. I am Nate, the talking snake, and I'm prepared to be of service to you."

When the old timer managed to speak, he stammered. "How is it that you can talk? And what in the devil is that thing in the center of the street?"

"I talk," rejoined the reptile, "because I am Nate, the talking snake. And 'that thing,' as you so rudely put it, is the lever which holds the world together. Should anyone ever throw it, old man, the entire planet earth would instantly split down the middle like the plates of a newborn child's skull."

"You're shitting me," said the aged prospector.

"Not that, but the consequences of the lever being thrown would certainly prove equally unpleasant. As to that service I offered you, I suggest you raise a few signs, run a few advertisements—tastefully, if you please. Because, between that lever and yours truly, we can turn a pretty penny in your behalf."

Well, the old fellow was crude, untutored, and dirt-poor, but not stupid. He acted upon the counsel of Nate, and money quickly flowed into the town, as thousands of people came to rubberneck at the talking snake and the lever which held the world together.

One day, however, the old-timer got drunk on expensive booze and roared into town in his brand new six figure sports car. Dimly, the old man perceived that the automobile was out of control and that he would have to choose between hitting the lever which held the world together or running over his benefactor, Nate.

Unhesitatingly, the aged prospector aimed his speeding car to the right and bounced high over the smooshed and serpentine body of poor Nate.

There is a moral, crystal clear and logical.

It's always better Nate than lever.

When Senator-cum-Professor Baldwin arrives, what it boils down to is this, I guess:

I'm going to introduce him to a talking snake . . .

Part One

Upon the corpse, hung from the pole,
They directed the Pulse and the Radiance;
Sixty times the Water of Life,
Sixty times the Food of Life,
They sprinkled upon it;
And, Inanna arose.
—King Gilgamesh of ancient Erech

A person of credit informed me that, being once oc-
cupied with others in search of treasures in the neigh-
borhood of the pyramids, they found a pitcher closely
sealed; on opening this, and finding honey, they ate of
it. One of them remarked a hair that stuck to his
finger; he drew it towards him, and a small infant
appeared, the body of which still seemed to preserve
its original freshness . . .
—Abd al Latiff, AD 1200

One

December, this year

"Oh, boy, oh boy! Two whole weeks away from school!" Peg Porter was exultant as she did a little dance in the snow, her face radiant as she gave her older brother a smile and looked to him for agreement. "Isn't it heaven?"

"Heaven?" Eric Porter gave her a surprised, scornful look. "Oh, yeah. It's just peachy." Doggedly, he plodded ahead of her, trying to maintain the balance of the burden in his arms. But the library books formed an unwieldy leaning tower that made it hard for him even to tromp angrily in the snow. Eric settled for sounding disgusted. "Whoopee. And hot dog, too!"

For a moment Peg remained in his wake, not so much depressed by her brother's attitude as seeking another grip on the shimmering edge of her fantasy world. At nine, she was still too young to believe in an absolute reality. When obliged to meet it head-on, depending upon her mood, she tended to react either with asperity and a quick departure to her room, or gentle persistence.

"Well," she called thoughtfully, "at least we don't have to get up and wade through snow every day for two weeks." Eric didn't pause in his grumpy, male stride and she tried again.

"And we don't have to worry about weekly tests. And all."

Turning his head slightly, Eric glanced back at his little sister with an expression that changed when he saw how small she looked. He really wanted to snap another putdown at Peg but her optimistic attitude was appropriate, and his bleak one wasn't. He put a lot of stock in what was appropriate. "I guess you're right," he said, waiting for her to catch up. Geez, she had such tiny little legs! "But I wouldn't count on much real fun."

"It's Lynn, right?" Caught up, she raised her winter-reddened face to his, considering it in her feminine fashion. "Well, maybe Lynn likes Christmas." The words seemed exactly right to her and she grinned. "*Everybody* likes Christmas!"

For several moments Eric didn't reply. He trudged on, toward the library, anxious to get the errand over with and read. Or watch TV. He envied his sister's flair for seeing everything in a rosy light and forgetting all the crappy stuff ten minutes after it had happened.

Like the way Grandfather Baldwin kept jumping out at them from around corners, any time they spoke much louder than a whisper. "*Hush!*" he'd hiss at them, pressing a finger to his lips. "You'll disturb Lynn if you aren't careful." And if they protested that they weren't making any noise, he'd say something like he did to Peg earlier this very week. "You'll turn out like your mother unless you learn to place Lynn first. It was just that kind of neurotic unwillingness to accept the requirements of genius that sent her over the edge."

Which was when Grandfather would tiptoe upstairs, prowl noiselessly down the corridor to Lynn's room, and pull the keys from his pocket. Keys Eric and Peg, had never seen—just like the interior of Lynn's room. But they'd hear the way the door creaked, then the old man's careful whisper, more polite and humble than that of Mildred, the maid. "Lynn, dear," he'd go, until Eric felt his own nose wrinkle. "Is everything all right in here?"

Who cared if old Lynn was all right? Crap on Lynn, thought Eric, as he led the way round the shopping center at East 38th Street, picking their way through winter-stalled cars. *I'll "disturb" Lynn, all right—with a baseball bat!* One good swing, and pow—life might be okay again.

Because it wasn't okay any longer, not since Eric and Peg had returned home. It had taken a long while just to get used to not seeing Mama and Dad, and to live with their cousins. The letters from Mama had helped some, but there came the time when they stopped. When the brother and sister were told, very cautiously, that Mama had fallen ill.

Then it was another long while before they were summoned back to their house, only to find their lives—their world—ruled by a very tall old man who was more like a drill-sergeant in the Marines than the grandfather they'd yearned to know. The only time Grandfather was ever red cheeked "like Santy Claus," as Peg had expressed her hope to Eric, was when he lost his temper. And instead of being "all roly-poly with a nice, soft beard," he'd been thin and arrow straight.

But even that had been tolerable, at first.

They finally had their own rooms; the food prepared by Mildred, the housekeeper, was delicious; even old Mildred herself was nice enough. They'd been told to be quiet, and that was okay since Mildred said it was for Mama's sake.

But Mildred had lied. Grandfather made that clear, a few months ago, when he began getting all dreamy-eyed about the relative they never saw, a person named Lynn who, according to the old man, was just about the smartest kid in the world. A kid who needed not only privacy (they never saw Lynn come downstairs for a meal, or anything else) but a constant, nearly daily exchange of books from the neighborhood library. And Grandfather Baldwin had said it was "merely natural" for children to "pitch in and help others in the family," since they could "easily" take the books back and pick up new ones.

Children are almost always pedestrians and the ice storm that had sheathed the shopping center like a rink did not represent a serious problem as they saw the small building at the end of North Eastwood, gray and lifeless on such a miserable day. Peg Porter, seeing the myriad ice crystals everywhere she looked, made private mental choices for a tiara. Eric, passing beneath trees that dangled dagger-like icicles, did not share her fantasy that they were bowing humbly to the little queen at his side.

"I wish ole Lynn was under one of those trees," he said, reaching the glittering sidewalk. His darkly handsome face became a mask of youthful vindictiveness. "I'd shake the damn tree till all the icicles fell off and one of 'em stabbed ole Lynn right in the heart!"

"Eric!" Peg pretended shock and surpressed a rising giggle. "You should never say things like that because it might come true." Decorous, prim, she reached out for the door of the one floor library and held it for him. "It's unhealthy and—and neurotic, like Grandfather said I was." He glowered at her, stopped in the door. "Besides, you don't know Lynn is such a bad person."

"Oh, yes. I do." He bobbed his head, hard. "Without Mama being up to take our part, we're always wrong about everything—because of Lynn. Grandfather always sticks up for Lynn. We're servants, Peg, just the way Mildred is."

The nine year old shuffled through the door after him, surprised. It hadn't occurred to her Mildred was a servant and not a member of the family. "Eric," she called from behind his back, as he lurched toward the distant check-in table, "tell me: Why did our Dad go away? Why did he leave us alone?"

"You ask," he said with adult weariness, "too many questions."

As wistful as she was annoyed, she watched him pile the books on the table, saw that Miss Earhart, the librarian was busy with another customer. She touched her brother's arm, and whispered. "Did something awful happen in Mrs. Edmonds' class today?"

Eric sighed but did not turn. "She saw my long list of books to take out and thought I was passin' a note." He hesitated, pained. "So she snatches it away from me and reads it out loud immediately. And the class and Mrs. Edmonds get real quiet, and she goes, 'Who are these

37

books for, Eric?"

"What did you *say?*" Peg asked, all-earnestness.

He reddened. "I lied, I guess." He glanced quickly at her. "I told her they were books I wanted to read myself."

"You didn't!" Peg buried her giggle in mittens.

"So then all the guys look at me like I'm a damn bookworm or something, and Old Mrs. Edmonds gets really cold and goes, 'They cannot conceivably be your books, young man. Your reading level is, to put it mildly, much beneath these titles.' Can you imagine that? So, well, I finally had to tell her about Lynn. Gettin' books all the time for a smartass who makes me look like a dumb servant!"

"It's your fault." Peg peeked at him. "You couldn't even pronounce the names of those books!" She ducked an elbow he fired at her. The library existed, scantly, as part of a neighborhood shopping center suffering from the current recession. Stores opened, and closed, with such rapidity that residents in the area had no chance to become faithful regulars. From Monday through Friday, the single story structure was filled by children from both the neighborhood grade school and John Marshall High School, and it had been there as long as either Eric or Peg Porter could remember. It was, in a meaningful way, the only landmark in their experience. Although Peg was the one who adored reading, both children customarily liked going to the library. Its staff consisted of pleasant, helpful, smiling people who were determined to encourage youngsters' reading and who, for the most part, were young librarians on the way up in the Indianapolis-Marion County library sytem.

But it was Miss Earhart, the head librarian, who was their favorite. Stick-thin, with flower adorned spectacles and hair that had remained dark much longer than nature intended, she gracefully placed an armful of newly arrived books on the table and leaned on them, bestowing undivided attention on the children.

"My pets are back again," she greeted them, striking Peg that instant as having the appearance of an amiable, underfed owl. "Did I ever tell you that O'Henry's real name was Porter?"

"Yes, ma'am," Eric replied, disposed toward the factual in preference to the tactful. "Lots of times."

"We want to read his stories sometime," Peg said with a distasteful grimace for her older brother. "Maybe he's another relative."

Miss Earhart's face crinkled in an artificial anxiety they were meant to identify. "Don't tell me my two little sweeties are going to take out more books for the holidays?" She rested her thin palm in the center of her fleshless bosom. "Why, my poor old librarian's heart couldn't stand the shock!"

Eric felt his sister's intense, appraising gaze upon him. "No, ma'am," he said slowly, reluctant to leave his lie behind. "These books we've been gettin'? Well, ma'am, they ain't ours. Aren't, I mean." With a sudden, peevish yank, he produced the new list of titles and gave it to the woman. "But here's another bunch we need."

Again Miss Earhart feigned surprise. "And

here I thought my favorite new borrowers were turning into Quiz Kids!" Studiedly, she peered over her rims at them and finally looked down at the list. "But do confide in an old lady, children. Who *are* the books for if you aren't reading them? And why doesn't he have a library card of his own?"

Peg spoke up, sparing Eric. "They're for Lynn."

Miss Earhart waited but that was all the information she was being given. "Hm-m. I certainly hope we can satisfy the needs of your . . . Mr. Lynn." A quick, darting glance. "Does he understand that this is merely a branch library?"

"He don't pick 'em out," Eric replied. "Grandfather Baldwin does that."

"And yet," Miss Earhart murmured, frowning distantly, "they're read by, ah, Lynn. Isn't that the oddest thing?"

"Lynn is smarter than anybody." Peg crowded the counter, vaguely sensing the family was under attack. "And Grandfather wants Lynn to become a true genius." Her eyelids batted as she retrieved the exact phrase. "A ver-i-ta-ble genius."

"Well, isn't that nice! Still, you come so often for him." The librarian pinched her spectacle frame at one corner and raised it. "One might say your grandfather is a bit of a taskmaster, hm-m?"

"But he means well," Eric put in, again exchanging sibling glances. "He says all this will —will 'benefit society one day in the not-so-distant future.' "

The woman sighed, spread the reading list

before her, and squinted down at it nearsight-edly. "Let's just learn what is available to your Grandfather and, ah, Lynn. Before this paper is positively *crumbled* right out of existence." A dark brow raised. "And so it goes. First higher math, microbiology, bacteriology, even nucle-onics, as I recall." A glance. "Even psychology; and epidemiology, am I right?"

The words meant nothing to him. "Sure, yeah," Eric agreed. It was hot in there. Sud-denly he yearned to work a jigsaw puzzle. Or watch TV.

"But my dears," protested Miss Earhart, "it's everything! The world's knowledge!" She raised her hands. "I can't even detect this Lynn's line of study. Today," she marveled, reading, "we have volumes on ESP and tele-pathy, a book on holography and another on quantum math — plus such diverse biogra-phies!"

"Diverse?" asked Peg. She associated the word, dimly, with something dirty.

"Indeed, my girl!" The librarian cocked her head. "Why, they range from Mozart to F. Scott Fitzgerald! Yet there are other books sought, too—here are titles concerning prehistory, mag-netism and hypnotism, even a dissertation on the Geneva convention!" She looked utterly confounded. "There is simply no continuity of discipline I can perceive—not a jot!"

"So," Eric said, getting hotter, "old Lynn just skips around, huh?"

Suddenly the librarian's attitude altered. "Why, you poor little loves!" she cried, and laughed merrily. "Here I am, pumping you, just like the old maid I am, and you don't know any

41

more about it than I do!" A swift breath. *"Do you?"*

"No ma'am," Peg said beneath her breath. "But if we don't get 'em back real soon, Grandfather's going to be mad at us."

At once Miss Earhart jabbed her pencil in her hair, turned. "Let me round up what I can then, and I shall send down to Central for the rest. All right?"

"I hope you've got most of 'em." Eric spoke tightly, looking worried, and it made the librarian stop. "We aren't supposed to let Lynn down."

"We all do our best," she retorted, peering curiously at the boy. "Eric, Peg: Why doesn't Lynn come get the books himself?" She stared at them, saw the embarrassment creep back into their cheeks. Something about it troubled her, deeply, but she couldn't have explained the feeling. "Well, do tell him to drop by. I'd simply adore making the acquaintance of a real, live genius!"

It took awhile, and there was animated conversation between Miss Earhart and her assistant, a brunette college girl who worked part time. But eventually they were released, staggering out on the shadowy streets with a sensation of welcome for the biting, winter breeze.

"I hated that," Eric said, heading back across the shopping center. "All grown-ups can do is ask dumb questions!"

"I know." Peg felt so sympathetic she'd taken three of the books to carry, and trudged in his wake. "I almost told her we aren't even allowed in Lynn's room, but then she'd have asked a whole bunch more questions."

The wind was building up. It made it hard to talk and neither of them resumed the conversation until they'd edged their way around the mall and reached the long block home.

"When I get to high school," Eric said with soft ferocity, "I'm goin' out for *everything!* I'm gonna look out for me! Man, things are gonna be *different!*"

"How?" inquired the sister, watching her cold breath escape.

" 'Cause I won't have t'stay home all the time!" he replied passionately. "I'll be away from Grandfather, and Mildred, and Lynn—I'll do it my way!" Laughing hoarsely, he sang a line of melody, his unchanged voice cracking.

But Peg's frightened voice sounded at his elbow. "What am *I* gonna do, Eric!" she asked. She tightened a long, woolen scarf around her neck, shivering. "I mean, it's a long time till I go to high school."

"Not so long," he shrugged, knowing he was lying. He shifted the stack of books with care. "You'll just have to become a regular female pest. Date boys and all."

Sobered, she walked silently at his side for more than a minute. It was spooky out. They were the only ones on the street and it was getting dark. The image of life without Eric around was the sharpest invasion of reality Peg could recall. It made her thoughts turn to the source of their discontent. "Eric," she started, her voice devoid of her customary cheerfulness, "Eric, tell me something: Who's Lynn?"

"I dunno," he said, turning into the walk leading to the Baldwin house. He glanced at the second floor, toward the room in which Lynn lived. "But if Miss Earhart thinks it's strange the way we get books from the library all the time, I wonder what she'd say if she knew the rest of it."

"What?" Peg inquired, approaching the front door of the silent house. She glanced intently at her older brother. "What . . . 'rest of it?' "

He didn't look down as Peg fumbled for keys to the house. He answered her very carefully, under his breath. "I wonder what Miss Earhart would say if she knew we'd *never seen Lynn* in all our lives!"

Two

The family Baldwin resided disdainfully on the fringes of a neighborhood named Central Eastwood, old tenants learning to despise the upwardly mobile. It had sprung up—or crawled, perhaps, to its knees—some fifteen years ago, before Eric and Peg Porter, grandchildren of the distinguished Senator, were born. In common with a sprinkling of other neighborhoods within a beer-belch of distance, Central Eastwood seemed to some to have been constructed basically because there was a region on the far east side of Indianapolis which remained lushly wooded, mainly occupied by small animals or birds, and mostly visited by young people in quest of lover's lanes.

Presumably, aspiring builders had taken a dislike to small animals—or birds, or trees; there was so much free-floating hostility going around at the time that any stripe of hatred was possible—enough to take a chance on selling hastily conceived, prefabricated housing. An even tinier Peg had once referred to "prevaricated places" and no one had thought to correct her.

Soon after word of construction, or assembly, was spread, all the teetering structures were snapped up. The snappers were people whose economic level was so precisely between middle-class and lower-middle-class that they appeared obsessive about beginning a new monetary level. And ambient about Central Eastwood, once fully tenanted, there was an alarming aura of briskly moving time—an early hint of unsettledness and impermanency, of prompt and inevitable deterioration.

Most outsiders, driving languidly through the neighborhood, sensed such attributes at once. The more sensitive ones, disliking the reminder of unfortunates with no better choice than trying to survive, stood on their accelerators and rushed out of Central Eastwood. Other drivers were sullen and envious residents of still less inviting neighborhoods and sometimes slowed their pickup trucks in order to make out the frequently ascending FOR SALE signs.

In Senator Baldwin's view, the adjective "transient' was rather too exact a word with which to describe the people moving into and out of the neighborhood taking shape around him. Some residents, to his surprise, dug down deep for extra jobs or put their kids to work and succeeded—if in nothing else—in remaining. Those who departed were frequently replaced by hardcore personnel of the U.S. Army base, at nearby Fort Benjamin Harrison: men who rented for their families, then, after a scant period, were ordered off to other bases and other prefabs, leaving Central Eastwood behind —like target houses in an area cleared for nuclear testing.

And the visible consequence of this very modern set of circumstances was that certain homes in the region were aged well beyond their decade and a half of existence, while others, which the owners had struggled to save, became precious middle-class jewels, guarded by the neighborhood vigilantes like the bank in a Gary Cooper movie. By and large, when Peg and Eric Porter returned home to it, the Central Eastwood populace was a polygot of blue collar workers with their motorcycles and pickups left in the yard or parked backwards at the crumbling curb, young kids with infants and no sureness about the color of their collars, and owners who'd paid off the mortgage by hook or crook and when, amazed to find themselves almost elderly but real property owners, fully intended to die there. For them—and the others, if they were fortunate enough to stay—the area houses were probably the only ones ever owned by anybody in their families.

So the American dream was sustained, around a man who'd once been a candidate for the nation's highest office, even if there were times when the dreamer seemed to have devoured a pint of pickles and a quart of ice cream before retiring.

And so even his neighborhood annoyed the great Adam Baldwin, who'd purchased his non-tract home with cash many years before a single ambitious realtor concocted plans for conquest. He felt, not without some justification, that the neighbors on whom he looked down would never understand the special quality of the Baldwins. It never occurred to him that he was, himself, incapable of understanding theirs.

Thirty years ago when he'd bought the big white brick two story on three acres of scrupulously maintained grounds, farmers down the road had whispered that the Old Man wanted the place only to retain a legal Indiana residency. Without it, he could not have been the Hoosier state's senior senator. None of them admitted the awe in which they held the aging giant nor discussed their wonderment at his ways. They'd never heard of a man who was so renowned in scientific circles that he could use his fame and contacts to achieve high office. By the time he won a Pulitzer Prize for his books on prehistory, he was so strange to them that he might have come from Mars, or belonged to the Mafia.

If they also whispered that Adam Baldwin's only lack of experience in subtle crime lay in the area of not being a Mafia don, it was all right with the man himself. Because he remained the only hold-out in the entire region and, when they greedily accepted generous offers from the aspiring realtor in question, they also moved on and soon forgot him. Until, of course, he ran for the Presidency of the United States and suffered the only failure in his lifetime.

At that agonizing point of defeat, though the former farmers did not know it, Baldwin himself had felt he was the victim of terrible injustice. How, after all, could one man manage to blackmail all the registered voters in a country? He'd made all the requisite promises a dozen times over, crossed the palms of political bosses in every precinct and hamlet drawn to his attention, and been compared—not unfavorably—to the late Adlai Stevenson. It hadn't occurred to Baldwin that the reference was a mortal blow.

Returning from the unpublicized trip to Iraq, some sixteen years ago, reportedly a wiser and sadder man, the Senator had surprised no one by his overt actions: after disposing of the property in suburbs around Washington, D.C., in California and New York, he had settled in to his now aging Hoosier home, presumably retired and never to be heard from again.

Like virtually everything that was publicly known about the former professor, the rumors and reports were nothing but wishful thinking —and a wholly unwise assumption that they could know the ways a genius thought.

Peg Porter, unlocking the massive front door for her brother Eric, knew very little more about her grandfather than anyone else. She stepped aside as Eric staggered in, starting to lose his precarious grip on the library books. After he'd dumped them on a highly polished table, just inside the marble foyer, each child hesitated at the threshold of the high-ceilinged living room, intently listening.

"Can you hear him moving around?" Peg spoke in low tones, breathing hard from the extended walk home. "I can't hear his cane, can you, Eric?"

Eric, massaging his aching arms, moved to the foot of the stairs and looked up. It was full of shadows at the next landing. "Nope, I don't hear anything. He's probably messing around in his study or laboratory or whatever he calls it."

Peg knew what he meant. The ostensibly retired professor and statesman had converted the attic into an immense, well appointed and ornate room which served both as a combination study and office, where he supposedly kept records related to household expenses, and a partial laboratory. She and Eric had been allowed to visit the office part, a few times, usually when they were called on the carpet. But like Lynn's bedroom, they had never seen the small lab.

"I wonder if Mama is up," Peg mused. She joined Eric at the stairway. "We haven't even seen her for ages."

"She asks about you." The voice, behind them, made the children jump. Mildred approached from the corridor leading to the dining room and kitchen, wiping large hands on her apron. "But she's asleep now, bless her heart."

"Is she okay?" Peg asked quickly.

"As good as can be expected," replied the housekeeper, lowering one thick, black brow. "Do hold down your racket so you don't disturb her rest. Or—"

"Or Lynn's, yeah," said Eric, sighing and turning toward a chair in the living room. "I know."

Peg watched Mildred follow him but remained at the stairs, one small hand on the bannister. She had no idea how old Mildred was but it was funny how she always seemed to be so big, working in the kitchen or across the room, but was actually kind of short. Mostly Peg had the impression of a rawboned, sturdy woman who might like to be their friend, if they paid her instead of Grandfather Baldwin.

Distantly, Peg imagined, there was the tiniest of noises from deep on the second floor. She gazed up into the massed shadows at the landing, hoping it wasn't Grandfather, wishing it were Mama coming down for supper. But the sound was an odd, electronic beep, nearly like the noises video games made, and that meant it was probably Lynn. Her heartbeat accelerated but she still craned her neck to stare into the darkness.

What in the world was going on up there? Who *was* Lynn, really?

Expending effort, sensing the redistribution of weight and mentally running through a recitation of the day's caloric consumption, Lynn pushed a small, green button and watched a video screen rise into view. Touching a second yellow button, the offspring settled back as today's international news was offered—both by audio and video. It had been flown in, as usual; it wasn't especially different from yesterday's, but it was the inside report from various think-tanks established some time ago at Lynn's request, and it had the advantage of approximating the truth.

Lynn's lovely lashes momentarily brushed a rounded cheek. Instantly the housekeeper's most recent tray of food rose beside the object upon which the offspring reclined, indicating that the sensory apparatus—machine-wise as well as Lynn-wise—continued to function in a satisfactory manner. With powerful muscles in the wrists and the top of the hands, Lynn snapped the meat bone in two and gnawed contentedly for minutes. Protein was important. So was the vitamin injection which had to be self-administered next, unless the Senator's presence was desired.

It wasn't; not then. The old man grew more boring by the day. So did the news of battles, of impending wars and impending peace treaties, of nuclear build-up here and nuclear disarmament talk there.

So, in point of fact, did everything grow boring for Lynn.

But something interesting was developing, elsewhere in the house; something unsaid that would soon be said. Something which might provide the chance to try certain quite special talents of which even Baldwin knew very little.

"I'm starvin', Mildred," Eric said, sagging into a living room chair with an attitude of irremedial malnutrition. He sucked in his cheeks, looking haggard. "Could you maybe fix us something to keep alive on until supper?"

"It's called 'dinner' in this house, young Mr. Porter," replied Mildred, hands on hips. "It don't make no matter to me but your grandfather has corrected your manners a thousand times." Unexpectedly, she smiled at him and gave Peg a hug. "Maybe I can make a cup or two of cocoa, even some peanut butter sandwiches."

"You're champion, Mildred!" the girl declared, using a word she'd picked up from a British program on television.

"I'm not even a challenger in this house full of geniuses." The housekeeper jabbed her finger at them. "But you get out of those wet shoes and cold overcoats before the Senator puts us all down for the count!"

The children watched her brisk departure and Peg sighed as she unlaced her shoestrings. "Honestly, I don't know whose side she's on."

Eric, sunk in a vast leather chair, opened his mouth to release a yawn. "What different does it make?"

"I just wish she would be," Peg sat on the bench before the electric organ, dangling her damp socks and looking wistful. "I mean, she's a woman like me and I could use a friend."

The boy's bright eyes appraised his sister's face. Recently he'd grown more aware of his older-sibling lot in life and noticed something important. Peg still teased him but she was aware he neared the brink of higher education and seemed to be looking to him for guidance. He liked that, he thought, so long as he didn't have to do anything heroic to establish his authority. "It's just that Mildred has a lot to do for Mama, and Grandfather Baldwin."

"You left out Lynn," Peg answered without visible rancor. She picked at a scab on he elbow. "I think she spends more time up there than she does for the rest of us. She's always feedin' Lynn." Peg's eyes, rising to meet Eric's, were surprisingly tearing. "I wonder what it'll be like if Mama dies."

"She's not gonna die!" Eric, agitated, jumped to his stockinged feet and threw his wet shoes in the general direction of the stairs. "She's gonna get well, Peg, I know she is!"

Peg watched him pad toward her and her mop of yellow hair shimmered as she looked down at the keyboard. "I don't think Mama is *ever* coming downstairs again."

"Sure, she is!" Eric stared down at his sister, blinking back tears. "I'll bet when spring comes, she'll be a lot better. She'll be with us every single day and—and things will be just the way they were before—before Grandfather sent us away!"

Womanlike, the girl raised her head and

looked expressionlessly into Eric's eyes. Awkwardly, she reached out to pat his arm. "I don't even remember before," she said at last. "I don't remember anything but living with cousin Sue."

That surprised him. He kicked the bench, none too hard. "Well, I don't remember anybody playing this dumb organ, either." Switched off, the powerful instrument stayed silent as he paraded his fingers over the ranks of ivory keys. "Old thing is just in the way. Like us." Abruptly, he looked back at Peg. "D'you ever think about Daddy?"

"Sometimes," she said distantly. "I can't remember him much."

"Maybe he'll come back someday," Eric said impulsively. "Christmas is coming, remember. Maybe he'll . . ."

"No, Eric," Peg said soberly. "Daddy isn't allowed here, remember. Grandfather said he wasn't even to telephone us. And Mildred's supposed to tear up any letters or cards we get from him. It's just us now."

"Sure," the boy argued, "but we're older now. If we ask Grandfather what he did, maybe he'll explain it all. And let us write him sometime."

"That will happen only when hell freezes over."

They jumped. Grandfather Baldwin had been standing at the foot of the stairs for some time, and now he leaned heavily upon his Malacca cane, frowning. As always, it seemed to both children that the cane would break one day and throw the old man to the floor. Privately, Eric couldn't wait; but he didn't think it would be soon.

Because the retired United States senator looked no less sturdy, healthy, and august than he had when they first saw him. No one, Eric thought, could meet him and not automatically call Grandfather "sir." With his imposing stature and severe but dignified limp, he might have been a Prussian general pausing in plans for an invasion.

"I think we've heard quite enough speculation about your biological father, children," he observed, his voice deep and sonorous. The knuckles on the faintly bending cane were white. "But since you are so eager to know why he isn't welcome in my house—and obviously so ready to affix the blame to your grandfather—allow me to enlighten you."

Peg sneaked off the organ bench and did her best to disappear into another massive chair. It wasn't enough that her grandfather had achieved almost everything in the world and was famous, brilliant, and admired by millions. He also had to be a powerful old giant, like someone out of the books she read. He'd told them once, that his "persona" had contributed to his climb, to "leadership of influential congressional committees as I made my Napoleonic surge up the power structure." Although he'd never struck her, she was terrified of him.

"When your mother fell ill, children," the old man rumbled, taking Peg's former perch on the organ bench, "your spineless father deserted her utterly." Furrowed brows narrowed. "He had opposed her and opposed me in every fundamental, scientific step of advancement the two of us sought and even dared to question . . . special plans, linked to Lynn. Now, I have willingly assumed the responsibility of acting not only as your grandparent but as a surrogate father. Logically, whatever regard you persist in holding for *Mister* Porter is rightfully mine." Grandfather clapped his cane on the floor, jarringly. "And should that ignorant fellow have the temerity to contact this house in any fashion, it will be the last time he disturbs our tranquility!"

"But does he know that, Grandfather?" asked Eric.

The old man's smile was enigmatic and freezing. "Oh, he *knows* it all right, young man. We made the warning perfectly clear."

Peg wrinkled her nose. Daddy was still Daddy and always would be. And who did Grandfather mean by "we," anyway? Him and Mama?

"As you mature, children," the Senator droned on, "you will become Baldwins through and through. Accordingly, you will have the intelligence to learn that matters of strictly biological parentage are of no special moment." His eyes glittered. "It is those bonds we voluntarily form which are significant. Ah, Mildred!"

Eric glanced up, saw the housekeeper returning with a tray of hot cocoa and sandwiches. Seeing her employer, an expression crossed her broad, middle-aged face which the boy could not identify. "Afternoon, Senator."

"I trust you saw to our Lynn's three o'clock meal?" he asked smoothly.

"Absolutely, sir." She placed the tray carefully on a coffee table, avoiding his eyes. "Trust Mildred, Senator. I'm like clockwork."

And so it had been, Mildred reflected as she poured, for longer than she cared to admit.

Originally, she'd been hired by the Senator's daughter, the distinguished scientist Elizabeth Baldwin Porter, and it had been a time of pride. Mrs. Porter was respected in her own right, one of the first internationally famous lady scientists since Madam Curie. Even now, with that poor girl virtually bereft of her senses, there were still endearing, unforgettable moments when Mrs. Porter regained her composure and seemed freshly brilliant, even beautiful.

And upon such an occasion, with her own thoughts full of the time that old Senator brought Lynn into all their lives, Mildred had found the courage to ask Elizabeth about it. Why she hadn't told her father he demanded too much; how she'd permitted the banishment of her own husband, her own children? And those lovely, soulful eyes of Elizabeth Baldwin Porter had turned to Mildred. "It's Father's last project, don't you see? His final chance for immortality—and that's all he ever wanted, Mildred. Because he's the greatest genius who's ever walked the earth and he's entitled to it."

In a way, Mildred had understood what Mrs. Porter meant. The Senator was getting along now, out of both politics and university life. Most folks had written him off and some probably even thought he was dead.

But then Mrs. Porter, before lapsing into another of her silent reveries, had said, quite distinctly: "With Lynn's development, Mildred, Father can have all the power he's yearned for. We don't even know how far Lynn can be advanced. But Father must have his chance—even if *all* of us go down with him."

The Senator had moved toward the foyer and

was squinting at the library books brought home by Eric and Peg. As he identified the titles, he tossed them rudely aside. "What's *this?*" called his stern voice. The children hurried to help him. "Three of the books I asked for are missing!" Face crimson, he looked at another volume as if he held something obscene in his hands. "This, for God's sake, is a substitute! Lynn is so far past Van Schliemann that this book is an insult!" Pivoting slightly, he hurled the offending book against the fireplace screen and raged at Eric and Peg. "Who suggested this substitution? Who did this terrible thing?"

Eric stepped back. "Miss Earhart," he said swiftly, "the librarian. I guess she thought it might do."

"Miss Earhart didn't mean any harm, Grandfather." Peg touched the sleeve of his suitjacket. "Why, she even wants you or Lynn to visit her at the library. When you have time."

"That's right!" Eric put in. "She has some questions to ask."

Grandfather's bald head spun. "What? How *dare* she! What kind of questions?"

"Nothin' much," the boy answered. He hated the way Grandfather looked eager to hit someone. "Stuff like Peg and me always going to the library and why you or Lynn don't do it sometimes."

"And especially why Lynn is studying," said Peg, quickly, reacting to the fury mounting in the old man's face. "Grandfather, it's okay, she's nice! Why, I bet she even tells the other library ladies how smart Lynn is!"

"Indeed?" The word was as impressively

small as he was large. He stared down at the girl, long fingers clenching and unclenching on his cane. She felt almost hypnotized, but eventually the redness suffusing his features started to subside. With a smile that did nothing for his eyes, he patted Peg's shoulder. "All right. We shall forget it, for the time being. I think that's best." He beamed upon Eric. "Thank you for carrying the books home. Be good enough to ask Mildred to bring them to me in Lynn's room —but only after you've had your little snack. All right?"

Relieved, Eric nodded and watched the tall man turn and, slowly made his way across the large front room to the stairway. Eric found he was perspiring, as he retrieved the unwelcome library books and put it back on the table; he avoided his sister's gaze, tried to stop trembling. Teachers could be so bossy, but he'd never seen anyone like his grandfather! It was as if not one doubt had ever crossed the old man's mind, as if he were absolutely sure about anything, and everything. *Tap-tap*, went the cane on the steps, as Grandfather ascended; *tap-tap*, the sound diminishing as Grandfather drifted unseen down the second-story corridor.

Then Peg's eyes met Eric's. Together, automatically, they waited. Listened. Heard the faint sound of a key, turning in a lock, being withdrawn . . . a doorknob being turned, the creak of a door as it opened . . . *tap-tap*, as Grandfather went inside.

And finally, from within, scarcely audible, there was a sharp snap, as a lock, inside, clicked into place. . . .

Now they could drink their cocoa, eat their

sandwiches. Yet when each of them sat before a tray, quiet as trapped mice, the cocoa was cold —and so were their appetites. Winter wind breathed against the windows, trying to get in.

Jittery—she thought of it as restive—Miss Earhart locked up her library for the night, paused beside a rest room as she saw her reflection in a mirror. The face, caught offguard, was unfamiliar.

Once upon a time, she had used a first name primarily—Sandra. There'd been a time when friends called her Sandy; but now there weren't any actual friends. Co-workers; acquaintances. That was all.

In those old days Miss Earhart's dreams and fears had been basically the same as those of her female companions, but they'd been emphasized in different ways, somehow. Not once had she tested the emotional waters of romance to see if she really wanted to be nothing more than a librarian who lived alone, and kept a cat.

In time, when Mr. Right could be found in her circles, he began to assume the characteristics in Miss Earhart's mind of one of the characters in the books to which she paid professional homage—and not a particularly prominent, or favorite character. And as time passed, with those who'd called her "Sandy" widely dispersed or deceased, Miss Earhart was content to see Mr. Right in no more prominent a light than that of a character she'd read about as a girl—Sherlock Holmes, perhaps, Nicholas Nickelby or Rhett Butler. Except that she'd read books about them more than once.

Not that life as a librarian disappointed Miss Earhart. Books had been her primary passion anyway, and the pleasant, well-scrubbed youngsters who visited her branch library were easily imagined as her surrogate children. Telling herself she was one of the early, liberated, independent women, Miss Earhart forgot how to cry.

Whatever else, she'd side-stepped the indignity of romance, the likely ugliness of it—and certain fears had lurked in her mind longer than the images of Holmes, Nickelby, Butler, or even Mr. Right.

The library was still brightly lit, as familiar as her gloves, say, or the bracelet Mother had given her years ago. Gathering up an armful of late-arriving volumes from Central, humming a slightly romantic melody from "The Sound of Music," she adjourned to the stacks. Soon, she'd be home with Kitty and able to remove her girdle.

She was facing the Ks, in the Biography section, thinking of the slots into which she slipped the books as so many gobbly little birds, when the lights went out.

Immediately Miss Earhart's heart skipped a beat. When certain pains had begun, about a year ago, she hadn't visited a doctor but she'd requested certain medical books from Central and felt sure her self-diagnosis was accurate. She thought of that day, now, how she'd intended to eliminate all her bad habits and conquer her condition. Moving unhurriedly, she headed for the rear of the building where a second row of ceiling lights awaited her. One flick of her finger and the library would be illuminated again, as befitting a place that illumined the mind and spirit. Smiling, she stepped to the far wall . . .

And saw that the light switch was no longer there.

She stared at the wall with her owlish eyes, bewildered. She'd been at Central Eastwood Branch for years; she knew perfectly well where all the switches were placed. *My eyes,* she told herself, raising a pale hand. It batted against the wall like a bird with a broken wing, finding nothing.

Sandra, she told herself firmly, *you're tired. It's time to go home.*

But a customer stood motionlessly among the shelves, partly-shadowed; a man, making no sound. *He likes to laugh,* Miss Earhart reassured herself; *he's right next to American Humor.*

"Hello," she called, seeking her usual literate but whimsical inflections. "I'm afraid we're closing."

The customer did not reply. He merely detached himself from the stacks and, quite noiselessly, deliberately, moved toward the end of the row. He suggested height, and surplus bulk; he's burly, she thought, and called out again without thinking. "We open again tomorrow at eleven o'clock."

She might not have spoken, he seemed so oblivious to her presence. From twenty feet distant, he drifted along an aisle and then faced her, as burly, as powerful as she'd imagined.

The last rays of that afternoon's winter light pried through the windows and struck his face, completely hidden by a ski mask.

Even as Miss Earhart's numb fingers allowed the books in her arms to tumble to the floor she was reminding herself that she could not, dared not, suffer such nonsense. It was getting harder to breathe regularly. But her memory was fine; it was her memory of what Mother had said, about husbands who battered their wives, husbands who left the family hearth to do unspeakable things, that came to mind.

And the fear of being raped which had been present in her mind ever since.

The inflamed eyes peeping through the holes in the ski mask reminded Miss Earhart of none she'd ever seen before. But the distant bulge at the front of his trousers, where his legs were joined, reminded her of terrors she'd seen a thousand times in her nightmares.

With dignity, drawing herself erect, Sandra Earhart turned without a rush and began walking toward the front of the library. Toward the door at the front. The thunder of her heart, she told herself, was ridiculous and probably half her imagination—the way the man himself might be. She was overworked; she absolutely had to talk to Mr. Steele into an assistant for the days she worked late.

Humming, she looked straight ahead—even when she heard the footsteps behind her. Closing the gap, getting louder. Suddenly she was at the door, unaware she'd walked into it, aware that she was letting tears spill on her cheeks, reaching out to twist the lock beneath the library doorknob—and finding it stuck.

"Damn," she swore, aloud, perhaps for the first or second time. Angry, scared, half-blinded by the now steady stream of tears, she yanked on the knob, struck the door with her thin shoulder, pulled with all her might.

He was right behind her and she thought she felt hot breath on her neck.

Desperate, whirling, she saw the motion at the front of his trousers, realized his thumb and index finger were pinching the top of a zipper, lowering it. But what was that sound in her ears, was it the sound of music? Or was it a noise that went with the choking sensation at the back of her throat and the impression of organs inside her, slipping with a sick lurch and starting to stop?

What she saw did not register on her brain. Miss Earhart was against the door, sliding slowly down it to the floor where she rolled over on her back, her ankles twitching, a last impression of a painful penetration cutting through her body until it became lodged in her brain, and it stopped.

Then the library grew quiet, indeed. All the lights went on glowing, brilliantly; they'd never stopped burning for even a second. The body of Miss Sandra Earhart was the only thing remotely human in the library.

But that had been the case since she let out the final customer and locked the front door.

Outside, it was snowing, and a gust of wind effortlessly blew the door open. Nothing visible exited; no telltale footprints were left in the snow.

Elsewhere, nonetheless, someone or something—smiled.

Three

During the strange, forgetting years that Eric Porter and his sister had lived in the Toledo, Ohio, home of his mother's cousin Sue and her family, he and Peg had once been taken for an outing to the Cincinnati Zoo. There, on a day made memorable not only by the rich variety of beasts there were to see, but by Peg's record breaking consumption of junk food, Eric had noticed something that intrigued him mightily. For an adult, they probably would have seemed obvious. For Eric, who was younger then, the situation was surprising.

He had always supposed a zoo to be a place in which wild animals lived as naturally as possible. He found that the kinds which would kill and devour others were cautiously and completely segregated from their customary prey. Oh, he'd expected the creatures to be kept in cages, of course—primarily to protect folks who came to look at them. But he was vastly intrigued by the careful fashion in which the big cats were maintained in one capacious building, birds in a second, monkeys and other primates in yet another structure of their own. He had thought it peculiar, if not wrong; it meant that Beast A would never know that nature wanted him to eat Beast B, and that Beast B might never have to experience fear.

Later, while cousin Sue was holding Peg's dumb head, the boy had wondered if there was a clue to how people might learn to live peaceably with one another in the manner of zoos. Maybe, after a hundred years or so, Human A might forget that it was supposed to hate Human B.

But now that he and Peg had returned to the big Baldwin place in Indianpolis, Eric thought uncomfortably about the Cincinnati trip. Peg's bedroom, which housed a dippy little bird whom any old predator could hurt; Mama's room wherein a rare, exotic, warmly cuddly creature seemed to him to live; and his own bedroom, occupied by a swift, playful but cunning coyote or prairie dog named Eric—all were part of the second-floor wild animal menage owned by Grandfather. And down the hall, behind locked doors, he kept a being so rare and presumably dangerous that popcorn-munching patrons weren't even allowed to see *The Lynn*.

Since moving back, Eric had turned his own cage into a place as representative of himself and his fluctuating interests as possible. Peg, he knew, had done the same. Neither of them knew how long they'd be there this time but in lives full of upheavel and change, a child did what he could to accomplish a picture of permanence. Three of Eric's walls, consequently, were virtually papered with posters, ads, drawings, old coloring book pages which had turned out particularly well, and messages that appealed to him for one passing reason or another. Most of the decorations he'd brought back from cousin Sue's; some he'd acquired through Grandfather Baldwin's reasonably generous allowance. Athletes represented ranged from retired soccer star Pele—about whom he knew nothing—to I.U. players Isiah Thomas and Uwe Blab—about whom Eric knew everything. There, on one bright wall, Pete Rose dove into the same base eternally, grinning through a cloud of dust; below it, Fernando Valenzuela's forty year old face and twenty year old pitching arm would never age.

Reflecting a total ignorance of politics, Eric's position-posters seemed schizophrenic. Ronald Reagan and Ted Kennedy stood side by side with an ancient portrait depicting Mao Tse-Tung and Ho Chi Minh. Above them, an especially stylish swastika and a drawing of an Iron Cross shared space with a poster reproducing the cover of J.D. Salinger's *Catcher in the Rye* and several hauntingly grisly pictures of the Holocaust survivors. Over to the right, beyond a Kiss poster and a dreamy eyed drawing of Olivia Newton-John, Eric had hung a parchment-like representation of the Ten Commandments. On the other side, among computerized geometric patterns and a few crayoned designs of Peg's and his, Eric had Scotch-taped three incomparably beautiful photographs of galaxies ripped from Sagan's *Cosmos* in a spasm of impossible desire.

The remaining, fourth wall, however, was visibly reserved for Eric's bookshelf. Grandfather Baldwin had rested it there in a rare, grandparently mood, no doubt hoping its new owner would fill the shelves with scientific or political volumes and treatises.

Instead, half the glass-fronted shelves had been stocked with mementos of which the twelve year old had only the foggiest recollection. He'd squeezed into that space a field-goal-kicked football, confiscated during the one game he'd ever seen; a much-prized Cavalier Magazine (secreted, discreetly, behind an old biology album of boring leaves); some rocks, grubby pennies bearing dates that seemed acient to Eric, the mousetrap in which he'd personally caught his first pest; and—the worst criminal offense of all—a glossy 9 by 12 photograph of his mysteriously vanished father.

Raymond Charles Porter, smiling, was forever frozen in his early thirties. Long ago, Eric recalled, Mama had said he looked like Daddy. Their dark hair and coloring were certainly similar, but Raymond Charles Porter's nose was sharper and Eric thought the mouth was wider, handsomer than his own. Sometimes, he imagined the chilling circumstances behind the taking of the photograph; sometimes he believed he saw fear in his father's features— and then he'd change his mind, sure that terror and Raymond Charles Porter were utter strangers.

It was, that photo, Eric Porter's most prized possession. Peg craved it mightily, he knew, but *she* had one of Mama tucked away and Mama was right down the hall, even if she might just as well be wherever Daddy was. The possibility that Raymond Charles Porter might have died was one that occurred quite distantly to Eric, from time to time; much in the same way that a grown man sometimes remembered his own impending mortality. He tried not to think about that.

He did keep a handful of books on the shelves,

delighted by the insight that Grandfather Baldwin probably didn't approve of any of them. They ran a short gamut from Tarzan, the Hardy Boys, and a Smurf paperback to a volume of Arthur Conan Doyle's *Collected Tales of Sherlock Holmes*, from two Ray Bradbury paperbacks and a shocking novel called "Slice of Life" by a man named Kisner to several comic books and an exceptionally pristine King James Bible (casually left with him by Mildred Manning, the housekeeper).

Peg, who was visiting him that Tuesday evening before Christmas Eve, her cat in tow, broke his concentration. He knew her sigh was intended to do just that. "Don't you ever get tired of gasping like that?" he demanded, looking down from where he sat crosslegged on his bed. "You sould like a dumb fish gagging on a beach!"

"I saw your stupid diary once when you were gone and you have a dirty mind." Flat on her stomach on the carpeted bedroom floor, she'd been playing with Krazy, the yellow cat, but deigned to give him an arch look. "It's not my fault there's nobody t'play with but Krazy and you."

Eric leaned over the edge of the bed, scratching the animal behind one pointy ear. Scarcely more than a kitten, it arched appreciatively. "Well, don't feel alone," he muttered. "I made a couple of neat, cool buddies at school but I don't dare ask 'em home. They might *speak*, or *cough* or something."

"I been thinking." She looked reflective as she kept her gaze on Krazy, batting at its ever-present ball of yarn with swift, silent paws. The yarn, like the cat, like Peg's hair, was basically golden—no accident on Peg's part. "About Lynn, who's young like we are. And I'd go absolutely *loony* if I had to spend all my time in one little room!"

"Maybe Lynn's already loony," Eric remarked. "Well, don't forget Grandfather goes up to visit all the time. He even tape records everything Lynn says, or something. And gives tests, I think, on what they've been studying." Eric shook his head.

"But Eric, he handles those old tapes like they were gold, or something." Her gaze fell upon her brother's wall, and the parchment religious replica. "Or maybe big stones with the Ten Commandments on 'em." Abruptly, she looked up, shuddering. "Like he has to save everything Lynn says for all eternity."

"Or everything Lynn thinks. Or figures out." Wind was gusting against the sides of the house, making sounds as if it were talking to itself. Sticking a pencil between the pages of his diary and sitting up, Eric hung his legs over the bed. For a moment he studied Peg's somber face. "You're wonderin' how come Lynn is so damn smart when we're kids, too, and nobody wants t'save *our* thoughts. Am I right?"

"Don't swear," she said absently. "What I was really thinking was, I don't believe it's—it's right, for any kid to be treated like a god. Even if it's the oldest child."

"I don't either," Eric agreed. *If Lynn is the oldest child*, he thought, unwilling to challenge their mutual opinion. "I just wish we could figure out what's going on around here. See, since I'm older, I remember the way Grandfather was before we went to Toledo. He was never really super nice, but he used to be okay —know what I mean? There were times when we could all laugh together." He squinted at the window as if trying to see into the past. "When Daddy was still here, and Mama was okay. Before he made a real, long trip somewhere . . ."

Feeling Peg's eyes on him, the boy stopped. By now, he sensed it when either of them had reached the place in their discussion where common sense told them to stop. Somehow they'd each felt there was an unspoken boundary, and an enigmatic, dangerous land into which they dared not move. Usually, Peg told him to change the subject, or started into another topic on her own.

But this time she was merely getting to her feet, picking up Krazy and pretending she didn't realize it was her cue. He knew, that second, that he had to go ahead—to venture into the forbidden past. Because they both sensed the future seemed likely to be even more hazardous.

"It's hard to read some of the stuff I put in here, a long while ago," Eric said softly, thumbing the pages of his diary. "But I believe Daddy was sent to Viet Nam, and that's when Grandfather sent us to live with Sue and Bernard in Toledo. So if I'm right, Daddy didn't run out on our mother. He had to go." He hesitated. Wind was drifting the noiseless snowflakes at a dizzying, unreal angle and the stark silence of the steady, shimmering whiteness was unnerving. "Grandfather'd just got back from his long trip, to some other country. And it was about then that Mama got sick, and took to stayin' in her

71

room. I remember how she cried, how she told us she'd always adore us, no matter what happened. How we weren't *like* Lynn . . ."

Peg saw her brother's lips close, clamp shut as if he didn't dare proceed. Holding Krazy against her bosom, she hurried to Eric and sat next to him on the bed. "Did you see Lynn then?" she whispered.

"Once, I think." He blinked several times, frowned. "I don't want to talk anymore now."

"But you got to, Eric," she insisted, her breath pepperminty on his cheek. "You *got* to!"

"I was so little then," he said, looking across the room at the door, imagining what existed down the hall. "Younger'n you. I think Lynn was seven or eight."

"Tell me, Eric." Her blue eyes were intense. She was squeezing her cat and didn't notice the way it was wriggling, trying to get away. "Tell me! What was Lynn like then?"

The temperature was ten degrees colder in the room; he'd have sworn to it. "All I can see in my mind is—fat. Just whole, big rolls of fat." He scratched his head. "It was only for a moment, when Mama and Grandfather and some guys I didn't know were carrying Lynn somewhere, just fussing over him and holding something against his mouth and—and Lynn was makin' odd, weird sounds." Eric laughed, shot her a glance. "Sort of like when you sigh and gasp all the time."

Yowling, clawing the air, the cat writhed successfully and, startling both children, dropped to the floor. Giving them a dirty look, it pushed its ball of yellow yarn against the door.

Peg's nails dug into Eric's arm. "Eric," she

said under her breath, "is Lynn our sister, or our brother?"

"Peg, don't!" he exclaimed, not meaning the way his sister was scratching him. "We don't dare pry into any more of it. Grandfather told us never to discuss Lynn the way we would our friends, or anybody else. Lynn is special. A genius. We're—we're lucky to have such a smart kid in the family, even Mildred told us that. Remember?"

"How can it be bad just to know whether our genius relative is a boy or a girl?" she demanded. Peg jumped up, tears of frustration in her pretty eyes. She reached down to grab the cat before he could dart beneath Eric's bed. "Why does everything have to be a deep, dark secret?"

"Dammit, Peg, you'll get Grandfather mad at us!"

"He's already mad anyway," she snapped, snuffling as she turned toward Eric. "Aren't you even curious?"

"Maybe it's like Lynn has a split personality or something like that," he offered, wanting to placate her. "And one of her personalities is the smart one."

"That's stupid," she informed him scornfully. "Next thing, you'll say he's a machine!"

"Well, maybe he is!" Eric exclaimed, piqued. "Or maybe he's got a terrible, cruddy disease— one that's catching, one that might wipe out the whole world!"

Peg kissed Krazy's head, then opened the door behind her without turning to it. "I'll tell you one thing," she said softly. "They aren't protecting us from Lynn. Because we don't count. But maybe they're protecting Lynn from *us!*"

Eric saw her leave, slamming the door behind her. He sat still another moment, holding his diary. "I don't know if Lynn's a brother or sister, a boy or a girl—or if he's got some weirdo disease, or two heads and six personalities—or if he's a machine or an extraterrestrial from some planet in a faraway galaxy." He said it aloud, meaning it for Peg, because he hadn't dared say everything to her when she was there. "And you know something, little sister? I don't *wanna* know!"

Peg hadn't heard him. But it was just possible Eric's words *were* overheard . . .

Four

It was, fundamentally, a midweek morning in late December—cold and blustery for much of the world, one more incremental step toward spring. However, the day was also a special one for most people living in what geopoliticians and international travellers called "the West."

And in Indianapolis, those men and women fortunate enough to enjoy gainful employment might ordinarily have regarded it as little more than "Halfway through to the weekend." The difference was that this happened to be Christmas Eve. Already most of the midwestern city's half million residents were either doing their last minute shopping or, astonished by the boss' generosity, headed home for the holidays.

And for most children in town, it was a morning when the possibility that Santa Claus really existed became freshly enhanced, regardless of what Barb or Bobby had been claiming for the last three or four weeks. Only a fool tells the gift-horse he has bad teeth, and it is nearly always adults who are fools. Children have a stronger self-interest than that.

Which, in part, was why Peg Porter hadn't gone downstairs yet. She didn't hold the slightest happy expectations of jolly old St. Nicholas being on his way, but by the same token there was still the remote chance that Mama might have got well or that Daddy could have defied Grandfather Baldwin and come home. Not yet ten, Peg was at the age when sitting still seemed to be the safest guarantor of not rocking the boat, and when abrupt, precipitous movement got kids into trouble. If she stayed put, as long as possible, who could say what might happen?

Besides, when she glanced out her bedroom window, there was a drab grayness to the farthest reaches of her vision; not a glimmer of cheery red and green in sight. She shuddered, hugged her arms around her small body. Gray was everywhere: In the silent streets, in the sky, even in the sparse wintry grass showing in embarrassed patches where snow had melted. Somehow, she thought, not at all glad about the discovery, the lack of color matched her own morning mood. Sometimes nature chose to cooperate, as if to avoid incongruity; sunshine painting the sides of the old house would only have obliged her to seem sunny.

Tugging on a pullover, annoyed by the way it messed her blonde hair, Peg frowned to herself. She'd told herself firmly, for weeks, that she should make the day before Christmas and the grand day itself nothing more than any other days. Yet deep inside, she had to confess, there was a silly, childish expectation of joy that she had not chased away. Quietly observant, as well as practical, Peg had sensed that Christmas was that rare occasion when human beings had a chance to be truly different from other animals. Although she liked pets and adored Krazy, her kitten, in an oddly mature, distant fashion, she knew that they always looked after themselves first. So did people, except at special times. Like Christmas.

Oh, there'd be a few gifts tomorrow. Down-to-earth, "sensible" things like sweaters and gloves, maybe a new stocking cap. And it was also true that she and Eric had arranged a small surprise of their own, hopeful of hinting about the way Christmas should be. But it wasn't only the question of exchanging presents. She knew, because cousin Sue and her husband Bernard had told them, when they all lived in Toledo, that a person's spirits were meant to be raised at Christmas—that it was a time for hope, optimism, believing things would get better.

And those were things as completely beyond Peg Porter's ability, then, as the aging Senator Baldwin agreeing to sing in a church choir or ring a bell on behalf of the poor.

Yet the goofy thing was, Grandfather had been smiling a lot lately, like a man with a secret, a man with utter confidence that what he wanted was just around the corner.

Peg looked in her mirror and saw the question in her mind flashing curiosity from her eyes. She wondered if Lynn would be smiling, today or tomorrow . . .

Basically, Peg's bedroom was a feminine version of her brother's. The posters were, by and large, of a gentler, more whimsical nature. Puppies and deer and kittens and golden ducks cuddled, here and there, against her walls. Peanuts people—particularly Lucy, Peppermint Patty and long-nosed ole Snoopy—frolicked beneath words of kindergarten wisdom, fantastically happy and wearing inane, cartoon grins.

There was a placard advertising the glory of athletics at John Marshall High School, which she yearned to attend someday; a calendar of Hollywood monsters from old movies; and a string of greeting cards she'd been saving for years. A few of the names signed to them meant nothing to her any longer. Still, without knowing who'd sent them, Peg rather liked touching and opening the cards, reminded of pleasant days or events if not of vanished friends' identities.

There was also a framed photograph of Eric Porter at the age of five, smiling with uncertain bravado from a decrepit, snarling pony. Where had they lived when that picture was taken? Peg shook her head, sighing; she felt overwhelmed by the past, sometimes, old before she was ten.

After she'd dressed in the pullover and skirt combination, Peg shoved a hairbrush remorselessly through her yellow locks, distantly watching her face and the motion of her small hand hoping to see recognizable traces of her Daddy in her own pert features. But that was eons ago, absolute centuries; if he'd left his mark upon her facially, it was shadowed by the complexities of her own baffling experience in life.

Afraid she'd miss breakfast, she left Krazy asleep on her bed and headed downstairs.

In the corridor, however, she paused, alone for the gray length of it. Eric's bedroom was directly across the hall and she thought of tapping, getting him up to keep her company. But he might not share her gloomy mood and there was no point in wishing it off on him. Feeling lonely, unwanted, Peg turned away from Eric's room and slowly continued down the corridor.

I knew where I was headed, all along, she told herself, being honest as she approached another door. *Because there are things I want to know.*

Lynn's bedroom. Quiet, at first. She'd never seen the inside of it, not once. If she wasn't supposed to think about her relative, was it wrong to think about Lynn's room? What was it like? what was kept in there? Tentatively, she placed her palm on the surface of the door and left if there.

Instantly, there were vibrations. She could feel them running through her small fingers. Strange, trickly, almost electrical vibrations which momentarily gave her the panicky feeling that her palm had adhered to the door.

Then she heard a flurry of staccato clicking sounds, rather like those of a typewriter being pounded at a furiously maniacal pace; and then, as if a switch had been thrown, the clicks would cease before starting up again, unchanged. Listening intently, Peg decided it wasn't actually typing at all. But what *was* it, what was Lynn *doing?*

Alarmed, nearly frightened, she withdrew her hand and let anger replace the apprehension. People sometimes joined Pen Pal clubs and exchanged letters with strangers they had never met. But when the letterwriter wanted to imagine something, about the unseen correspondent, there were enough clues to picture *some* characteristics—an image of vivacity or plainness; eyes of a certain color; height and weight. With Lynn, however, there was a greater strangeness — an unfathomable, uncrossable distance — that could not even be measured by miles. It was as if Lynn dwelled on another planet, or something; and yet, here she was, right outside Lynn's room!

On impulse, Peg snatched the doorknob in both hands and turned it.

The door held. While the knob rattled, there was the impression of one lock, at least, perhaps two or three, firmly barring her admission. Since she'd made no discernible noise, Peg pressed her ear against the door to hear.

She caught the slight sound of breathing. Heavy breathing. And an impression that, despite how quiet she'd been, Lynn had heard her and stopped doing anything, to listen back. An impression of a formless, faceless Being seated in a chair, staring at the locked door and perhaps seeing straight through it.

"Lynn?" she called impetuously, to shatter the silence. "Lynn, can I come in, please?" She paused. "It's just Peg." Little old harmless you'll-scarcely-know-I'm-there Peg. At times she thought of herself in those terms, as a small, indistinct, insignificant and almost invisible creature, and she'd always hated the feeling. Now, she wanted to believe in it, and to move away from the sealed room, down the corridor away from the shadows to a light, *any* light, revealing the ordinary, the known.

But she could not leave then and have any self-respect; so she hesitated, her nerves screeching, in a silence like an ominous fog, slithering from beneath the door and threatening to devour the last traces of Peg Porter.

A new noise. Peg doubled her fists, tense. Had Lynn believed she'd gone on? Or was it that

Lynn thought she wasn't worth worrying about? What was that sound, now, anyway? It suggested the turning of pages, rapidly; very, very rapidly, as a near machine-like rate. Yet if that was what was happening, there was no way Lynn could be reading them—Lynn or anybody else. The world's finest speed-reader would not be able to catch more than a glimpse of a single line or two!

Because there were some skills that were just beyond human ability.

So maybe Lynn, like Eric, enjoyed showing off. Peg wrinkled her nose in disgust. In her mind's eye she saw a frail, bespectacled, ill boy of twenty, his overworked and enfeebled eyes faraway and detached, probably holier-than-thou in every glance he gave anybody. Satisfied with the picture, Peg tossed her head and took a step away from the room.

The door opened with a howl of creaking menace. Mildred, the housekeeper, came through the door and turned quickly, locking it, her movements so sudden that the child was unsure whether she'd imagined an odor from within the room—something old and musty, that touched the tip of the tongue like dry cotton or a graveyard kiss. With her partly combed, gray-steaked hair, Mildred looked faintly manic.

"Margaret Porter!" she called in a whisper, hands on hips. "How dare you shout at Lynn that way!"

"I just w-wanted to say Merry Christmas."

A fleshy arm shot out; Mildred had Peg by the arm, the meaty fingers digging into the skin. "Lynn has work that it much too important to be interrupted by old-fashioned sentiments! The Senator would have a *stroke* if he saw you trying to get into Lynn's room!"

"I didn't mean any harm." She was being rushed, virtually dragged, down the hallway toward the stairs. "I just wanted to meet Lynn."

Mildred didn't reply until they'd reached the second step from the first floor; then, pausing, the housekeeper turned to Peg with softened features. "Look, darlin', it isn't my fault. I have my orders." She slipped her sizeable arm round Peg's shoulders. "But I am sorry there's so much you haven't been told."

"Like what?" pried Peg, following the middle-aged woman to the kitchen door. "For example?"

Mildred scarcely glanced back. She didn't even tense. "That's for your grandfather to decide, child. They don't tell old Mildred much because I'm simply paid to do my job and follow instructions the best I can. You'd be wise, Marrgaret,"—she rolled the *R* and winked as she bustled into the kitchen and toward the stove, "if you did the same!"

"But I'm not a servant."

Mildred's back stiffened. The instant Peg said it, she wished she hadn't. Even to a person as young as she, it was clear that the housekeeper was proud of her loyalty and unquestioning industry. "I'm sorry," Peg said, rushing across the floor and touching Mildred's calloused hand. "I really am. But why *can't* we know more about Lynn? Why does Grandfather have us bring so many books and why does he record everything Lynn says?"

Mildred squared her shoulders and slowly

turned to the child. "I'll say this much." She kept her tone of voice low, her jaw outthrust. "Lynn is . . . different than you, or I. Geniuses have their own ways." Her gaze flickered above Peg's head, searchingly. "And Lynn is the genius of geniuses."

"I thought genius kids went to college," Peg argued.

"You forget that your grandfather was a professor. And he, child," the woman's eyes widened, "he says Lynn already knows more than the entire faculty at any Ivy League university. And that," Mildred caught a breath, tweaked Peg's button nose as she turned back to the stove, "is all you'll get from me! What would y'say to some breakfast then?"

"Nothin', Mildred," Peg replied, her tone agreeing with the lightening of mood, "because I don't talk to food!"

As she set the table, one of her regular chores, Peg giggled at her joke and, with the wholesome fragrance of good cooking filling the air, her own spirits rose. At least she was away from school for awhile. There'd be a chance to learn embroidering, something she'd planned for months, and time to talk with Eric and play with Krazy. It mightn't be such a bad vacation if she forget about Christmas.

By the time Mildred filled a plate and Peg was perched in the breakfast nook, Eric ambled in, rubbing sleep from his eyes with his knuckles. "H'lo," he managed, his yawning mouth cavernous.

"You're really a believer in holidays, aren't you?" Mildred grunted, giving him a sharp look as she slid a glass of tomato juice beneath his nose. She reached for his plate, winking female to female at Peg. "Your sister has been up for hours!"

Eric took his seat, clearly awkward in the way he handled his growing legs. Accepting the plate of bacon and eggs, he reached for the Heinz catsup bottle and glanced up, sleepily irritable. "Why shouldn't my sister be as weird as everybody else around here?" He pounded on the bottom of the bottle; huge gouts turned his eggs red.

"Well, at least *I'm* not crazy enough to spoil good food with catsup," Mildred exclaimed.

"No one in my home is crazy, or weird," Grandfather Baldwin's large hand grasped Eric's shoulder, the fingers vise-like. Fully clad in a business suit, white shirt and somber tie, the old man had limped in unnoticed. "Your view of this household, young Porter, is diametrically opposed to the facts in the matter. Intelligence of the highest order—painstaking and pragmatic planning—fill the very molecules of the air you breathe."

Since the old man's fingers had relaxed, Eric forked eggs into his mouth and merely nodded. He'd heard this speech before and it always drew near the threshhold of vital information, facts the boy craved, before withdrawing, tantalizingly. But Eric also knew that the ex-Senator was in a pompous good mood. "Is it smart t'stay in your room all day long, not even knowin' anybody?" he asked pointedly.

Grandfather, seated, turned to study him. The whitening brows furrowed. "I suggest you remember this, boy: Genius comes in a grand diversity of forms, in countless guises. Such brilliance resides in this house of Baldwin that it may one day become a national shrine! What proceeds herin, Eric, may one day alter the entire course of history!"

"I don't do bad," Eric said shortly, chewing. "I got all A's and B's except for a C in English. I'll go to high school before long."

"Precisely my point." Grandfather smiled despite himself. "No one crazy, weird, or ignorant is in my charge—not even you!" Abruptly, harshly, he laughed. He reached into his jacket pocket for a slip of paper. "Now, then, I have an errand for you to run when breakfast has been completed."

"Don't tell me," Eric groaned.

"Another list of books to get?" Peg asked incredulously. "But there's no school today!"

"There is," the old man said, arching his brows, "an open library." He tilted his head and, while they could not see it from the breakfast nook, the children knew he indicated the table in the foyer. "You'll find a stack of books to be returned. Here is the current list of what Lynn will be requiring today."

"It's not fair." Eric said it flatly, tonelessly. He stood, glaring down at the old man. "This is our vacation." He glanced at Peg, working at appearing defiant but feeling his confidence wither. "We aren't gonna do it."

Adam Baldwin did not reply at once. Nothing about the expression on his long, leathery, distinguished face changed nor did his hands move from their place on the table. "Don't challenge me now, boy," he said softly. There was almost a note of warm concern clinging to the frosty warning. "Don't do that to you and your sister."

Eric hesitated, then snatched up the book list. Peg, who hadn't spoken, bounced soundlessly out of the nook and, pushing him, followed her brother down the corridor to the front room.

"One of these days I'll say 'no' and mean it," Eric said, striking the air with an impotent fist. He approached the foyer, cheeks crimson. "I mean it, Peg—someday I'm gonna fight back!"

So furious he was trembling, Eric seized the stack of volumes to be returned to the library and the top book fell to the floor. Swearing, he stooped to retrieve it and it fell open.

On the flyleaf of the library book the boy saw that a note had been hastily scribbled in pencil and just as hastily erased. Part of it remained, a strange combination of apparently foreign words and tiny diagrams, like enigmatic pictures.

Across from the note, he saw three browning stains that might have been blood, a peculiarly sweet *stink* arising from them—and a *single fingerprint, very wide and blackly filthy*.

But what really surprised him was the appearance of the fingerprint. He'd seen them many times and had always been impressed by their detail, the way a human's whorls curved in and out in endless complexity.

The fingerprint on the page of the library book showed only four or five broad, almost clumsy lines. It was as simple and lacking intricacy as the pawprint of a great ape.

Five

As always, he paused to listen, inclining his large head, summoning his once impressive senses to be alert for the slightest suggestion of another, unwelcome presence. The precaution was wise, but it had never borne fruit. It was always quiet in the long, gray hallway on the second story—or had been, since he'd brought Lynn here to live. And sometimes he wondered why that was, that uncanny quietude, since there was no obvious, acoustical reason for the absolute silence which seemed to gether itself outside this room, midway down the hall. It permeated the house, it followed him sometimes when he went downstairs, or to his third floor study, like a cool, moist hand pressing against his soul.

Perhaps, reflected Senator Adam Baldwin, perhaps the absence of sound is something radiating from Lynn—something that emanates from the door or the very walls and, meeting the relatively normal atmosphere in the rest of the building, tenses in anticipation of conflict. Perhaps it was not even possible for a being as extraordinary as Lynn to exist in an ordinary room of an old house in the ordinary midwestern United States without the laws of nature mumbling a mute protest and heightening the pitch of the squeaking floorboards, or darkening the tall shadows which, even to the old man, seemed to be thrown by watching, invisible shapes huddled in the corners.

Of course, he was being foolish. There'd be no intrusion today, no interference now or any other day. There was no reason for anyone to come, pounding upon the downstairs doors and flashing badges of authority, because nothing wrong, nothing criminal, was going on here. Perhaps they existed in a state of total liberty to proceed as they pleased, Lynn and he; which would be only right, would it not, considering that there was no authority alive in the world which was higher than their conquest of the future, their scientific pledge to make the world right for the right people.

Yes, there was no problem with outsiders and there'd be no problem. With the children at the library, only he and Lynn and two other people occupied the house just now, in any case. Mildred had her chores to do, simple fool, and her loyalty—her fidelity to a science as far above her intellect was farflung galaxies were above her dyed head—was generously rewarded, fully assured. As for Elizabeth, his daughter, the poor girl was doubtlessly under sedation again, lost in her mother's nightmares. Horror-twisted reflections of how she had ultimately failed her famous father and that prodigy, that offspring, she'd been asked to raise as her own.

I overestimated her, the former presidential candidate thought for the thousandth time, fumbling for the proper key to Lynn's room. *I believed I had made Elizabeth as capable, genuine, and detached a scientist as I, but I did not take into account her inability to conquer her own absurd femaleness. I had imagined her competent to rise above the psychological drives common to a hundred million hormone-bound bitches, and if she has been irreparably harmed, it is only my fatherly pride in a brilliant daughter that is my responsibility.*

Because the fault resided in her own sexuality, and the ultimate blame—the responsibility for ruining Elizabeth, taking her from her own father's wise care—belonged to that fool Porter, and his common lusts. How I wish I could have slaughtered him, instead of merely watching as Lynn punished him and sent him running! But Lynn had been right, even then. It was the release of human emotion that would bring inquiring, prying strangers to the house—uncomplicated, common busybodies who lacked the foresight, the intelligence and the will, to put a perfect future ahead of simple human life!

The Senator unlocked the door, glanced around once again, then quietly entered the room and carefully locked the door behind him.

As always, turning, he shivered involuntarily in the frigid temperature of Lynn's room and, as always, he strove not to show it. He was not anxious to display his own aging infirmity, his own human weakness, to the towering genius who acknowledged his presence in no way whatever.

He hesitated, waiting as usual for the youth to speak first. When there was only the ongoing image of long-standing familiarity—Lynn reading, Lynn studying, Lynn hard at work upon their mutual quest—Baldwin blinked his eyes several times and looked away, shamed.

Throughout his life he had regarded himself as a man of dedication, immensely more devoted to the fulfillment of his dreams and plans than anyone he'd ever met.

Until Lynn, who lived—pure and simple—for the day when triumph was theirs. Never wasting a word, never trying to be amusing or gratuitously sociable, never giving a thought to anything or anyone but the difficult task that lay before the two of them: seizing control of first one government, then another, and reshaping a world full of danger, of potential devastation, into a globe as docile, vulnerable, harmless and peaceable as the housekeeper, Mildred. Such commitment as Lynn's was incredible, even . . .

Inhuman. Unasked, the world leapt to mind. Instantly, Adam Baldwin expelled it, dimmed his thoughts into the half-awake conglomeration of pointlessness typical of ordinary human beings. Glancing at Lynn, he hoped that his critical description of the offspring had gone unnoticed. It was hard to tell whether Lynn had taken notice or not, considering the way the youth's great head remained bent, in concentrated study.

Faintly trembling, the old man removed a newspaper from his pocket and quietly sank into a chair against the wall. Machines on either side of him whirred, and clicked, the language that they spoke an electronic buzz of otherworldly data exchanged so swiftly even he could not guess their meaning. But Lynn could; Lynn did not even have to guess, Baldwin knew, because Lynn had been the one to think of the right questions—questions no man had ever dared conceive. The old man remembered something he'd read in a computer journal, years before—an assertion by a prominent DP authority: "Once we reach a certain level in the advancement of computer capability—a level we all know is accessible—we will be limited in the amount of knowledge we gain only by our human limitations of imagination. It would be possible to take a quantum jump in what we know about the cosmos itself, even Him whom we call God, greater than any ever taken by the species of this planet—if we simply knew the right questions to ask such computers."

Now, there was Lynn. Lynn knew all those questions. Lynn was formulating questions for the computers Adam Baldwin had privately refined, and evolved, and they were questions that had never occurred to the most profound brains in human history.

Because the genetic source of them had never been clouded by modern morality or the accumulated prejudice and faith of what contemporary fools called "civilization." A source that existed outside history, before timid, traditional, bleeding-heart civilization.

The old man spread the newspaper across his pointed knees, read a story on the obituary page, and gasped.

The librarian—that Earhart woman who had insisted upon asking Eric and Peg so many questions about the reason for the continuous series of books they were withdrawing from the library—was dead! Startled, Baldwin raised the newspaper closer to his aging eyes, scanning the story quickly from benath lowered brows. He was truly amazed, because he was a scientist and did not believe in coincidence, in what the psychologist Jung had termed synchronicity. He found it hard to accept that the one person posing a problem for them, since Lynn had banished Porter from the house, was so obligingly . . . removed. It seemed almost miraculous, ordained.

It is good, is it not? Sic itur ad astra.

The Senator looked up, a trifle blankly, when Lynn communicated. But Lynn did not look up. "You read my mind? You know, now, that the librarian we discussed has passed away?"

I said that it was good, n'est ce pas?

The Senator squirmed. "But what does that mean, exactly?"

It means, in totidem verbis, that I took care of it. Und so weiter.

"In so many words? And so forth?" The Senator, clearing his throat, folded the newspaper. Carefully, stalling, he tucked in the edges and slowly slipped it back into his pocket. "Let me make sure I understand you, Lynn." His laugh was a trifle nervous, he realized, inhaling. "Kindly follow this line of reasoning, all right?" A pause. There was no reply. Lynn was not looking at him; calm, at ease, Lynn was reading. "You have the intellectual capacity to, um, house such an involved mass of subject matter that I cannot always follow your reasoning. Yet you are, ah, so very direct." Another pause. A weighty arm moved, lanquidly, and a book— finished—sailed into a corner. At once, Lynn, unperturbed, began reading another. "Are you saying that . . ."

That I eliminated the librarian. Killed her.
The slightest flicker of long, lovely lashes and a

brief, uncouth scratch. *Force majeure, pater.* Full lips, smiling. *Honi soit qui mal y pense, sic passim; et cetera, et cetera.*

"Speak in English, dammit," snapped the Senator, leaning forward in anger, "or stop speaking in ciiches!"

Her functioning is ceased. The tone was obliging yet taunting. *She is no longer a problem.*

Now the old man considered, cautiously veiling his thoughts. "Lynn, we only began to discuss what to do about her. We saw her as a potential problem, nothing more." He shrugged. "I hadn't decided what we should do."

I decided.

"Yes," Baldwin replied carefully, forcing a smile, "you certainly did." He felt a muscle begin working at the corner of the mouth. "And I would not be so foolish as to question the accuracy of your judgment, Lynn, of course not!"

Il n'y pas a dire.

"I disagree, there is much to be said." The old man arose, struggling for self-control, and a control well beyond that. "The point is, you had no authority to arrive at such a conclusion alone. Taking human life needlessly, or at least without civilized discourse, a consideration of all the options and alternatives, is impudent, an impulsive act which . . ."

What does Lynn know of 'civilized discourse?'

"Yes, I follow that," replied the old man, being very reasonable, "but allow me to finish. It is an impulsive act which, however logical or even correct the decision may prove to be, denotes the essential immaturity of the person

93

reaching the decision, performing the impulsive act."

Recoge to heno mienstras que el sol luxiere. A mischievous smirk. *I am a child.*

"Precisely!" cried Baldwin, heartily. One could always reason with the superior person, with a first-rate mentality. "Well, we shall let it pass this once, Lynn. In the future, however, I want your word that you will not take such sweeping steps on your own. I made sure you were acquainted with the concept of law, did I not? Surely you memorized all the legal books with which I furnished you?"

Of course. Every finding, precedent, case on record, for hundreds of years. Every rule, regulation, codicil and clause. Law is what passes for order at a certain time, at a certain place, under certain rulership. This is Lynn's time, and place, and rulership.

It was pointless arguing about it just now, the Senator saw. Lynn had moods like this; there were times when the offspring's immature handling of impatience to be on with it, on to the levels of achievement the two of them sought, merely required a firm, paternal hand—but not necessarily this moment. What had happened was over; it could not be undone. Tomorrow would be soon enough to reestablish the terms of their relationship.

The Senator straightened, got his cane under him, turned to the locked door. "You're progressing admirably, Lynn, in the main." He spoke judiciously, always somewhat more complimentary than to Eric or Peg. Genius required tender, loving care, kid gloves. "Just remember what I said. Is there anything you'd like Mildred to bring you?"

Food.

Something in Lynn's voice made the old man look back.

He wished he hadn't. Even after one had managed, as a consequence of daily exposure to the offspring, as a result of lengthy periods of time in which one reasoned with oneself about the proper place of sheer appearance, to get used to the way Lynn looked, there were moments when it was just too much. Moments such as this, when the naked hunger, the unconcealed greed that motivated Lynn, rose to the impossible eyes—pursed the pink, full lips—caused a rumbling from the unmatched belly that sounded somehow like the carnivorous growling of a huge hyena, gone stark, staring mad with lusting appetite.

"You've already eaten one extra meal today, Lynn." The Senator attempted to keep the reproach and disgust from both his tone of voice and his easily absorbed emotion. "We must consider your physical well-being, your bodily health as well as that of your intellect. Do you understand?"

Ingenii largitor venter, the creature replied. Quietly, as close to removing the menace as possible, Lynn added, *Send food.*

Adam Baldwin stared a moment longer. Flatulence, as thickly oppressive as the stench from mammoth containers of gas, wended its way across the bedroom toward him. He found it absolutely nauseating, dizzying.

"Very well, then," he said thoughtfully, at

last. "I'll send Mildred up with a tray, shortly."

A Lynn hand rubbed the Lynn belly in anticipation. *I love you, pater.*

"Well, I love you too, Lynn," responded the old man.

Sighing, he unlocked the door, let himself out, laboriously locked it after him. He smiled sweetly, secretly. He did love the discovery of his lifetime, too—rather adored the incomparable child, worshipped Lynn for the future which lay ahead of them and for a brilliance unequalled in all the annals of time. Loved that terrible creature because, together, they would surely shape the governorship of the world.

"The belly is a prodigal dispenser of genius," Lynn had quipped, in Latin. Grandfather Baldwin's secret smile broadened, overtly, as he limped toward the distant stairway and the common universe he had always detested. Indeed!

How could a foster father possibly worry over temporary lapses, insignificant mistakes, or stay angry at all, when his offspring had a sense of humor like that!

They might not resemble one another—thank God! But Lynn was still a chip off the old block.

Six

"I want to sneak into Lynn's room. And I want you to help me."

"What? How?" Eric, reddening, craned his neck in surprise. Dawdling, in no hurry to reach the little branch library and haul another stack of books home again, they'd stopped on a corner near the shopping center. The boy stared with consternation at the look of total determination on his sister's serious face, and stomped in a miniature mountain of snowy slush. "I mean, you're really gettin' crazy like the rest of 'em! Why, Grandfather would skin us alive if we did a thing like that."

Margaret Ann Porter's eyes flashed. "What you mean, Eric, is that you're afraid of Lynn. You don't even know what he does, or how big he is, and you're chicken!"

"I don't even know if Lynn's a he," Eric protested, crossing the street with the light. He walked fast enough, purposely, to make Peg hurry to keep pace. "I know both girls and boys who are named Lynn." He gestured over his head at her. "It's like Chris and Jean and Jamie. Or Jesse, Sidney and Blair. Y'can't tell the boys from the girls without a program!"

"Well, if Lynn isn't a boy," Peg argued, rushing after him, making slurpy footprints in the sidewalk when she slid, "are you still scared?

'Cause that means he's a girl!"

Eric stopped suddenly. As he turned, Peg collided with him. She'd been running and sliding with her head down and he gave her a scornful, big-brother glare. "Look, you've still got your allowance, haven't you?"

She nodded.

"Let's see a movie before we go to the library. Okay?" He made a face. "And if you'll stop talkin' about breaking into Lynn's room, I'll buy the popcorn. All right?"

Without thinking it through, Peg nodded reluctantly. And when they reached the two-screen movie house with prices reduced for the afternoon, she recognized her error in judgment at once: One side of the theatre was showing a Sylvester Stallone movie—she saw Eric's eyes light-up as he read the outside poster—and the other had a Christmas special, "Galactic Santa Claus." Peg's own eyes widened as she read the legend beneath the title: RIDE BY ROCKET WITH RUDOLPH & SANTA HIMSELF. ST. NICK IN STRANGE LANDS ON THE OTHER SIDE OF THE UNIVERSE!

"Look, Eric!" she exclaimed, pretending to make the discovery on his behalf. "It's a science-fiction flick! Just the kind you like!"

He didn't even bother to answer. With a derisive laugh, he stepped up to the box office and bought two tickets for another look at guys beating on guys. Peg sighed and followed him inside.

Still short of ten, she'd never figured out why she always lost the battle of choice—not only when the two of them went to the movies but with nearly everything. She didn't know whether it was because Eric was older, or because he was male and she was female. Even when she was waging one of her rare, valiant fights, it simply meant she'd give in eventually —let him have his masculine way and tag after him like a little kid. Probably, Peg reflected, because nothing much was important enough, to her, to risk putting up with days of awful silence between them. She loved Eric too much, enjoyed his company too much, for that. But it sure didn't stop him from insisting, or just taking it for granted the way he was today.

Sometimes, Peg mused as they ventured down the aisle of the dark theatre, it really sounded nice to be both a girl and a boy at the same time. Because she'd still be pretty but have a boy's muscles, if she had to fight. Actually she could, as a rule, make Eric do what she wanted if she was willing to cry and act hurt enough. But that was sort of humiliating, and, whenever she resorted to it, all the fun was taken right out of the win. If she was a boy as well as a girl, she'd be much tougher minded and then she'd have all the weapons she'd need to win any argument with him at all!

Instead of doing what she was doing when the movie began.

The film, from her standpoint, was boring and dumb. Old guys without any shirts and without having shaved for two of three days, making muscles and flashing hairy chests and pretending to hit each other or fall down a lot. Seven minutes into it, she climbed over Eric's elongated legs to go to the ladies room and, nine minutes after she'd returned, climbing over them again to get the popcorn refill to which she was entitled. Coming back to squint at him in the dark and politely ask, big eyes luminous, if he wanted a refill too.

When he'd threatened to "bash" her often enough to be convincing, Peg settled into her chair and began guessing with startling accuracy, who'd win each fight scene and what would be happening later in the flick. Exasperated, Eric responded with macho stares at her predictions proved right.

Then, during a scene on the screen which a person Peg's age would not have been permitted to see a decade earlier, she flung her arms around her brother, digging in with her nails and panting passionately in a sequence of gasping heaves.

At the end of the movie, Eric, who'd manfully ignored most of his little sister's antics until then, saw that an ad was being shown for "Galactic Santa Claus." Smiling his most brotherly smile, Eric snatched Peg's popcorn box and poured the contents over her hair and lap.

By the time they'd left the theatre to the relief of the other patrons, brother and sister were tickling each other and giggling.

That still left the walk to the library, a longer one now that they'd veered from their path to attend the movies.

Once, when grandfather had been in an especially talkative, good mood, Peg remembered, she'd begged him to make Eric go by himself. The aging giant had instantly assumed a quasi-comical pose of pompous importance and adopted a tone of conspiratorial confidence. "These errands are a matter of immense importance as well as the utmost secrecy, troops," the old man had replied. "We all depend upon you, the soldiers of tomorrow!" And, jabbing a long finger at Peg, "And in our grand army, even young ladies can become generals!"

She thought about that as they approached the library branch, breathing hard from the greater walk. Grandfather'd been kidding, of course; she knew that. But the talk about armies, soldiers and generals tended to upset her. Daddy had been wounded in Viet Nam, she recalled, and she hated the idea of violence, of killing. God didn't want things that way, in Peg's opinion. And besides, Grandfather was kidding on the square—for real—when he talked about the "utmost secrecy" of their library mission.

Somehow, she had to know what was going on in Lynn's room, and soon.

That college girl who assisted on weekends and during vacations—Agnes, Peg thought her name was—greeted them from the library desk as they entered. Agnes was alone. Eric put the list of desired books on the counter—it looked even longer than usual—and grinned at the college girl. "Hi! Where's Ms. Earhart this afternoon?"

Peg, idly looking at the new volumes which had come in that day, didn't see the older female's expression. But she heard what Agnes said, and the tremulous quality of her voice: "Oh, didn't you hear? I'm afraid she died last night."

"Oh, Lordy," Eric gasped.

Peg stared in horror at Agnes. She'd liked Ms. Earhart so very much. "That's terrible! What happened?"

For a moment the college girl's lashes batted frantically, as if fighting off another flood of tears. Already, Peg saw, her eyes were bloodshot from crying. "They said it was a heart attack," Agnes replied at last. Abruptly she looked away, into the shadowy library stacks. "But she looked like she was . . . scared to death."

Eric swallowed. "She was awful nice to kids." He'd turned pale, seemed almost on the verge of weeping, or of violent trembling.

"Can you get this new list of books for us?" Peg inquired quickly.

"I guess so." The older girl sighed heavily, glanced down at the list without picking it up. Peg guessed she was frightened. "But it's a drag when we have to send down to Main for them."

Before, Peg had paid little attention to the names of the books Grandfather Baldwin requested. Now she moved to the end of the checkout desk, reading the list as the college girl scanned it with mild irritation.

In no particular order, either alphabetically by title or author or in a logical sequence of scientific discipline, the list puzzled Peg as it had the late librarian. It was as if someone had come up with an idea, a *possibility*, and Grandfather had swiftly scribbled it down: Bron's *Advanced Suggestion;* Horseley's *Narcoanalysis;* Cavendish's *Encyclopedia of the Unexplained;* Wilson's *Mysteries;* and Walker's *Man & The Beasts Within* were there. So were Wellard's *Search for Lost Worlds;* Ardrey's *Territorial Imperative;* Campbell's *Masks of God: Primitive*

Mythology; and Grave's *White Goddess.*

Peg saw the titles *Manual of Psychotherapy* by Yellowlee; *Biology: The Science of Life* by von Frisch; *Origin of Consciousness in the Breakdown of the Bicameral Mind* by Julian Jaynes and *The Right Brain* by Thomas Blakeslee; *A Study of Gnosis, Praxis and Language Following Section of the Corpus Collosum* by Akelaitus; and an article called "Paleoneurological Evidence for Language Origins" by Holloway. Besides these titles, carelessly, perhaps, Grandfather had written a notation: "It's about time *L.* learned of self." The titles, incomprehensible to her, swam before her young eyes: *Man on His Nature,* by Sherrington; *New Mind, New Body: Bio-Feedback,* by a woman named Dr. Brown; *The Book of Time* by John Grant; Lyall Watson's *Supernature;* Gabor's *Inventing the Future;* and *Before Civilization* by Colin Renfrew.

By the time Agnes, perspiring and pale with anger, put two books by J. B. Rhine and something called *Cellular Slime Mold,* by Bonner, on the check-out desk, there were three other patrons tapping their toes and frowning at the children.

"Could you give us a box to take these in?" Eric asked, oblivious to the circle of impatient adults. "Or maybe two? Miss Earhart used to keep some back by the restroom."

"Eric," Peg warned him, seeing the college girl's cheeks fill with color.

"Okay." Agnes folded her arms across her breast. "But why don't you kids try poisoning your minds awhile with television? There are some really rotten things on cable after midnight!"

"The books aren't for—"

"Eric!" Peg cried, elbowing him.

When they left the library, eventually, it was with an enormous white container between them—a box nearly too awkward for children to carry. "She did this on purpose," Eric growled, half-lurching through the shopping center. "Just t'get even."

"Girls don't get even, not ever," Peg said from her corner of the box, already panting. "They just try to hold on."

A thin new carpet of snow was covering the streets of Central Eastwood and, with the street lights turned on, the combination of white glare and awkward labor was almost more than Peg and Eric could handle.

"This'll just have to hold Grandfather Baldwin and his precious Lynn awhile," Eric said, speaking for the first time in ages as they turned into the lone lane leading to the old two story house. "I saw a sign sayin' the library will be closed until after New Year's Day."

"Great!" Peg exclaimed, relieved. "Now you see there's a reason for learning to read."

"I read," Eric argued, huffing and puffing. There'd been no one in the walkway since the snow started, judging from the bright clarity beneath their own feet, and he felt strangely isolated—unwilling to return home. "I read all the damn time!"

"Don't swear!" Peg corrected him, backing toward the front door. "It's sure a shame about Ms. Earhart. I just hate her being dead and all."

"Me, too," Eric sighed. Balancing the container against the side of the house, he fumbled for the front door key. "She was okay." His gaze met his sister's above the heavy box. All four eyes were sober. "I didn't even know she was sick."

"I didn't either." The child grew thoughtful. "But I guess it happens a lot to old people. Heart attacks."

"Agnes said she looked . . . scared." His back was to her as he inserted the key in the lock. "Would a heart attack get you all spooked?"

Peg paused before replying. Looking down the block, she saw wreaths and Christmas trees standing in vivid splendor before picture windows and, here and there, a house bearing just *trillions* of multi-colored lights twinkling a cheery greeting: MERRY CHRISTMAS TO ALL! And, YULETIDE JOY!

Overhead, as Peg looked up at her own house, she saw yellow light spilling from Grandfather Baldwin's study on the third floor, as if a toilet had overflowed. Here, they were back from the street and, without a convenient street light, the old house was shrouded in shadow. Motionless ribbons of darkness curled around a great brick chimney and, more-or-less directly below that, Lynn's room lurked—illuminated always, at all times, but now completely hidden by a frosting of ice upon the large pane. Was Lynn up? Did Lynn rise? Or for that matter, did Lynn sleep?

Eric's animated face peered back at her from the squeaking door. "Okay," he whispered, "I'll do it. I'll help. We'll slip into Lynn's room some-how, all right?" He put his arms around the case of library books once more and Peg saw, in

105

his familiar features, a look of determination—and one of deep apprehension. He finished hoarsely, "We're gonna find out what's going on around here!"

Part Two

"My brother, withhold not from drinking and from eating . . . from following your desire by night and day; put not sorrow within your heart, for what are the years of a man on earth? The place of the dead is a land of sleep and of heavy shadows, a place wherein the inhabitants . . . slumber on in their mummy-forms, never more waking to see their brethren . . .
   —The poem of a dead man's *ka* (spiritual double), several thousand years old

Woe unto you that desire the Day of the Lord;
To what end is it for you?
For the Day of the Lord is darkness and no light.
                                   —Amos

Their terror is awesome, their glance is death.
Their shimmering spotlight sweeps the mountains.
They watch over Shamash, As he ascends and descends.
                                   —King Gilgamesh

Seven

Mildred Manning met Eric and Peg just inside the living room. She began taking the books from the box, helping the children pile them on the marbletop table in the foyer—and the first thing she said to them was, "Hush!"

"But I didn't say anything, Mildred," Peg protested.

"Then don't." The housekeeper glanced meaningfully across the room and toward the stairway. "Senator Baldwin believes he is drawing near some sort of breakthrough, some new level they've been working for. He insists upon absolute quiet tonight."

"Tonight's Christmas Eve," Eric put in, looking resentful.

"That's beside the point in this house, young man," replied the woman, giving the stacked books a last judicial nudge with her finger, to straighten them, and dusting her hands. "As you well know."

"Ms. Earhart died," Peg said softly, walking deeper into the huge front room.

"That won't interest anyone around here," Eric said loftily, trailing after his sister. "But maybe y'better tell Grandfather about the library, Mildred. It'll be closed until after the first of the new year."

"I'll make sure the Senator gets your message, but I doubt he'll be purely pleased with it," Mildred said. Hands on broad hips, she stared after them. "Who's Ms. Earhart, Margaret?"

"Nobody." Peg dropped into a chair, looking sad and rebellious. "Nobody and nothin'. She *was* our friend, the librarian."

"Something scared her to death," Eric said, looking at Mildred as he removed his coat and galoshes. "Or somebody."

For a moment the woman did not answer. The muscles of her face remained lax, expressionless; but a glint in her eyes, while unrecognizable by the children, gave them an odd lustre. "I can't imagine what could frighten a grown woman to death in this neighborhood, or during the Christmas season." She strode at a brisk, businesslike pace into the center of the room and paused. "And as you said, young man, this *is* December twenty-fourth. And Santa Claus cannot possibly come until you're both sound asleep."

Peg tittered, hiding her mouth. Eric made a rude sound with his tongue and throat. "C'mon, Mildred," he grumbled. "We gave up all that kid stuff while we were livin' with cousin Sue and Bernard, in Toledo. Maybe because jolly old Saint Nicholas forgot where we'd moved to."

The housekeeper laughed, projecting a new Mildred Manning or certainly an unfamiliar one, and touched the boy's forearm. "I was teasing. But how would it be"—she hesitated, looking from one cynical young face to the other—"if we all decorated a Christmas tree together?"

Peg was instantly on her feet, joyous. "You're kidding! A real tree?"

"Where is it?" Eric demanded, filled with excitement. Suddenly his fine brows curved downward in a doubtful frown. "Don't tell me grandfather finally decided to buy a Christmas tree for us! Are you sure ole Lynn didn't wave a magic wand or something, and make the tree grow down here?"

Mildred trod toward the dining room, completely ignoring Eric. Her gesture, however, encouraged them to follow her and both kids detected an air of mystery. "Come along," she urged. And then she stopped in the doorway to the dining room, nodding in appreciation of her own common sense. "This is just about as far as we could put it—as far away as possible from bein' underneath your granddad's study."

Standing, nearly leaning, since it had been procured late in the season and the best firs had already been picked, in one corner, farthest from the entryway, the bare Christmas tree might have been close to five feet in height. At least four and a half feet, Peg thought, adoring it on sight. Because the tree remained damp from the snow and drizzling rain, and glistened, it seemed for a moment to be too lively a bright green for anything but an artificial tree. Both children despised phony things. But as they approached, tentatively touching it and circling around it in a ritual-like dance motion, they found that it was, indeed, a bona fide Christmas tree—ready for decoration!

Nearby, on the dining table, Eric saw,

Mildred had placed boxes of old ornaments and tinsel. Another corrugated box contained strands of lights, growing like fairy buds from the emerald cord. To the delight of each child, the housekeeper had made a platter of fat ham sandwiches and a pot of her tastiest hot chocolate. The cups and saucers, shining, were also on a tray.

"How marvelous of our grandpa!" Peg declared enthusiastically, fairly bobbing up and down. "Why, I didn't ever think he'd remember Christmas!"

Her brother's blue eyes narrowed suspiciously. "Well, I don't think he did remember it," Eric stated firmly, turning to Mildred. "Who got the tree for us, really. Did you buy it?"

"On my salary?" she replied, and laughed. "And how would I get it in here?"

"I bought it."

From the kitchen stepped a small man and woman, lost somewhere in their thirties but apparently, judging from their happy smiles, content wherever they found themselves. Each of them wore clothing which, to Peg, looked like new traveling garments; and they headed toward the children in an avid rush, especially the welcoming woman.

But it was the man behind her, her husband, Bernard, who had spoken. While she hugged and kissed them, the man reached over to take their hands in his and crush them in a hearty, glad shake.

Eric, trying to choose between pretending to wince and chuckling out loud, felt tears rushing to his eyes. They surely were not because of any excruciating pain since cousin Bernard, an accountant, was scarcely taller than Eric himself. He was a grinning near dwarf who might very well have appeared ugly except for black, well kept wavy hair, more charm than any man Eric had met, and a range of emotions within himself that Eric was only beginning to identify or perceive.

While he and Peg had lived with their mother's cousins for a sizeable segment of their brief lives, and had never been mistreated or neglected in any manner, the boy hadn't realized until this moment how fond he had grown of them. Nor that, since the "real home" he'd yearned for in Toledo had proved to be a source of living nightmares, he'd missed them. It was weird, Eric thought, thinking you didn't like somebody much when it was just because you wanted so badly to be somewhere else. Now that he considered it, Bernard and Sue had treated them very nicely, taking them on little trips, giving them paternal advice, apparently happy to regard Eric and Margaret Porter as the children they'd never had or as honored guests.

Mama's cousins, it developed, had been given a larger Christmas bonus from their respective employers than they'd anticipated and, concerned not only about the children who'd been their wards but Elizabeth Baldwin Porter, too, they'd decided to drive over to Indianapolis for Christmas.

"It used to be a real celebration when we were children ourselves," said cousin Sue, accepting a cup of cocoa from Mildred and beaming upon Peg and Eric. "The only one who didn't seem to understand, really, was Uncle

Adam." Sue laughed merrily, hugging Peg against her side. "I'm afraid your grandpa was a bit of a stick in the mud. But I guess it takes that kind of seriousness to climb the ladder of success the way he has!"

"Marrying into this family," Bernard commented, taking a sizeable bite from a ham sandwich, "I have a somewhat more direct outlook on the Senator." The little man's gaze flicked to the housekeeper, who stood back from the dining table with her fleshy hands folded. "Where is that master politician and all-round genius, Mrs. Manning? Dissecting frogs? Or beating cadavers and sending slices to the President who defeated him?"

Mildred colored. "I'm sure the Senator will be down shortly, sir," she averred. "I informed him that you and the missus were here even before you went out to buy the tree."

Cousin Sue exchanged a look with her husband, Bernard. "Why don't we begin decorating the tree—all of us in this room—since Uncle Adam has no interest in it?" She glanced down at Peg, then Eric. "Would you like that?"

They would, and they did. The five of them worked together, giving Eric a stronger sense of family-life than he'd ever known before. He'd helped Bernard and Sue put up their own tree but this was in *his* house! Other than a brief chortle of laughter, or a random squeal of pleasure, they didn't speak much until Mildred warned Eric about literally *throwing* the tinsel on the tree.

Devouring sandwiches and cocoa, they finally finished the pleasant task and stepped back, regarding their labors with pride. "Gosh, this is wonderful," Eric said, his smile trying to reach his ears.

"It's beautiful," Peg said in a hushed voice. Her eyes gleamed with tears. "Thanks, everybody."

"Would you two like one more piece of good news before you go to bed?" Mildred inquired. Boy and girl alike nodded energetically. She smiled above them at the visiting cousins. "I informed your Mama that her family had come for a Christmas visit. And she'll try to come downstairs tomorrow morning. For a while."

Eric and Peg hugged the woman, then, wordless in their happiness, hugged the other adults. Finally the boy glanced up at Sue. "I d-don't even remember when I saw her last. Gee, this is just fantastic!"

"It's also bedtime," the housekeeper said, glancing at her watch. "After ten."

"Time for Lynn's late-night meal," Peg said, slowly turning to peer questioningly at the married couple.

"Time for old Lynn's feeding," Eric stressed, making an animal-clawing gesture with his fingers.

There was no immediate, vocal reply. He saw the cloud cross cousin Bernard's small face, the look he gave his wife, helpless, concerned, even angry. "So the old professor kept his little secret after all. And went on keeping the mysterious 'Lynn' on the premises, even though he told us on the phone that Lynn was gone."

"He asked us to send you two kids home," Sue added, her expression anxious. "Of course, that's where any children *belong:* At home. We'd never have let you leave Toledo if we'd known Lynn was still living here."

"Why?" Peg demanded.

"Yeah, why?" Eric repeated her query. "Is he dangerous or something? Who is Lynn, anyway?"

"Eric," Mildred cautioned him, looking in the direction of the stairway.

"We were never told," Sue answered. In common with many petite women who succeed in controlling their weight, the cousin looked much younger than her thirty-odd years. Eric realized, just then, that he had a crush on her. For Peg's part, if she couldn't grow up to look exactly like Mama, she'd delightedly settle for resembling cousin Sue. Her wavy, dark hair made her seem more a sister to Bernard than a wife, and her thin nose, widely-spaced dark eyes, and generous mouth added to her attractive appearance. At five feet three or so, she might have been two inches taller than her husband. Now, she seemed to gaze not at the freshly decorated tree but at the shadows behind it. "Elizabeth merely told me that her father had brought home a child from his travels and asked her to raise it. Then, when there was some kind of misunderstanding with her husband, we weren't surprised by Elizabeth asking us to take you two kids awhile. Uncle Adam was always hard on the men who wished to date her. He really preferred that she remain single, follow in his king-sized footsteps."

Later, when the children were getting ready for bed, each of them heard Grandfather Baldwin go downstairs to play host. Listening, hoping for information, they heard the affable conversation sounds of greeting and caught snatches of idle conversation.

Idle until, to Eric Porter's surprise and intense interest, all cordiality began to slip out of the overhead adult tones.

And he distinctly heard his short cousin Bernard saying that, if Uncle Adam wouldn't let them know the story behind Lynn—or even visit Lynn in his room—he had no choice but to worry about Eric's and Peg's safety. And heard Bernard say, bold as brass, that he and Sue were not leaving the Baldwin mansion until he found out exactly who—or what—Lynn was.

Another time, that might have frightened Eric for the pleasant, smiling people who were his mother's cousins. One did not, as a rule, give orders to Senator-cum-Professor Adam Baldwin. And one did not risk the wrath of the enigmatic relative who dwelled behind locked doors on the second floor.

But tonight—this Christmas Eve—was different. Because tomorrow morning, on Christmas Day, he and Peg would get to see Mama again. Nothing else could matter at a time like this.

Nonetheless, Eric hoped they'd be more careful about crossing Grandfather in the future. It did not do to make him lose his temper.

Mama! thought Peg, flopping atop her bed and bouncing. This was going to be the finest Christmas of them all, there was no question about that.

But she certainly hoped cousin Bernard would be more discreet about what he asked the old man, while he was staying in the Baldwin house. It was hard to be sure about a dreadful thing like this, and Peg didn't know if it were her imagination or not.

Still, she thought Grandfather would stop at nothing in having his own way, and she wanted no harm to come to Sue and Bernard. Maybe this time she'd ask about the chances of returning to Toledo with them, before Grandfather or Lynn got around to killing the cousins in order to be certain they'd never start any unfounded rumors. And if Senator Baldwin didn't, Peg thought sadly, somehow she believed Lynn would.

Eight

Only on Christmas morning are most Americans willing to set aside differences of long standing or even, here and there throughout the nation, confess to themselves that their distinctions might be too fine, too divisively exaggerated. Most commerce grinds to a halt not because people have no money to spend but voluntarily, and because the money that has been spent is, for once, on behalf of others. Only at Christmas do the most commercial of men and women adorn their faces with out-of-practice grins and experience the nobler emotions, along with the special holiday dinners dear to their particular family traditions.

Only the relentlessly aspiring, the militantly driven, continue adamantly on their chosen way.

By nine-thirty on Christmas morning, Eric and Peg Porter were poking at the paltry display of presents beneath the tree in the dining room. When they heard cousins Sue and Bernard entering the spacious front room, bidding a good morning to Mildred Manning, the children rushed to greet them.

Eric, in particular, was relieved to see that the little man and woman were safe and well. After listening to the way Bernard dared to question Grandfather about Lynn and the "project" going on upstairs, he'd been plagued by worry and found it hard to sleep. Now, as he shook Bernard's small hand and hugged the petite and fragile Sue, he told himself how foolish he had been. Perhaps there was nothing really dangerous about either the aging senator or the mysterious relative in the locked room. It was even possible, Eric decided as he took a seat, that what the old man planned was genuinely humanitarian, something that would benefit people and not harm them.

Peg, the boy thought, looked prettier than he'd ever seen her. It would not do to tell a sister such a thing, of course; but she almost made Eric ache with joy to see how eagerly she awaited Mama's visit. *Strange*, he mused, *thinking of someone who was ill in the mind as coming to visit them.* It was as if their mother had gone, unwillingly, to some far country to which only a handful of people were ever admitted—a bizarre, upside-down country where nightmares came to life in some sort of shadowy, alien reality only one person at a time could ever recognize.

But Grandfather Baldwin was the first to join them that morning. The housekeeper had instructed them that he'd be down shortly, after checking with Lynn, that he'd actually looked forward, too, to seeing his daughter once more. The concept of that—of the old man hiding behind his cold stare and austere dignity a range of limited emotion, including the capacity for affection, for fatherly love—seemed impossible to grasp when Eric heard Grandfather upon the stairs. *Tap* went the cane; a pause, as he lowered his giant's bulk another step; *tap*;

and finally, with a sound that almost suggested gliding instead of walking, a steadier *tap-tap* as he drew nearer the living room.

Sue, was closest to the hallway leading to the staircase and saw him first. "Merry Christmas, Uncle Adam!" she cried.

Then all of them saw him.

Remarkably, he'd donned a rumpled sports coat and a pair of jeans so sky-blue and unwrinkled that Eric was sure he'd never worn them before. When in the world Senator Baldwin, the former professor, had bought such casual trousers was beyond the boy but fascinated him. As Grandfather, smiling broadly, worked his way toward them, the scratchy sound rising from the blue jeans as his powerful old legs rubbed together was mesmeric.

So was the pile of Christmas presents in the arm free of his cane. "I trust it will be a Merry Christmas for all of us," he said slowly, depositing the gifts in Mildred's arms. "Never let it be said that Adam Baldwin is not an admirer of Charles John Huffham Dickens. I make it a point to avoid appearing Scrooge-like, one day of the calendar year."

"Oh, Grandfather," cried Peg, rising and rushing to him. Happily, she gave him a hearty hug, scarcely reaching his waist.

Absently but with a kind of unpracticed, rough affection, the old man patted at her back and shoulders, his gaze moving from Sue and Bernard to his grandson's startled face. "Come, come, Eric," he exclaimed, making a noise that might have been laughter, deep in his throat. "I've neither been visited by the spirits of Christmas past or present nor have I been quite the ogre you've imagined. I have had my eye firmly upon an unending cycle of Christmas *futures*, for mankind throughout the civilized world." He paused blinking, as the thought occurred to him. "It is even a remote possibility that I have neglected my, ah, true grandchildren since Lynn does not appear to perceive the special meaning of Christmas."

Eric was astonished. Arising slowly, he went to the old man to shake his hand. "Does that mean there won't be any more books to get from the library?"

Grandfather released the small hand peremptorily and old ice tinkled behind his frosty eyes. "I said nothing about abandoning the most important project of the century, did I?" Directly, he gazed at Bernard, the man who had challenged him on Christmas Eve. "There are momentary setbacks in every stage of scientific advancement, my dear family, times when the, um, the *subject* of a scientist's inquiries seems to be going willfully in its own independent direction. But a true and dedicated scientist finds the means to regain control, and set the direction as he pleases."

"Grandfather," began Peg, impulsively tugging at his oak-like arm. "Sir?"

"Yes, Margaret," he said gravely, even kindly. "What is it child?"

"I just remembered, all at once, that it was you who used to play the organ, wasn't it? It really is your organ, isn't it?" The words came tumbling out, so eager she was to melt away the remnant of glacial self-interest isolating her from her grandparent. "I remember now that after you left the Senate and all, you used to play for hours and hours."

Eric grinned at the look on the old man's face. Clearly, he was taken aback. "What you say is true," he confessed after a moment.

"Couldn't you play some Christmas music for us?" Peg asked. Another tug at his arm, this time in the direction of the huge Hammond. "Please?"

"Well, now. Really." The old man's face was pinkly illuminated by the flames burning in the fireplace. Mildred had a Yule log burning brightly and, judging from drops of perspiration on Grandfather's face, it was warm in the room. "It's nice that you remember, Margaret. And nice of you to ask. Of course. But . . ."

"You just came down from Lynn's room," Mildred put in, making herself speak up. She looked flustered, to Eric, but pleased—probably glad, with the rest of them to see her distinguished employer in human guise for a change. "That means you won't disturb anybody if you play."

"*Do*, Uncle. *Do* play." Bernard spoke softly, a teasing smile moving upon his small-lipped mouth. "I've never had the privilege of hearing you."

The Senator obviously saw the defiance and challenge, even derision, of his niece's husband. Abruptly, pivoting almost nimbly despite the unsteadiness of his thick malacca, he found his way to the organ and lowered himself to the bench. Half-smiling, bemused, the old man turned on the machine and let it warm itself on the more-pleasant vibrations in the house. It murmured to itself like a great cat, the sound a distinct purr. Krazy, little Peg's yellow kitten, jumped out from behind the instrument in fright and ran from its gigantic opposition.

"It has been so very long," the Senator said slowly, mulling it over. He snapped his wrists, briskly, and paused, apparently abashed. "I'm not at all sure a performance is—"

"Yes, my father. Do play it—for me."

All heads in the front room spun simultaneously, to face the white-clad figure which drifted gracefully from the foot of the stairs and entered the large room. The housekeeper crossed herself and jumped to her feet.

The mother of Eric and Margaret Ann Porter, the daughter of the United States Presidential Nominee Adam Baldwin, stared for a considerable time at her seated father. It was Peg who had the unspoken sensitivity to realize how incongrous he must appear, to her Mama, and must himself feel. Some women made sons of all men and the famous ex-professor had became a small lad about to perform. Besides, the world of music, if not a diametric opposite to the chillier worlds of science and politics, was surely no close kinsman. But while Mama's expression was steady, impossible even for either Peg or Eric to read, the brilliant turquoise eyes shining from her pale, extraordinary face with the high cheekbones, the widow's peak, the subtle daub of lipstick on a mouth that once might have been sensual, were unwavering and seemingly rational.

She had, Eric saw, but felt the comparisons more than thought them, some of Grandfather's height. As she waved Mildred off and walked unhurriedly to the center of the room, there was a trace of his dignity and poise, as well. Her forehead was high, her nose acquiline, her mouth small, refined, and trapped in the parentheses of laugh lines—feminine renditions of the great professor himself. But where he exuded joyous command and a flat lack of willingness to *give* so much as an inch, Elizabeth Baldwin Porter seemed to all those present strangely broken, obliged to muster the cracked courage to display her former command of manner and as fragile, perhaps, as exquisite, old china.

"Elizabeth, my dear!" Grandfather found his feet, grabbing for his cane. His tone of voice was so tender it verged upon the apologetic, yet stopped short of that. "I am so delighted you can be with us this morning. And a Merry Christmas!" Pulling himself together like a marionette fleeing its strings, he gestured to his housekeeper, his daughter's nurse. "Mildred, assist her to the couch, won't you? Children, give your Mama a hand—quickly now!"

"Dear, imperative father!" The woman started toward her cousins, first, smiling back at the old man even as her hands went out to Sue and Bernard. "He always makes such a fuss over the very things that are beyond redemption." Squeezing their small hands, she accepted a kiss on each cheek and stood, turning to her children.

"My little birds," she murmured, fingertips gently touching their soft young faces. "How long I've left you neglected in your nests! There is so much to make up to you, so much"—her glance rose above their heads to meet the

125

Senator's baffled eyes—"to tell you."

Peg, Eric saw, had her face buried in the folds of Mama's immaculate white robe. Then he felt her gaze upon him and he was lost in adoring, clinging to her wrist with his hands as if he might never release her. "You don't ever need to say you're sorry, Mama," he whispered. "All you have to do is stay. Never go again."

"Sweet Eric!" She sat between them on the couch and saw how drawn she was, beneath her makeup, to assume yet another disguise—this time from a lie he knew to be inescapable. "I had to descend those trying, imprisoning steps on such an occasion as this. It is, you know, the celebration of a Saviour." She stared expressionlessly across at her father, who braced himself with both big hands on his cane. "The first of two, if I can still detect modern mythology through the miasma of my illness, and my dependency."

"Don't, Elizabeth." It wasn't a command. The aging Senator was almost begging.

"Oh, have no fear, Father." Mama laughed, played with Peg's hair. "I possess, even now, the scientist's sense of appropriateness. It is Christmas, and daytime. It is only in the dark, after midnight, that one should discuss the *other* Saviours." Suddenly she laughed. "Can you picture Lynn upon a cross? Can you, Father? Just think of it a moment, if you'd like a moment of Yuletide merriment. Why, if they ever decide to put Lynn to death, it will surely be done by a data processing man who removes the tubes—or employs a harpoon!"

Bernard, hearing the note of bitter hysteria in her high-pitched laughter, cleared his throat loudly. "Eric and Peg were perfect children with us," he said. The girl, turning to watch him, observed that his feet scarcely touched the floor. His composure around her towering grandfather amazed Peg. "No trouble, really. We'd be glad to take them back to Toledo with us, when we go."

Eric caught his breath. Bernard's comment was pointed, obvious; he only needed Mama's permission and they'd be safely out of the Baldwin house.

But Mama, her sweet, chestnut hair pulled back from her forehead, did not immediately appear to hear. She was beautiful even now, but he realized how she'd aged. It showed in the subtle dulling of the transluscent skin, the effort required merely to turn her head and focus her remarkable eyes. *Mammoth*, he thought; *they're huge now, they make you forget everything else about her face. Mama has eyes that have seen too much; if her mind forgot it all, the knowing would still be there in her eyes.*

And they were fixed upon her father's face, virtually attached to it. She had heard cousin Bernard, Eric knew then; she'd known exactly what he was saying—and yet she was checking Grandfather! The boy couldn't believe it! After the old man and Lynn had made her so ill, made her need the drugs he provided, she still looked to him for the final word.

Mama stirred then. "I thought you were going to play your organ for us, Father," she said, more evenly than Eric would have expected. "It might bring a measure of gaiety into the old house. Or remind us, perhaps, of things we have all forgotten."

Before Grandfather nodded, and again took his seat, Eric noticed the glint of satisfaction in his eyes. *Damn him!* The boy swore to himself. *He knows he's still in charge here!*

The selection was "Jingle Bells." Swelling ocean waves lifted massively from the organ, the roar of subterranean surf washing over them, the ponderous sounds splashing sonorously, nearly deafeningly, in all their ears.

Peg caught Eric's attention and made a face behind her raised palm.

Adam Baldwin's musical touch was as heavy and killing as stone, the usually jolly melody heaving itself upon the still air in the spacious living room and sinking into, permeating, the sofas, the chairs, the old, rich carpeting and the floor beneath it. At the end of a single chorus, Grandfather segued into "Silent Night." The familiar melody, simple in structure, profound in its reverence was ladled from the mighty Hammond like shovels full of sand drawn from a seaside grave. One by one, as if they heard some dark, evil music being disinterred and poured over their troubled nerves, they glanced to one another in embarrassment.

Mama was on her feet. Her customarily contralto voice, shrill, penetrating above the deep and orgasmic surges of black melody, seemed to reverberate against the walls of the wide room and echo in the shadowed corners.

"That is quite enough!" she said loudly, with Baldwin power, in almost a scream. "Kindly desist from that damnable blasphemy!"

A final chord of rippling cacophony sounded as the old man slammed his palms down. "But you asked me to play for you," he said, gaping at her with a puzzled stare. Suddenly, he frowned, and the familiar martinet blazed from the sizzling eyes and twisted mouth. His long fingers, which had clawed in shock above the keyboard, spastically fought with the organ's variety of controls and the instrument died, at last, with a groan of animal anguish. "Damn you, Elizabeth, you asked me!"

"Ah, but it did not occur to me, father dear," retorted Elizabeth Porter, lids batting but voice still under tight control, "that we might be entertaining that diabolical *creature* on the second floor. Maybe I'm being ridiculous—perhaps I am as mad as you'd like to believe—but the carols or hymns of any religious faith should never be played in the presence of monsters Satan himself would refuse to accept!"

"Lynn was your responsibility too!" Baldwin raised the cane, smashed the tip on the floor. "There was a time when I believed you loved Lynn, and what we intended to do, as much as you love me—or your miserable Porter children!"

"Oh, no," snapped Mama, pointing. "You wanted to believe that. But that was when all I loved most in the world was you, Father—when I believed you knew what you were doing and that I, too, needed to sacrifice for the common good! I'll never believe such things again. Father—no matter what happens!"

A palpable silence crept into the front room, a new and unmerciful irritant to their stunned nerves.

Eric, helping Mama back to her seat on the couch, broke the quietude. His active young brain was working a mile a minute and all he could see, then, was that Mama might bolt from the room at any instant. "Can I give you something Peg and me made?"

She glanced back at him from the other side of the solar system. The hair of her widow's peak was faintly damp, and she looked drained of all color. "Of course, my little boy." Then she reached for Peg's hand and gripped it tightly. "I'd love to see anything you two darlings made."

Immediately Eric dashed at top speed toward the dining room, and the Christmas tree. He was back rapidly, something secret held in the hands behind his back. "Actually," he began, making a small speech, "Peg and I made it mostly for fun and I s'pose Peg really made most of it. And it isn't for you, Mama—we got somethin' else for you, a really expensive, neat hairbrush. But y'see, we thought maybe the problems in this house had to do with the way our relative doesn't even know us, or get to play with us. We thought, maybe, we might make things a little bit friendlier. So this present is for Lynn."

Unwrapped, he held the gift up. He displayed it so that Mama and Grandfather Baldwin could see the knitted pair of garish Argyle socks.

"I dunno if eleven is Lynn's size or not," Peg said from the other side of Mama. She saw with terror the dreadful expression coming into her mother's face and yet there was no choice now but finishing. "We can make 'em either a little smaller or a little bit bigger, if Lynn's feet are different from Eric's."

"Oh my dear God!" Mama's eyes were wide

open now, gaping. Abruptly, she was lurching to her feet, her thin frame trembling as if from some ague. When she saw her son's happy grin of pride starting to fade, she still could not keep from saying the words rushing to her lips. "Dear Lord in heaven, have mercy upon us all for what we've done! Forgive, forgive!"

Mildred brushed past the children, taking Mama by the elbow and leading her away. "It'll be fine, Missus," cooed the older woman, supporting the younger. "Sh-h, it's all right."

Mama looked back at Eric and Peg, her voice low, childlike. "How sweet to buy me a hairbrush. Do I still have hair, I wonder?" Her laugh was harsh, unpleasantly close to hysteria. "Tell Mama, children—do I have something on my head except these millions of evil, hungry worms?"

No one spoke until she'd rounded the corner, gone with Mildred to the staircase. "Is it true I have hair, Millie?" she wondered. "There, there," came Mildred's voice, genuinely caring, strongly firm. Muffled steps on the stairs. "Can you *see* it, Mildred, through the worms and the snakes? Do you see my pretty hair?"

It was silent in the room only for a moment.

Then, tearing his gaze from where his daughter had last stood, Senator Adam Baldwin whirled to face his grandson. His movement was so swift he tottered upon his cane, nearly losing his balance. "You—you miserable *Porter!*" he wheezed. It sounded obscene, the way he said it. He snatched up the socks and hurled them into the fireplace. "This is your final warning, both of you children!"

"Hey, take it easy, Uncle," Bernard called on

a placating note.

"What's wrong with giving Lynn a pair of socks?" cousin Sue demanded. Protectively, she hugged Peg to her. "Does that 'creature' Elizabeth referred to have no feet?"

Baldwin stopped only briefly, looking down at the small couple from his great height. "Oh, there are feet, all right. Feet and legs to bestride the world, to encompass the cosmos!" He turned, pointed at Eric and Peg. "There'll be no Christmas dinner for either of you. Go to your rooms at once! I'll notify Mildred when you can come out."

"The presents . . ." said Peg, moving away from him, tears in her eyes.

"Later!" he roared, slapping his cane-tip. "When you deserve them. *Go!*"

Half infuriated, half terrified, Eric vaulted the steps in three leaps. Behind him, midway up the flight of stairs, Peg began crying, the anguish and embarrassment trailing after her all the way to her room.

Opening his own bedroom door, Eric paused when he heard cousin Bernard shouting: "The instant we can speak with Elizabeth again, we mean to take those poor kids out of this mad scientist's laboratory!"

And the oddly softer response of Grandfather Baldwin: "I'll be talking with Lynn soon, Bernard. And you're welcome to take the brats—if any of you, at all, are permitted to leave my house . . ."

Nine

That long afternoon of December 25th was all but unendurable for the Porter youngsters, alone much of the time in their separate bedrooms. Winter wind howled outside the windows like a chorus of demons in ebony robes, singing dark hymns to Something that smiled and tapped a cloven foot. Eric, alternately pacing the floor in anger and lying face down upon his unmade bed, realized it was not that he sought permission to rejoin the adult world. If Grandfather Baldwin would be there —if the endless enigma of the being named Lynn was to drone into yet another chapter—he wasn't sure he ever wished to go downstairs again.

But what he did desire was to be somewhere else, in a different place entirely, gone from this house of mystifying riddles and impenetrable shadows. Away, forever, from the constant impression of not only unasked for obligation and duty, but ominous threat—from the ceaseless feeling that, if he barged in upon something he should not see or even asked the wrong question, his life or his soul would be placed in jeopardy.

Grown-ups who were fed up, who simply didn't want to remain any longer, could leave. But the reason for that marvelous freedom was not alone the greater economic liberty afforded by adulthood, Eric saw. It was that grown people had a whole variety of options. They knew lots of other folks, they knew what other places existed and how to get to them. At his age, twelve, he'd be hopelessly lost if he were taken downtown and left.

At mid-afternoon, however, Mildred Manning tiptoed upstairs and slipped quietly into Peg's room. She carried two trays of cold turkey sandwiches with side helpings of cranberries and a dinner roll apiece. Peg, knowing full well that Eric would refuse to eat, begged Mildred's permission to go to her brother's bedroom. The housekeeper's broad face revealed her many misgivings but eventually she agreed, and was rewarded when she saw the boy's smile as Peg joined him.

An hour later, the rawboned woman returned to Eric's room, unlocked it, and awkwardly placed their Christmas packages on the bed.

"Not interested," Eric mumbled, yawning.

"Me, too," Peg agreed, despite peeking at the shape of one gaily-wrapped gift.

"Aw, kiddies, it's Christmas," Mildred coaxed. Bustling, she turned on a few lights to make Eric's room less gloomy and beamed upon them. "It's a time for forgiveness and I'm sure your grandfather is only doing what he thinks best."

"Did he buy them?" Eric demanded. "Or just give somebody the money for them?"

The housekeeper frowned. " He sent me to K-Mart last night," she confessed. "Fortunately, they were open late for last minute shoppers. But the thought . . ."

"No way," he countered, crossing his arms on his chest.

"One or two wouldn't hurt," Peg said hopefully, eyes big. "The gifts from Bernard and cousin Sue, at least."

Eric, who was seated on the edge of the bed, struck out with one foot. The pile of presents tumbled to the floor. "We aren't gonna be bribed," he declared. "It's a bedroom sit-in! I'll go downstairs in the morning if Grandfather lets me. But he ain't gonna turn me into a little kid again, all full of tears because he spends a few bucks on us at the last minute!"

Mildred paused. "You're no little kid, Mr. Porter," she said at last, smiling. "But I hope you don't live to regret the way you're actin'."

"I thought it was nice of us to make ole Lynn some socks," Peg said.

It was evening, at last, and they'd played with Krazy, the kitten, until they were bored watching him chase his ball of golden yarn. Neither Peg nor Eric had mentioned Christmas morning.

"I did too," the boy confessed. He sighed heavily and lay back against his pillow, ruminating. "What do you suppose we did that was so awful?"

"I hated the way Mama . . . changed," Peg said softly, cuddling Krazy close. Her head was lowered to keep Eric from seeing the tears in her eyes. "The way she got sick again." Then she looked up at Eric, boldly. "But I can't see how it was our fault! What's the matter with the kid anyway?"

"Wait a minute!" He held up a cautioning

arm, listening. "Hold on!"

The house was silent, except for a murmur of adult voices so distant they could not be sure it wasn't their imaginations. And except for a noise closer than the downstairs speakers, as close as the room down the hall.

A humming noise, not human, unidentifiable, and faint—yet distinctly *there*. And, now and again, a series of swift and breathless little *clicking* sounds. Cuh-*chink*, chet-chet; cuh-*chink*, chet-chet . . .

Eric's eyes grew large. Knees under him, he leaned forward on the bed toward his sister, seated on the floor with Krazy pressed to her breast. "Know what I think, Peg?"

"What?" The word was scarcely audible.

"Wait!" He got up noiselessly, and padded to the locked door in his stocking feet. For a drawn out second he cocked his head, intently listening.

Then he pounded his fist into his other palm. "Sis, I don't think we have a living relative at all!"

"What?" she demanded, incredulous.

"I mean it!" Eric's eyes gleamed. "I think Lynn was invented."

"Come on!" She giggled, but the sound was highpitched and nervous. "That's silly!"

"No, it's not! 'Cause machines don't have feet!" Eric stood over her, his lineless face earnest. "If Lynn's an android, or a robot, it'd explain why Mama got so upset. Because she sort of raised him, like a real kid—but if he doesn't have feet, or hands, she must of got to the place where he scared her!"

Peg stared up at him another second. Then,

dissolving in hilarity, her usual respect for the older sibling vanished and she rolled on the bedroom floor. "That's ridiculous, Eric!" Tears of derision coming to her eyes, she curled into a ball and laughed up at the boy. "That's the silliest thing you ever said!"

He looked down at her, irritated, and saw her expression of amusement would not go away. Reddening, he shrugged and sat down again.

"Okay. Maybe you're right." Then he gave her a hard glare. "But if Lynn isn't a machine of some kind," he said, "you tell me, what he—or she—is!"

In time, Mildred came to unlock Eric's bedroom, collect Peg, and take her to her own room.

Eric, left to his own devices, saw that his watch had stopped. Standing in the center of the floor, he shook his hand to get it running again. Grudgingly, the tiny hands began to move, at last, and he felt better about it.

Until it dawned on him that he had no idea what time it really was. Undressing, changing into pajamas, he found himself shivering with something worse than cold. During the winter, when there were days that remained essentially dark without a glimmer of reassuring sunlight, it was possible to lose all track of time. Whether it was actually a sensible hour to go to sleep or not, Eric didn't know. And, pulling the covers up to his chin, he shuddered and squinted at the shadows lying in the corners before finding the nerve to switch off the lights. Perhaps it was still daytime, perhaps he was going to go to sleep in the evening, and awaken when it was still pitch dark, no better than the middle of an impossibly long night.

And maybe, if a person lost track of time too long—if the days became nights and the nights became days—he'd really be lost *in* time, left adrift in a cold, careless universe in which he floated perpetually on the outermost edge of decades, never quite a part of anyone or anything, ever again.

Frightened, lonely, Eric Porter dropped into troubled sleep.

. . . And came awake, terrified, with the feeling of other skin touching his forehead.

And the skin *moved down,* to his opening lips.

And bestowed a sweet and tender kiss. That instant he knew, without question, it was a mouth which meant him no harm.

It was too dark in the room to see, however, and when a hand touched his cheek, caressed it, cool and gentle, he squirmed despite himself.

Then, "Don't be afraid, little boy," a voice said. "I've already hurt you enough."

"Mama!" he squealed.

"Sh-h," she cautioned him, her tone soothing, reassuring. Dimly, now, he could make out her adorable face in the shadows. The wonderful, remarkable eyes, the widow's peak of her hairline, the sad, distant smile on her lips. "I had to explain, the best I could, my little one. But my best is not very good, these days."

"Mama," he said quickly, struggling to sit up, "let's turn on the lights!" He was eager, starving to talk with her.

"No." The word was tender, regretful, but firm. Her hands urged him to lie back. "What I

138

must say is said better in darkness." She sighed, the sound like wistful wind through a stand of weeping willows. "When my father brought Lynn to me, you and your sister were so very young, not yet individuals. I tried mightily to please Father, to love Lynn as my own child. That is my terrible mistake, my sin; because I came to marvel, to admire that—monstrosity. And to neglect my flesh-and-blood, my darlings who were my real children."

"That's okay, Mama," Eric swore, and nestled his head against her warm, maternal cheek. He felt that he was starting to cry like a big baby, but he didn't care. "I forgive you."

"I know you do." Her eyes were near and, despite the bedroom's darkness, he could tell they were filling with tears too. "But I can never forgive myself. The horror of my neglect, you see, is not limited to you and Peg." Abruptly, her hands squeezed his cheeks, the nails pricking, almost painfully. "Tell her for me, son! I must get back to my own room, before they find me—loyalty is everything to the two of them. But tell my daughter, Eric, all I've said. Tell her that always, from now on, it is you two who are Mama's own darlings—my own, true children! Not—not Lynn!"

He nodded, but she was gone, apparitional in her silent departure; then, in the dimly-lit corridor behind the door, Mildred Manning's familiar voice, whispering, reached the boy's ears: "Is that better now, Mrs. Porter? Do you think, perhaps, you might be able to sleep a little now?"

The reply was muffled, unintelligible. There was the crisp sound of a key being turned in the

139

lock of Eric's door, and then the sound of feet, shuffling up the hallway.

And the old house fell still.

There is consciousness. There is unconsciousness. But all things, some say, possess boundary lines. And there are borders, edges, cuspal interfaces—and, too, a space of the mind itself between waking and sleeping. Sometimes it is hard to detect, even when one finds herself there.

Peg Porter had not yet become one of those who strive to live, for awhile, in that oddly magical, mental space where all things, good or evil, are possible. She was too young to know anything of Yoga and the other eastern disciplines, or hypnotism, or even the hypnogogic state; and so, Peg had never wondered for a moment if a person who passed through the portals leading to unconsciousness but, refusing to enter it, discovered it was hard to turn and locate again, the doorway to reality, consciousness, the universe of living. . . .

She had always come back.

Even by three A.M., however, she remained in that rare, narrow world, like a waif abandoned upon a doorstep. Most of her senses informed her that she was asleep until, as if to establish the fact beyond all doubt, there was a time when her mind said to her, "I'm asleep."

The lie brought her quickly, if barely, to wakefulness.

Thinking of a chum at school who owned a chow. *It is black as Choy's tongue*, she thought, blinking against the darkness. Which meant, of course, that it remained night; such small, practical judgments as that were always duck-soup for Margaret Ann Porter, who liked standing ankle-deep in reality.

Experimentally, she moved her arms and legs, learned she had them still and that they functioned upon command. Softly, heard by no one, she giggled. Funny to think of it like that, "ordering" her body to do things. Because it seemed to her that she merely had the thought and everything did what it was supposed to do. Science was a funny subject. It told you things in a voice like God's and teachers said you were stupid, and failing, if you'd rather believe your own body.

Cuh-chink; chet-chet; cuh-chink, chet-chet.

She squeezed her eyelids together and refused to hear the sounds down the hall.

Instantly she saw in her mind's eye Grandfather Baldwin's organ and a *Thing* seated before it, clanking, clicking, taller than Grandfather, taller than the house or basketball players or maybe even the sky—an immense, metallic, towering chunk of steel with moving parts, with great, gigantic digits instead of fingers—appendages which, striking the keyboard, brought a shower of white and black keys like cosmic snow.

Cuh-chink; chet-chet;. cuh-chink, chet-chet; cuh-chink, chet.

Peg sat up, staring into the darkness, experiencing real terror for the first time in her life.

The house was full of forms that moment, for her; there were rows of iron robots and faceless phony-fleshed androids—columns of them—parading from Lynn's damn-damn-*damn* bedroom and marching down the hallway, toward her room! Dozens, no hundreds of monstrosities, three abreast, stuffing the half-lit hall with their uncaring and merciless, metallic might. *Cuh-chink, chet-chet; cuh-chink, chet-chet.*

And there was nothing left but the distant, madly-spinning parts (*cuh-chink! cuh-chink! cuh-chink!*) surrounded by a half-starved, utterly insane, yawning SILENCE which seemed avid to swallow the world.

She listened to it, alone in the center of her bed, eyes huge, hearing only the gradually agitating but also gradually running down sound of otherworldly machinery, and the awful, aching absence of any other sensation.

"Mama," Peg begged, blind with more than the darkness of her room. "Please . . .?"

And the metal sounds ceased. Slowly, like a white sheet drawn over the immobilized features of a corpse, a normal silence returned.

And from halfway down the hallway, as clearly as she'd ever heard anything, there was the whining voice of someone cursing, in a language she'd never heard before.

Ten

The next chilly morning, when Grandfather told Eric and Peg with a grim and stoic expression that they might go downstairs "if they pleased," they left their rooms gladly enough, but wearing the impassive faces of long-term prisoners, or military enlisted men. People who had finally grown accustomed to being heedlessly prodded from one location to another. If their blank expressions disturbed the old man, he didn't show it. He simply stood at the top of the steps, buttoning a vest he'd donned for added warmth, and watched them descend.

But he joined them and Mama's cousins for breakfast, his entrance momentarily leaving the usually cheery kitchen colder than the temperature in the old house. It wasn't, however, until they'd nearly finished eating that Grandfather casually rested a powerful arm on the back of the breakfast nook and informed the kids that they were "temporarily grounded." Obliged, as their holiday respite continued, to stay in a place they'd learned to despise, and fear.

Bernard, who, judging from his size, might well have been another somewhat world-weary boy taking his morning meal, looked up at the ex-senator at once. His glossy black hair was a trifle askew, as if he'd had trouble sleeping; and while he clearly disagreed with the old man's continuing punishment, he did little more than hold Sue's small hand and give it a comforting squeeze.

"I don't think it's fair," Eric opined, several moments later when the conversation had awkwardly meandered into other, safer channels. Everyone turned to look at him in surprise, including Mildred, working at the stove. His cheeks were pink well up on the bone and his eyes hot as he peered directly across the wooden table at his grandparent. "We didn't even know we'd done anything wrong. It just isn't fair to keep us chained up in this dumb house."

"Eric," Peg said softly, touching his tautly-muscled forearm.

"You're scarcely 'chained,' young Mr. Porter," Grandfather stated, stressing the name of his hated son-in-law. Furry white brows came down and he appeared hawk-like to Eric as he hovered above his breakfast plate, the predatory fingers of each large hand clawed on the edge of the table. "You have complete run of the place, access to everything. Except . . ."

"Except ole Lynn's hole-in-the-wall, or laboratory, or whatever it is," Eric mumbled. "You'll sure send us on errands if you feel . . ."

A sudden clamor from the ancient doorbell, muted with age for the past year but still audible, made everyone jump. It rarely rang; few people came, any longer, to see Adam Baldwin.

"See who that is, will you, Mildred?" Grandfather ordered after a steely glance in the direction of the front of the house.

"My hands are full right now, Senator," the

housekeeper replied, and Eric thought he detected a faint tone of rebelliousness in Mildred's voice. "There's only one of me, you know."

"I'll go," Peg volunteered, before the old man could rebuke the housekeeper. Hopping down, she disappeared through the kitchen door and they heard her small, running steps as her heels clicked on the foyer floor.

"Oh, hi, Eddie!" Peg's sappy voice, in her brother's view. The one she got when older men showed up.

"'Lo, Peggy," said a boy's voice. Grandfather, Eric saw, kept his gaze fixed upon the distant direction and seemed anxious. "Got another big delivery for Mrs. Manning."

"Bring it on back," said Peg, clearly drawing nearer. "It's nice t'see you."

Eddie Dobbs appeared in the doorway. No one paid him any attention but Grandfather, who looked back down at his plate when the teenager, arms loaded with sacked food wrapped in white paper, stepped into the kitchen—and Eric, who rather looked up to Eddie. Slightly older than Eric, Eddie had a job that paid good money and more independence than anyone Eric knew. Krazy, Peg's cat, materialized at the teenager's feet and rubbed her side against Eddie's calf.

After Eddie assisted Mildred in emptying the sacks, he went back to his delivery truck for more. By then, the housekeeper had unwrapped a few meat packages and revealed a variety of porterhouse, sirloin, and T-bone steaks. Each was of top quality, nearly two inches thick. Eddie Dobbs whisteled. "Looks like you're feeding a lion," he muttered.

No one said a word but Eric's eyes locked with his Grandfather's. Then the old man said, simply, "We've a nice freezer. Most of the meat goes into it."

"I'd of sworn I brought an order like that last week," Eddie observed, making notations on his pad. He tilted back a cap he was wearing, put out a hand containing the pad, for Adam Baldwin's signature. "Sorry it's so much. Wow, more than three hundred dollars worth and it's all meat."

"Here." Grandfather scrawled his name, and something else, gave the pad back. "I added a generous tip for your trouble, young man."

"Thanks." Eddie did nothing but glance at the pad, apparently hesitant to leave. Eric, seeing Mildred put three raw steaks on a tray and quietly slip from the kitchen, realized that the other boy was full of questions. Questions he yearned to ask, but for which he lacked the nerve. Finally Eddie said softly: "You don't really keep a lion here, do you, Senator?"

"That would be against city ordinances," the old man said acidly.

"But what do you keep here, Uncle?" demanded miniature Bernard, his tone playful.

Baldwin did not remove his gaze from young Eddie and it became more intimidating as he started to rise. "Get out of here, boy," he said levelly, "or I'll draw a line through the tip I added to the bill. *Now!*"

After Peg had seen Eddie out, she stood in the doorway to the kitchen, sighing. "People are really starting to wonder," she said to nobody in particular.

"Let them!" Grandfather wiped his mouth on a napkin, eyes sullen. "It doesn't matter, you see. Because it's nearly *time*."

"Time for what, Uncle Adam?" asked Sue. She put out a hand to touch his wrist. "We're all family here. I think it's our business too."

He looked at the tiny, black-haired woman, appearing to consider her point openly. When he drew down his napkin, his lips were smiling. "Perhaps you're right, and an explanation of sorts is in order." He cleared his throat, primarily regarding his grandchildren.

Maybe, Eric reflected, *he can't look at Bernard right now.*

"And a way to begin—a way that modern people will comprehend, rapidly, is to say this: The triumph Lynn and I shall soon achieve will mean a literal fortune, and if there's a fault I do not possess, people, it's forgetting who makes my successes possible." He beamed upon the kids. "You children, you see, are going to become important leaders in the new world we're designing—admired, respected relatives of Lynn capable of getting anything you wish from life!"

"We're gonna be rich?" Peg squealed.

"Rich in power, Margaret," Grandfather declared smoothly. His expression was expansive, even youthful with avarice. "And power, my child, will get everything you want!"

"But we aren't poor now," said Eric, glancing at the cousins for confirmation. "I mean, you make sure we all get plenty to eat. The house is okay, we keep warm. What do we need with a whole bunch of money? Or power?"

"Yes, Uncle," Bernard interposed, sitting

straight and looking steadily across at the former senator. "What do they need with it? What, for that matter, does anyone want with so much power over other people?"

"Don't be imbecilic, Bernard!" Grandfather crimsoned. "It will merely be the natural product of our immeasurably important triumph!"

"Who," asked cousin Sue, "who is Lynn?"

He turned to her at once, speaking confidentially, easily. "I met Lynn as an infant during my world travels a number of years ago, Susan," he began. "A foreign boy, from a very old family, indeed. A frail, helpless child with the greatest potential for intellectual as well as creative development I've ever had the awed privilege to encounter. Orphaned, alone in the world, the little fellow needed someone to care for him and I saw soon that I was that person."

Eric, about to reply, saw Mildred coming back into the kitchen. The tray she'd carried was not in sight. He glanced back at his grandfather. "I don't wanna have a bunch of power. If I had t'tell folks what to do, they'd never get anything done. Besides, I'm too young. I might make the wrong decision and hurt somebody."

"That's right." Peg nodded solemnly. She'd only touched her breakfast and looked nearly as pale as Mama. "I don't want to be all different, the way Lynn is."

"Why will you not believe me when I tell you forthrightly that Lynn's genius does not represent a slight difference, but a massive one?" The old man struck the tip of his cane on the floor; the wooden table jumped. "That, with his aid, a new order is being created, a new *world* is being born? Can't you find the common wit to grasp my words, my meaning?"

"Easy, Uncle," Bernard cautioned, seeing the anger flooding Baldwin.

"This nation is first." The Senator did not seem to hear the little man. "It must be re-shaped, from stem to stern. We must do away with virtually every institution, every law—and start again. People will be grateful to the whole Baldwin family for generations yet unborn!"

"What kind of people?" Eric inquired. "Or do you mean all kinds?"

"Certainly not!" Grandfather shook his large head. "There'll be no further tolerance of in-grates and ignoramuses, people who cannot excel and, by the time they've passed through the reformed educational system, take further leadership roles." His eyes blazed with excite-ment. "For much too long a time, this country has abided people who contribute nothing but their bodily presence! Idlers, loafers, without ideas, abilities, the necessary skills of the future—a future drawing closer by the moment, and one which will give humankind either all that it needs, or total chaos."

"Who's gonna say what we need?" Peg asked, her eyes open with honest curiosity.

"Are you going to decide, Grandfather?" Eric, frustrated by all that had happened, did not care what he was saying. "Because all those ordinary folks were the ones who wouldn't let you be President?"

Instantly, Baldwin rose to his feet and slapped Eric jarringly across the cheek.

It might have ended there, but it didn't. Ber-nard, seeing that his wife's uncle meant to

149

strike the boy again, jumped out of the booth. In the same, swift motion, his palms hit the Senator just below the chest and knocked the old man back into his seat. Probably he hadn't intended to be so rough; perhaps he'd only meant to shove his host, but he'd lost his self-control on behalf of a harmless child.

"You underdeveloped little dwarf," said Adam Baldwin, sneering the words at the much younger man. "How dare you?"

Bernard, on his feet, colored. This way, he was scarcely taller than the slumped old man. "If I was out of line, I apologize." He caught his breath. "But I do not intend to let you bully these decent children while I'm around." He held out a hand, willing to help the former professor back into a seated position.

Eric, holding his breath, was surprised. Grandfather took the hand and struggled up, breathing hard. "I shall finish what I was saying," said the old man, all the obvious anger gone from his tone of voice, "and then see to Lynn's needs." He smiled; incredibly, he patted Sue's hand. "You have misunderstood me badly. All of you. You believe I am just another frustrated, dying fool of a madman with delusions of grandeur. A man with my credentials in scientific and political attainment does not suffer that kind of delusion. Nor am I a neo-Nazi, a member of the German Greens, a communist, or a fanatic seeking to prevent justice for the Jews or blacks."

"I didn't mean to imply," Bernard murmured, "any such subversive objectives."

The Senator stood, inhaling, balanced upon his cane. "There is no science fiction film in the

150

works, Porters—no exercises in experimental nonsense by an aged reprobate with a God-complex." His dry chuckle was humorless. "There will be a place for your doddering grandfather, yes, because I can make contributions no other man can offer. But kindly do not think of me as just another fool of a demagogue, another lunatic Hitler with the common instincts of a pervert."

"Forgive me, Uncle Adam," said Sue, brushing back a lock of her dark hair. She seemed a teenager, that instant, a few years older than little Peg. "But I must ask you in order to have some peace of mind about the matter. Why shouldn't we think of you in those terms?"

"Because," Baldwin replied promptly, turning toward the kitchen door, "of the answer I was not permitted to give to young Eric's question. Who's going to decide what people need?" He stopped, a majestic figure, his bald head gleaming. "Not I. Alas, no; not I!" Slowly, a smile crept upon his thin lips, and spread. *"Lynn* will decide, people. Lynn will decide *everything,* for *everyone!"*

They were heading upstairs, still absorbed by what they'd heard that morning, when they heard surreptitious footsteps padding down the second story hallway. Until then, both Eric and Peg, discreetly alone together in the living room, had been talking in whispers about Grandfather's embryonic revelations. Each child wished the old man had gone on to say more and sensed that he'd wanted to. His triumph and Lynn's appeared to be just over the horizon and, as it was true for most men, Grandfather Baldwin obviously looked eagerly forward to the days when he could speak fully, boastfully, about his victory—and his plans.

But once they had tiptoed the rest of the way up the steps, letting their heads show just enough for a cautious peek, they forgot what they'd been discussing.

Mama's cousin Bernard, crouched with his cupped hands to his jaw like an alert mouse, stood outside Lynn's locked door. Judging from his motionless posture, he was trying hard to hear exactly what was going on inside the mysterious room. When he made a quick, beckoning gesture with his arm, the kids darted forward to join him.

Nothing much happened at first. Eric had to supress a giggle with pressing fingertips, Bernard looked so comically conspiratorial. They exchanged grins; Bernard knew he was never going to play James Bond.

But then, once more, there came the incessant sequence of strange, metallic noises, and a monotonous flutter of swiftly-flipping pages.

Hearing brisk heels striding across the bedroom floor—headed toward the door, and them —Bernard drew Eric and Peg quickly across the corridor, into the bathroom doorway.

Mildred appeared, turning promptly to lock Lynn's room from the outside. The gleaming dinner tray she'd taken up earlier, bearing a trio of thick and juicy raw steaks, dangled from her other hand.

Except for several drops of overlooked blood, it gave every appearance of having been licked clean.

Eleven

That evening, when Eric came into the living room with a surprising hunger for dinner, he heard Peg rushing down the stairs behind him. She intercepted him near the organ, leaning close to whisper her news.

"Mildred said Grandfather Baldwin isn't eating with us tonight. Because he's gettin' closer and closer to what he's trying to do with Lynn." Her mind was racing so fast, her expression was so animated, that her eyelids were batting furiously. "And Mama isn't feeling well, and neither is poor cousin Sue, and I think," Peg paused, gathering her nerve, "I think Lynn is *doing* something to everybody already!" Her lips clamped shut, she glanced around to see if she'd been heard, and her brother thought she'd finished. But then she added, tears beginning behind her leashes, "And I absolutely cannot find Krazy anywhere!"

Eric, despite himself, laughed. "Heck, you can't find anything but crazy in this weirdo place!" Playfully, he batted at one of her blonde curls in a mock karate chop. "Peggo, you're mixin' apples with oranges." He said it in a kindlier tone, though, and started through the living room in quest of dinner. "Apples and oranges!"

She trotted after him, piqued. As always, his

big-brotherly ways took her mind off her fears. "Well, what does that mean? I didn't say anything about fruit."

"It's something I heard on TV," Eric called back to her, heading toward the dining room table. "It means adding stuff together that's not the same."

"But it *is!*" Her voice rose, so sharply and insistently that Eric turned back to her. She looked miserable, and stuck with maintaining her view—because it was better than having no understanding at all. "It *is* the same, Eric! Grandfather almost always eats, 'cause he's a big pig like you. Both Mama and Sue are sick, so for all we know, maybe Grandfather is too! Maybe cousin Bernard is next, or you—or me!"

"I feel great." Bernard, smiling, stepped from the kitchen entrance toward the table. He looked much more chipper than that morning, or the awful moment they'd seen the polished-off trays in Mildred's hand. His black hair was freshly combed and, nearing the children, he gave off a pleasant fragrance of a good musk cologne. "And I think Sue is just bothered by the monthlies," he added, looking at Peg, "if you know what I mean."

Eric watched the man take a seat at the table, feeling surprised and a trifle disappointed. Bernard had witnessed the same thing he and Peg saw. But he appeared relaxed, tonight, even jovial.

"I wish you were here with us all the time," Mildred said above Bernard's shoulder, reaching past him to rest a bowl of cauliflower on the table. "You make things seem—normal."

"Things are not always what they seem, Mrs.

154

Manning," he replied lightly, returning her smile. "Unless I miss my guess, there's not much about this house an outsider would call normal."

Eric and Peg, taking their seats, looked up at him in surprise.

"You look so great tonight," the boy offered, candidly. "I thought maybe . . ."

"Maybe I'd come up with a rationalization?" Bernard, finishing it for him, cast a warning glance at the middle-aged housekeeper. He waited till she'd gone back to the kitchen to bring more food. "Or gone over to the other side? Well, I can't see our Mildred as the enemy but you must understand she has her income to consider. And she lives here, too."

"That's what I told you, remember?" Eric asked Peg, excited now. "That ole Mildred's okay but she works for Grandfather!"

"I didn't mean she could necessarily be trusted, or relied upon," Bernard cautioned, keeping his voice down. "These days, a person really has to think about her job, even put it first."

"Then you really think something bad is going on?" asked Peg.

Bernard nodded. "I do, and so does Sue. Something that may be terribly evil, and dangerous. The trick is to find out what it is, while there's time to stop it."

The discussion waned until Mildred had done her customary, thorough job. A great deal might be wrong in the Baldwin house but no one was going to starve to death, not if it were left up to Mildred Manning. Something in her attitude seemed to say as much, that night, Eric

155

imagined; he had the impression that the industrious housekeeper and cook yearned to take her seat at the dining table and confide everything she knew.

Instead, when she was sure the three diners had everything they wanted, she paused at the head of the table, wiping her strong hands upon her apron. They glanced up at her, expectantly. Peg thought she looked nervous; certainly Mildred seemed near exhaustion.

"If there's nothin' else you'll need," the woman started, avoiding any direct gaze, "I'll be goin' upstairs." She hesitated, lips twisting as if she could not say all she wished. "I'll check in on my sweet Mrs. Porter, to see that she's comfortable, and then rest a bit myself."

"What are you saying, Mrs. Manning?" Bernard asked gently, peering cautiously at her. "Or what is it you *aren't* saying?"

Mildred blinked, looked directly at the little man. "I've an avocation since childhood, sir, and it sounds like pure foolishness to some." She nodded. "Numerology. Writin' down an endless string of figures, addin' them up, seeking counsel in an old and precious volume my mother gave to me before she died."

"And?" Bernard asked.

"Some allow that it isn't as fine a thing as astrology, and the modern folks talk about biorhythms and such. But I swear by my numbers, I do!" Her heavy head bobbed emphatically. "The poem of antiquity has it, 'So the potter sitting at his work, / And turning the wheel about with his feet, / Who is always anxious about his work, / And maketh *all* his work by number.' Why, life—excuse me, *everything!*— is number-

156

ing; truly it is! The Chinese of old performed numerology on a Holy Board they called *Lo Chou* and erected a great civilization long before anyone in Europe. The Phoenicians blended numbers into their ancient alphabet, y'know! Why, the science goes back beyond anything of the good Senator's science, back to bearded Pythagoras in Greece, prayin': 'Bless us, divine number, thou who generates gods and men!' And back to the Hindus, as well as the Egyptians." Her hirsute brows rose and she looked meaningfully, defiantly from one to the other of them. "Even to the long-forgotten Sumerians . . . and the dawn of civilization!"

Bernard, anxious to discuss his wife's uncle with the children, glanced rather impatiently at the hovering woman. He was, after all, the controller for a modern company, equally familiar with numbers but disposed to believe that they were fully under his control. Yet he'd seen certain anomalies himself, oddities, at best; and there was something so hypnotically earnest about Mildred's solemn words that he tempered his comment. "Mrs. Manning, is there a point to all this?"

"A point? Why, yes." Qualmish, but no less sincere, she tried to get her thoughts together. "I have done the science of names and numbers, counseled with the cosmic vibrations of man's destiny, ever since Senator Adam Baldwin brought Lynn to this house." Slowly, almost fearfully, she took a step back from the table, from them—as if they might be watched. She glanced in the direction of the staircase, troubled. "I'm talkin' about irreversible, unavoidable cycles which mold every one of us today. About the rhythms of this living planet Earth, and the strange, distant music of the spheres." Her weathered hand suddenly shot up, her index finger pointing firmly to the ceiling, toward Lynn's room. "And the ways we know are dyin', folks dyin', and soon t'be replaced. Replaced by ways far, *far older* than anything or anybody you know, or have ever heard of." She swallowed hard and turned to flee, her hoarse voice a detectable, rough whisper. "It isn't the future you must fear. It's the *rebirth* of a period when two plus two didn't always equal four . . . the unrecorded days before time began!"

She was gone; the dining room was quiet. Midway up the steps, Mildred's clumping footsteps turned to soft, stumbling paces which left aged, creaking sounds lingering upon the heavy air.

"That was quite a speech." Bernard tried to shake it off. He glanced at each child, poured himself another cup of coffee. "Want me to get you guys a coke?"

Peg shook her head. She looked worn out and drained, bewildered by data she could not conceivably grasp. But Eric said, firmly, "I want some coffee!"

"Are you serious?" Bernard, bemused, gave the boy a hard look.

"It's that," Eric replied with a sigh, "or booze!"

Chuckling, Bernard went out to the kitchen and returned bearing a second cup and saucer. Smoothing back his glossy black hair, he poured for Eric. "Today you are a man," he announced, clapping his shoulder. Then he sobered. "Now then, our private conference in the improvised War Room in convened. What the heck do we make of all this?"

"I told Peg I think Lynn's a robot," Eric remarked. "Or an android."

"What did *you* say?" Bernard asked the girl.

"I don't remember." Peg yawned. Her eyelids were drooping with sleepiness. "I just wanna go find Krazy and go to bed."

"He's probably down in the basement, lookin' for mice," Eric suggested.

She frowned. "He's scared of mice. Or maybe he doesn't like how they taste." She'd been slumping but now she sat up, trying to shake off her mood. "I'm sorry. We did promise t'try to find out the secrets in this old house." Wearily, she shook her head. "Sometimes I don't think I'd understand what's going on if I saw it myself."

"Oh, I think you might." Bernard sipped his coffee, looked thoughtful. "Those sounds we've all heard. I'm pretty sure they're machinery, very modern gadgets. Don't forget your grandfather is a first-rate, state-of-the-art scientist. He has the skill to modify machines, even computers, to program them the way he wishes in order to help the young genius with his studies."

"Or hers," Peg interjected.

"But instead of trying to figure out who or what Lynn is," Bernard continued, "we might be better off considering Senator Baldwin's plans. He's a known quality, at least. A brilliant, talented, ambitious man who seems to have wanted to know everything there was to know in the world, *about* the world . . ."

"And to run it," Eric put in. "Even if he does say Lynn will make all the decisions."

"There's much about this world that might benefit from one or two men taking charge," Bernard said softly, "*if* they were people who had the morality of the Apostles and the wisdom of Solomon."

"But how does anybody 'take charge' of something as big as a world?" Eric demanded.

Bernard shrugged. "The old man tried to do it in one of the two traditional ways: By election to power. The other way, conventionally, is through military might, seizure of the reins of power. Somehow I don't see the Senator acting conventionally after failing at the alternate means."

"But what does that leave?" Eric inquired.

"Intimidation; terrorism." Bernard studied the boy's face, thinking how bright he was, how unnecessary it had been for Baldwin to search elsewhere for genius. What was there about certain men who doubted the quality of their own families? "That could mean a thousand things. Weather control, for one. If a scientist chose not to use nuclear energy, but could threaten a volcanic blast such as that of Krakatoa, or the still unexplained Russian blast at Tunguska in 1908, he'd get the attention of a lot of governments. If he threatened to destroy the Van Allen belts, we could be laid bare to solar rays of enormous intensity. What can be done now with viruses and germs, lasers, tasteless chemicals." He paused. "Yet somehow, with all the diverse ways a brilliant team of scientists could plan a take-over by controlling the world, I think it's most likely that Senator Adam Baldwin and his unknown genius are involved in two fields. One of them is the human brain; the way people think—because, after all, the old man places a higher premium on the intellect than anything else."

"Coffee stinks," Eric said, putting his cup down. He'd tried sugar, milk, then more sugar, without being pleased. Looking at Bernard, he wrinkled his nose in distaste. "You grown-ups are all weird."

The little man laughed, looked at his watch. "We aren't getting anywhere, are we?" he asked gently. "Maybe we should adjourn and try this again in daylight."

Immediately, Peg jumped to her feet, too exhausted to think straight.

But Eric stood and stretched. "You said you believe Grandfather would use two things to get what he wants. What was the other one, Bernard?"

Dark eyes glittered. "Time, son; that's what. I think your grandfather has figured out something related to time." He looked at the ceiling, remembering. "There was a quote from St. Augustine about it: 'What then, is time? If no one asks me, I know what it is. If I wish to explain it to him who asks me, I do not know.' "

They left the little man at the dining room table with his coffee, thinking how like them he seemed to be, because of his size, yet how much more a father he made than their own, absentee one, or the unapproaching Grandfather Baldwin. It was possible, Eric thought, as they started up the stairs, to look up to someone for reasons most folks didn't seem to remember, or appreciate.

At Peg's prompting, they looked in her room for the kitten, golden furred Krazy, peeking beneath things and finding no trace of the pet.

Yet when they glanced into Eric's room, they discovered an apparently endless, yellow string of the animal's prized ball of yarn trailing from the doorway. This was a hunt children could handle! With a glad yelp, Peg rushed back into the partly lit corridor and, with Eric at her heels, raced in pursuit of the yellow marker.

It led to Lynn's room.

The door, as usual, was closed, presumably locked.

The string of yarn disappeared through the crack beneath the door.

And on the outside, lying on the floor, was Lynn's dinner tray—a tray bearing four miniature bones, chewed and broken into tiny shards. Beside them lay a tangled scrap of yellow, and it was impossible to tell the yarn from the pathetic patches of golden fur.

Part Three

In those days, in those years,
The Wise One of Eridu, Ea,
created him as a model of men.
—Mesopotamian text of ancient Sumer

When captured by the prehistoric king "were examin-
ed, bound, their throats cut and their entrails taken
out. Finally they were hewn in pieces and roasted in
pairs or baked in ovens. The meals of the king took
place three times a day and consisted of the juicy parts
of the poor captives. The 'horrid rite' was intended to
bestow . . . all the intellectual and magical tributes
which resided within them, and thus to increase his
own capacities and powers."
—Humphrey Evans, *The Mystery of the Pyramids*

Our fathers' age, than their sires
Not so good,
Bred us ev'n worse than they; a brood
We'll leave that's viler still.
　　　　　　　　　　　　　　　　—Homer

Twelve

"Lynn killed my cat! That dumb damn old Lynn killed and ate Krazy!"

Once, only once that night, did Peg Porter issue her forlorn and plaintive cry. But over the ensuing hour, as her revulsion and anger mounted, it was Eric who picked up the charge and repeated the awful accusation in a dozen inspired variations.

Originally simply sharing his sister's profound sorrow, the boy's emotions had veered to fury and such a hunger for vengeance that little Peg found him almost frightening, too. It was as if Eric had reached a peak—or plunged to the floor of a bottomless pit—and could not, would not tolerate another horrifying and inexplicable act.

But Peg also saw, with her shrewd, feminine wisdom, that it was as if her brother felt some kind of acute betrayal. That did not surprise her. Looking back, she recalled the moments at the branch library when Eric had grudgingly defended Lynn, and Grandfather Baldwin's endless commands. And she'd known, then, that Eric both wanted and needed to think of them as vital parts of the family—proper subjects for his complaints or Peg's, but not for outsiders. Now, therefore, from his boy's vantage point, Eric was seeing the seizure and slaughter of his sister's harmless pet as the intolerable, last straw. A straw of treason.

Yet she also realized, as Eric paced his bedroom floor, ranting so loudly she feared what might happen if Grandfather came to demand silence, that in its purest, simplest, most decent form, young Eric's rage was a response to his little sister's pain.

Strangely, the truth of the matter was that Peg, already, was doing her best to shove the terrible act to the dark recesses of her mind. While she was still red eyed from her initial crying, and a part of her secret heart would always be crushed by the loss, she remained more practical by nature and also more passive than Eric could be. What was done, she felt, was done. Krazy could not be brought back to life. And striking back either at Lynn or their grandfather simply didn't make sense, since that still would not put gentle little Krazy back in her arms.

"Eric," she said, now that it was nearing midnight and she needed sleep even more than she had when they were talking with cousin Bernard, "stop. Okay? We don't know what happened. Maybe it was an accident." She looked up from the edge of his bed, where she'd been sitting while he paced. "Maybe Krazy got caught in one of those machines."

"Oh, come on!" Eric shouted, pleading eyes raised skyward. "Come on!"

"And another thing." Peg leaned toward him, seeking his peace of mind. "We didn't—touch it. Maybe it wasn't Krazy."

He gave her a hard look, considering it nevertheless. "Be serious," he said at last.

"Or—or maybe Krazy sneaked in and scratched Lynn, and Grandfather hit him with his cane. Or . . ."

"Or maybe it'll be summer tomorrow," Eric snapped, "with a temperature of 196 degrees." He stopped near her, pounded his fist into his pillow. "I just don't see why! Why Lynn would just—just rip Krazy into tiny pieces that way!" He glanced at her curiously, feeling a thrill of fear. Fear of the unknown. "You don't really think Lynn ate him, do you?"

"I don't know." Her voice was just above a whisper. "Since Mildred takes Lynn food maybe a thousand times a day or something."

She sighed. Eric, who'd resumed pacing, stopped. Looking back, he saw how small she looked on his big bed, how unhappy. Her sigh had ended in a catch, almost a whimper, and he was reminded suddenly of why he'd become so upset.

"I'm sorry, kid," he apologized. He crammed his hands into his pockets, and lowered his head. "I guess I talk too much."

"Yes, you do," she answered simple. "I've been thinking . . ."

"About what? Lynn?"

Peg nodded. Her gaze drifted toward the door, as if she could see down the hallway beyond it. It was only because he was watching carefully that he saw her tremble. "I don't think any of the things we guessed are true," she began, pulling her thoughts together carefully. "And I don't think Grandfather is telling the truth when he says Lynn is a genius." She shifted her gaze to Eric's face. "I think Lynn is really, truly crazy."

167

"Huh? But that doesn't make any sense!"

"Doesn't it?" There was an edge to her tone; a challenge.

"No!" Eric snapped. "What about all the wonderful things Lynn can do, the special powers, the way folks get scared of . . ."

"Eric," she interrupted, "what did we ever see Lynn do ourselves?" She paused, waited for an answer. But he did not reply. "Just 'cause we thought Lynn murdered Ms. Earhart, somehow, doesn't mean it's true!"

"Well, no," he confessed.

"They lock Lynn's door, all the time. In movies, they do that to insane, dangerous people, right?" Her eyes blazed. "We aren't even allowed to see Lynn, and that would be true of a mass murderer, too!"

"But why would Grandfather, and Mildred, even Mama say how smart Lynn is?" Eric asked, puzzling over it. "Of course, Mama got upset just 'cause we made a pair of socks . . . as if Lynn would never, ever get to wear them!"

"Right on!" Peg laughed, clapped her small hands together. "As busy as he says he is, Grandfather always has time to bug us about our grades. And they're pretty good grades! Don't you get it?"

Eric shook his head blankly.

"He's ashamed of Lynn!" she exclaimed. "He doesn't want anybody—not even the rest of the family—to know Lynn's crazy! Or a retarded kid!"

"Yeah, I do get it!" Eric perched on the chair by his small study table, excited. "So what the old man does is make a big deal of Lynn, go the opposite direction—and let us all think he's a genius!"

Peg nodded. "So Lynn's really nuts, and eats cats and stuff." Her smile was one of sheer relief. " 'No one in this house is crazy,' Grandfather tells us, gettin' all worked up over it. But there's really nothing to be afraid of, Eric. Just a dumb, crazy, pathetic kid!"

A knock sounded on the door.

They were both startled. It was rare when anyone knocked on Eric's door, or Peg's. They usually just barged right in.

"Yeah, come in," Eric called.

They heard the scratch of a key turning in the lock; then the door opened.

It was former Senator Adam Baldwin himself, smiling, hesitant, almost polite. "May I enter, children?"

"Sure. I said it's all right." Eric glanced away from the aging giant, added a mumbled, "Sir."

Leaning heavily on his cane, looking older than they'd remembered him, Grandfather lumbered toward the chair Eric vacated. Clearly revealing the effort, he lowered himself into the chair and let the cane rest between his long legs. Tentatively, almost timidly, he smiled again at them. "It's been some time since I stopped by your rooms," he said.

"We've been here," Eric replied.

"Yes, you have been." Grandfather looked around the room at the posters, the diversity of expressed beliefs and slogans. "Can't make up your mind which side you're on, eh?"

Eric knew it was a joke; he heard the bantering quality in the rumbling, deep voice. But he didn't feel very affable. "I'm on my side," he said levelly. He looked away. "Mine and Peg's."

"I knew you were bright, a Baldwin at heart." That tone, those words, made both children look at him. But he was staring only at Peg. "My poor child. I understand your kitten is missing?"

"Not missing, sir," Peg corrected him. "Dead."

"Another practical rejoinder!" Grandfather beamed upon them. Even seated, he seemed taller, stronger, more in command. "Very well, I'll be equally plain: Everyone, all of us, think it's a pity. And I know it is difficult for you to understand. Even your Mama has become . . . overwrought." He hesitated, clearly meaning more than he was saying. "I'm concerned about her, and you. Permit me to say this precisely: If your cat does happen, ah, to be gone permanently, I shall personally be certain that he is replaced with another cat like Krazy. What do you have to say to that?"

Peg said nothing at all. She sighed.

Observing the honest response, Eric knew how she felt: a kid who loved a pet learned more about it than she would ever know about anything else until she was lot older. How the fur lay, where it turned or became darker, or lighter; the way it responded to certain pats, or gestures, or words. The way it could nearly talk, sometimes, because you got to understand it but before that happened, it got to understand you. It was the first real friend you ever had in your life, for some people it would be the only real friend; and stupid grown-ups thought such close friends could be "replaced"—just like that. It was as if Eric himself had disappeared, and Grandfather was promising Peg a "replacement." For little kids, their pets were the most real things in the world and considerably more genuine, predictable, and honest than adult human beings.

"What we really want," Eric said, aloud, distinctly, "is an enormous, very mean lion. A man-hating lion." He stood, confronting Adam Baldwin, man-to-man despite the fact that his Grandfather towered above him. "So we can slip it into Lynn's bedroom and make it tear Lynn up—just the way Lynn tore up Krazy!"

"You little fool." The words weren't loud, they weren't even especially menacing. The old man had the knack for conveying threats in the same tone and at the same pitch Bernard might use to say, "Have a good day." Baldwin had risen the instant he saw the vindictiveness in Eric's face and seemed on the verge of striking out with the cane he gripped in his massive hands. "You understand nothing of what is happening here. You are wrong, boy, if you experience even a moment's desire to injure your remarkable kinsman down the hall. Dead wrong."

This was the time when Peg generally whispered his name, Eric knew, when she cautioned him against going too far. But his sister said nothing. He felt her eyes upon him, and the old man; he sensed the encouragement she was sending the one and the detestation she sent the other.

"If I could," Eric said, "I'd get the lion and sic him on Lynn. Or maybe I'll just call the newspapers, and tell 'em what's happening. Or—or maybe the police would like to take a look around dumb ole Lynn's room, Grandfather." His hands knotted into fists. "Because maybe it isn't just cats Lynn likes to murder, and eat. Maybe it's . . ."

"Lynn is building tomorrows," Grandfather argued, eyes flashing beneath his white brows. "Yours, mine, everyone's. Tomorrows of peace and plenty, of order, law, nonaggression." He slapped the tip of the cane on the bare floor, the report like that of a rifle shot. "We're making dreams come true. And we cannot, we will not, tolerate interference!"

Slowly, the boy smiled. He felt he'd hit pay dirt. "You didn't like that idea, did you, Grandfather? My idea of calling the papers, or the cops?" His smile broadened. "Either I get introduced to Lynn—Peg, too—so we know what's going on around here . . . or I'm gonna call 'em."

"You don't know what you're saying!" Grandfather paled.

"Yessir, I do." Eric nodded hard. "I'm sayin' we're tired of livin' in the dark. We have some rights, even if we are kids—and there are laws against abusing children, right? Aren't there laws against it?"

"You've never been physically mistreated!" retorted the ex-Senator.

"There are other kinds of abuse," Peg said softly.

Grandfather, surprised, glanced at her. His granddaughter Margaret was female, and females, like Elizabeth Baldwin Porter, were supposed to support the views of a great man.

"Just introduce Lynn and me, all right?" Eric spoke quickly, to seize and use their advantage. "Let us talk to Lynn, find out why anybody would be mean enough to rip a silly cat to pieces. Let Lynn explain everything to us, Grandfather, and I won't call the police or the newspapers." His eyes were shining with the honesty of his pledge. "And we'll do whatever you want us to do."

"And if we don't get to meet Lynn," Peg said, jumping down from the bed and taking several steps toward the old man, "we'll find out everything about you and him—or her. I mean it." She swallowed. "I'll figure out a way t'get into that room, Grandfather, and the whole world will know what's happening!"

Adam Baldwin shut his eyes. He loomed above the children, his massive frame swaying like a wind buffeted oak. This time, his crimson face had stayed red and, when he opened his eyes, they were huge in the long, leathery head. He raised his cane, the knuckles white in his powerful hand.

"Very well, Porters," he said. His voice was dangerously gentle, the purr of some great, uncanny cat hunched on a mountain shelf overlooking a helpless world. "You will have your wish. It will be granted."

Suddenly whirling, he strode toward the bedroom door, everything in his manner bespeaking the resignation of a man who had done what he could to prevent an awful tragedy. With his hand on the knob, he looked back with flashing eyes. "Clearly, there is no alternative and you must be punished for questioning not only your grandfather but the most important scientific project of the century." Momentarily, so fleetingly, Eric was not certain he'd seen it, a look of regret crossed the famed and distinguished

173

face. "After that, well, I am certain you will be more cooperative and docile young people than you've ever been before."

"We aren't scared of Lynn anymore," Eric boasted, crossing his arms.

"That is because you haven't met Lynn yet," replied the grandfather, opening the door. There was a glimpse of his sinister, gleaming smile. "Tonight you shall!"

The door was slammed shut. The key was turned in the lock.

Thirteen

When a number of tense minutes crawled by
without any further contact from Grandfather
Baldwin—and without a summons to the
promised audience with the regal Lynn—an unfortunately adult cynicism surfaced both in
Eric and Peg Porter.

Clearly, each child felt, it was a case of just
one more grown-up falsehood. Boys and girls
were always taught to tell the truth, in even the
worst families, convinced that it was a virtue
for which they'd be rewarded. Then, when they
did, adults either criticized them for being
rude, laughed at their ingenuousness, or made
sure they found out fast what happened to
people who consistently paid homage to truth.

Maybe what happened to a bright guy like
Grandfather Baldwin, Eric pondered, was that
he started out being honest and got so hurt by
the convenient lies of his own elders that he
developed the habit of making up wild stories—
at least, when he couldn't simply keep every
aspect of his life a deep, dark secret.

When Peg said she couldn't keep her eyes
open another second, Eric realized that she
shared his convictions: Their door would stay
locked tonight, to keep them out of mischief,
and so would Lynn's—although for different
reasons. Probably Lynn didn't even know they'd

demanded to be introduced; probably Grandfather forgot all about it the minute he left them alone.

And maybe Peg was right and all that lived down the hallway was a crazy kid that Grandfather kept hidden away to avoid suspicion about the whole family.

Mildred had given permission for Peg to sleep again in Eric's bedroom. The housekeeper, acting as if she'd made some decision when they'd discussed things with Bernard downstairs, had been the picture of maternal sympathy. Knowing the grief the children shared over the death of Krazy, the cat, she'd authorized the sleeping arrangements even before the old man paid his late night visit.

Peg, relieved when her older brother gave the word, collapsed in Eric's bed and pulled up the covers without even saying goodnight. He had crammed his lanky, growing body into the sleeping bag brought from cousin Sue's, and the child, drowsing off, mused over the mysterious changes in Eric. A year ago, if an occasion developed when they were to share the same bedroom, Eric had made a beeline for the bed and mumbled something to her about "usin' the sleeping bag or puttin' the bod in a chair."

Now, however, he seemed to have a different, even protective attitude. He wouldn't hear of her sleeping anywhere but in his own bed, and yet he even more adamantly refused to share it with her. *Boys*, Peg mused, stretching, *are downright peculiar.* And then she was asleep.

After zipping up the sleeping bag—the Baldwin house was always airy, draughty, rarely warm on even the hottest days—Eric changed

his mind and sat up. An instant later, he un-
zipped it and, while he kept his legs inside,
leaned the upper part of his body against his
desk.

You are so damn dumb, Eric Porter! he told
himself.

He'd seen a billion movies, and read maybe a
million books or stories, and ought to
remember the way Bad Guys operated! But he'd
forgotten, and it could have been fatal!

Bad Guys didn't give in that easily to honest
threats. They never said "Okay" and then came
knocking at your door, smiling politely as they
gave themselves up! They fought back deviously,
sneakily—which was one of the reasons they
were Bad Guys!

It was just possible that Grandfather had
meant what he said, and that Lynn would "introduce" himself, or herself, yet that night. But
that sure as heck didn't mean a hearty hand-
shake and a clap on the back!

It meant an evil, sneaky attack—when it was
least expected.

Eric tried to see Peg, in the bed, and all he
could make out in the gloom of the room was a
huddled shape. The more he looked at her, the
more restless and apprehensive he got. For a
long as Eric could remember, he'd had this sort
of limited imagination about things that were
scary. He'd never once been afraid of those
perverts cousin Sue and Bernard had told him
about, or being run down by a speeding automobile driven by dopeheads or drunks. Even
the possibility of what germs could do—they
were exactly like the Bad Guys in movies, since
you couldn't see them coming and they always

bit you when you least expected it—only mildly troubled him.

But *the Unknown*. Well, that frightened Eric! Weirdo ghouls or gnomes slithering around under the earth, munching on corpses' ears; with gigantic clouds of swarming bees, the concept of ordinary Nature going shit-crazy turning on people instead of dumb flowers; unimaginable aliens from Planet 0099-X or Star System Galvanus, capable of taking over your personality or pretending to be your mother or father—they scared Eric badly.

But they weren't as bad as his Number One terror: Monsters somebody else had already imagined. Nobody knew anything about that fear, he hadn't even told Peg. Because they made an oddball kind of logic to Eric, especially those monsters he'd been able to see in comic books and movies. After all, somebody had seen them—if only a low-budget moviemaker or a cartoonist who lovingly detailed every scale, antenna, horn, hump or wing. Someone had seen them clearly, rendered them visible for a boy's awed eyes to suck into his unconscious brain. And unless he dealt very severely with himself, Eric was terrified that he might see them too.

So how the heck could he be sure that was just ole Peg lying under the covers?

Reaching, stretching his young body to avoid getting out of the sleeping bag and exposing his vulnerable limbs to the Things which might be lurking somewhere in the dark room, Eric pushed the button on his desk lamp. Then he hesitated. He could push it two more times and get quite a bit more light, but that might wake

Peg up (if it was ole Peg in bed). And besides, accepting all the illumination the lamp might give amounted to an act of cowardice and a guy had to be able to live with himself.

Reluctantly, Eric removed his shaking hand, drew back into the bag, and took another look toward the bed. Actually, it was so dark outside that the single push of the lamp's button removed a good deal of his trepidation. The lumpy shape beneath the covers had a thumb in its mouth and the eyelids weren't quite closed, idiosyncrasies of the small human being he called Sister. There was, he decided, a good chance it really was Peg—and if it wasn't, he had the light on now and he could keep an eye on the huddled form. If it didn't turn out to be a monster, he'd not have wasted his time because he'd know Peg was A-OK.

Eric grinned. Sure, that was Peg; yeah, who else? Nobody looked that cute but his dumb sister. The grin widened, approached paternalism. The blonde hair spread on his pillow was like some especially nice, first-rate look at the sun. The more he thought about it, the more he liked the idea of ole Peg sleeping in his bed, under his protection.

Nobody's getting to her, he boasted to himself, stifling a yawn. Captain Eric Porter, the most decorated soldier in the defense of the Martian colonies, was on guard. Nothing escapes his eagle eye. Nothing can stand against a man who knows every kind of martial art in the 73rd quadrant of the galaxy. Nothin' . . .

He fell asleep.

And the next thing he heard was a sound, coming from the window. Eyes snapped open,

Eric stared straight ahead, not at the window, for his back was to it, but at the locked door. Can't escape through there, he thought.

Scrabbit, scrabbit, went the sound behind him and he felt the sweat start everywhere on his young body. He tried to turn; couldn't. *Scrabbit.* The sound was midway between a tap and a scratch; like fingers with impossibly long, pointed nails seeking covert entry.

"Eric," came a whisper, and he'd never felt so cold. But it wasn't the entity at the window; it was Peg. He could see her from the corner of his eye without turning his head, which he felt he might never do again. He could see her press her fingers over her small mouth and the way her eyes were becoming huge, and he could realize, if he had to, that she was facing the window—that she could see what was there.

And all she'd succeeded in getting out—like the quick gasp of a prayer—was his name.

Panic welled up. Panic, and dreadful obligation. He knew he must look toward that window; he sensed, somewhere in the crippled cordon of nerves running through his body and making his toes twitch, that once he did look— it might be too late. *I won't look then*, he told himself firmly.

He looked. Somehow he was spinning around and craning his neck around the edge of the study-desk and seeing it—and screaming.

A figure was hunched outside, head and shoulders crammed against the windowpane. A muscled figure with the most hideous face Eric had ever seen—and yet it was immediately, terribly . . . *familiar.*

He was looking straight into the red eyes and

180

fang-lined mouth of a werewolf.

Silver bullets, they killed werewolves! His eyes shut, very briefly, as he despaired. That was just the reflex thought taught him by the movies; because he had no gun, no silver bullets, even if he'd had a gun. "God," Eric whispered, knowing he must not close his eyes again. The beast's face was a tangled forest of hair and fur, indiscriminately mottled in tones of black, brown, and an incongruously pretty light-gray. The ears came to a point, satanically. The nose was wet, dripping, and seemed to smell blood. "Please," Eric prayed again; because he'd seen, dangling from the rending mouth, a path of pale skin and red gore—the remnant of a previous victim whose throat the werewolf had torn away.

Noise, at his back . . .

But it was just Peg, vaulting from the bed, breaking her own terrified paralysis and running, stumbling, half-crawling toward the closet.

Even as the window shattered shards of glass shooting into the locked bedroom.

The whole head of the werewolf appeared in the aperture, unimpeded except for slices of glass clinging to the frame. Snarling, clawing with long yellow nails, the creature tore out the broken pieces, oblivious to the seeping cuts left in its skin—intent upon Eric Porter.

The boy sprang to his feet, charged. At the bedroom door, he turned the knob and tugged with all his might. When it held—when the beast growled—he yanked even harder until his shoulders and wrists ached. Hearing the little-boy noises he was making deep in his throat,

Eric willed himself to stop.

Looking back, he began them anew, louder. Because the werewolf was all the way into the room, landing nimbly, crouching now, great hirsute arms extending from a torn human shirt, its claws poised, ready. Eric saw the incongruous trousers tainted with the dried blood of its victims. Seeing Eric's gaze upon it, the werewolf snuffled, pulled remotely human lips back from sharp animal teeth, and took a step toward the boy.

"No!" cried Peg; and Eric glanced at her. Sitting on the floor of his closet, she was defending him. Incredibly, she was leaving the closet door open, so that he could join her there. The vivid blue of her eyes seemed to shriek with actual sound and Eric, desperate to protect her, tried hard to think.

The moon isn't full. How can he have turned into a werewolf?

How he had the presence of mind to remember the legend's details, Eric did not know. But when, half praying, he looked back—

The beast was gone.

Eric began snatching great gobs of air, sucking it into his parched lungs. *I imagined it,* he thought wildly; *but how could Peg imagine it too?*

Relieved, feeling faint, he gave his sister a smile—and realized the look of horror on her face had not vanished.

Crunching the broken glass beneath its feet, much taller than Grandfather and outweighing the old man by more than two hundred pounds, *the Frankenstein monster began an agonizing, deliberate, lurching march toward him!*

182

Eric's mind was aflame with fear. More than any creature in the entire pantheon of monsters, Eric Porter had shuddered before the evil, mindless, man-made Thing—a crazy quilt of dull eyes, ripped muscles, maimed limbs; the Creature Comprised of Corpses, animated not so much by Dr. Henry Frankenstein as by a satanic professor laughing hideously from some corrupting console in Hell.

He tried not to look, he really did. But his eyes wouldn't remain closed. And every time they opened, the Monster was a step closer. Eric gaped at it, momentarily frozen in wonder. Never before had there been such muscles! It pawed the air, more of the workman's shirt was sundered and, as it drew nearer, the zipper-like stitches where pieces of dead flesh had been rudely sewn together, flashed in the moonlight like a thousand grinning mouths. Oh why did I ever even feel sorry for it? the boy asked himself.

For one scant second, there was hope. Stupidly, the Creature paused in the center of the room, one mammoth hand-thing beating the air. It had lost its bearings! Eric ducked, dashed away from the closet, pressed his frail body against the distant wall.

Then, laboriously, Frankenstein's dark triumph again rolled in pursuit, oak tree arms groping. Eric cursed himself as he realized he'd separated himself from his sister, across the room in the closet, unprotected. She was making a noise an infant might make, clucking her tongue against the roof of her mouth.

And the slitted eyes of the Undead registered what it had heard. The huge head swiveled on its mountainous neck. Distantly, Eric could hear the faint hum of the cruel electrodes piercing that corded throat, but no other sound escaped it. A trickle of saliva worked down its grayish green jawline, stained its ruined shirt. Deep in his mind Eric realized that the creature's awfulness was not only from his expressionless face, its creeping menace, it mindless determination to create other beings-made-dead. It was horrible because it had no normal human attributes and because it was, except for the implanted electrodes, an utterly silent being. With no problem, it could destroy all the townspeople and never make a sound.

The damned Thing had veered—it was heading straight for Peg!

Drawn by her pathetic, terrified mewling noises, the monster had abandoned Eric and sought only someone still smaller, more vulnerable.

Eric forced himself to stand, braced against the far wall. His head was reeling; dizziness threatened to steal away his all-important consciousness. For a moment he felt he would surely drown in the sweat pouring from his temples. Mopping his face with his arm, Eric shook his head, wondered what he could possibly do. Why didn't someone come? He cast desperate glances in every direction, looking for a weapon, any weapon.

The desk chair! Grandfather had moved it; now it was out of reach. Damn the old man!

His baseball bat—but it was in the closet, at his sister's shrinking back; no way to get it in time!

Something, anything! Because the Frankenstein monster was closing in on poor little Peg, Tyronnosaurus Rex lurching above a puny scrap of sweet and innocent flower, its drab, dead pate scraping the ceiling, its monstrous back blotting out the closet door and Peg as it sidled forward into the final position before slaughter.

Then it looked back at Eric, and tried to smile. All but brainless, it had turned jovial with the certainty of its kill—and, as the cracked lips parted, the boy saw a crusted tongue, the stubs of yellow teeth, a black hole that might have been the entrance to Hell. Above the yawp, still worse, the gay glint in the blighted pupils chilled Eric to the marrow. *"Not my sister!"* he shouted.

And, careless of his own safety, Eric leaped at the creature. Aiming quickly for the back of its knees, hoping dimly to topple the monster as an axe could fell a tree, his principal plan was to make the pea-brain conscious of him—willing to turn from Peg and take him, instead.

He felt a crashing blow like thunder at the moment of impact, and lapsed into blessed darkness.

One living thing in the Baldwin house smiled, a moment later, and relaxed. Glad it was over, happy to stop thinking about ludicrous things such as werewolves and monsters created by a long dead poet's wife. Glad the childish affair was finished, and glad to turn again to the really important concerns of life.

Not long now. The reading machine was activated. When the idea-facts began to form again, they were whispered to the ever waiting recording device, priceless apparatus and inventions, methods and schemes ten thousand years in advance of that amusing concept called "evolution," diagrams and devices and laws and constitutions and mutations and modifications and offensive weapons and defensive weapons and scientific flights to worlds no man had suspected in his wildest fancy.

If Lynn had been asked *one* question—is there a way to stop it all, anything beyond the capability of your intellect—Lynn would not have needed a computer to analyze the query and answer it.

Another dark figure unlocked the door to Eric Porter's room. Hastening, it moved soundlessly across the floor, paused, looked down at the child sprawled in the closet door. Unconscious, but physically unharmed. Relieved, the figure carried Peg to the bed. The child was so small it was possible to lay her body across the foot of the bed, a decorous touch.

When Mildred Manning located and picked up the boy, however, she began crying. Why had they been so harsh? Anxious, she carried him in her strong working-woman's arms to the bed and, with difficulty, slipped his feet and legs beneath the covers. Moaning, Eric threw out an arm; his eyes rolled beneath his lids. "Poor kid," she said aloud, softly, and examined his injuries.

Satisfied he'd heal, Mildred fetched iodine, and bandages, and did what she could.

Her weeping continued, noiselessly now, without the outrage she'd long since expended. She did swear, now and then, using words no

186

one had ever heard from her lips. Part of it was because even poor Elizabeth had tried to help, even that poor, sick darling was badly upset. And it was such a worry, not knowing how far Mrs. Porter would go to defend the little ones— or how far the others would go to stop any further interference.

Arms hanging helplessly at her sides, Mildred took one final glance around the bedroom. They'd be all right, she decided. Physically, at least. Her gaze fell upon the window.

No buglar would walk in to harm them. She could tell that. Because the window was quite solid, and it was locked.

There was no broken glass beneath the window, at all.

Fourteen

Mildred Manning slept poorly that night, worse than usual. Generally, it was the nightmares that tortured the hard-working woman—searing images of an Adam Baldwin as tall as the INB Building and that bloated bastard Lynn, filling a television screen with their imperial bulk, standing beneath the blessed Presidential seal while they told folks just what to do, and meant it. Sometimes, too, her dreams showed a ceaseless, senseless parade of crazed, clownish numbers. Eager elevens and frolicking fives, tumbling tens and scrambling sixes, shouting inanely as they piled atop one another to make freshly alarming totals or subtracted themselves from lumbering, larger numerals only to flash death-dealing differences which brought the housekeeper at once to shrieking consciousness. She would have been hard put to say which kind of nightmare was more hellish: the ones portraying her cherished, cosmic numbers as a terrifying troupe of doom-cryers, or those which showed fatherly love for something still more monstrous.

But last night. Well, last night was unforgettable. Even after she'd done what she could for those poor children, even after she had taken Elizabeth Porter some broth and sat with the haunted woman, swearing that her little ones would be okay, Mildred had scarcely closed her eyes. Perversely, it reminded her of the fine times before her clever husband Andy took his life—when love, not hate, had kept her up. Nights before Senator Adam Baldwin found out what Andy had done and threatened to blacken his decent Christian name if she refused to work for him and care for that brilliant blob from Hallowe'ens past. That slimy, self-serving, madly brilliant thing which she had always tried to forgive—until last night.

Repeatedly, during the dragged out hours of night, Mildred had second guessed herself and tried to determine how far she could go before a dead man's name must take second place to the needs of the living. Surely Andy would not wish her to sacrifice small children for a being that was neither man nor child, that had never quite found a place among either the living or the dead.

But just what had happened in the boy's bedroom? She'd asked herself that in the dark, tossing miserably, and she asked herself that now as she was dressing for the day. Why had a normal boy like Eric Porter apparently hurled himself against the wall? Yes, of course; it was surely Lynn's work, somehow. But how could either Lynn or that old reprobate Baldwin cause a sensible boy to do something so crazy?

Later, she placed food upon the table in the breakfast nook, smiling nervously, guiltily, as Eric and Peg entered the kitchen. So far as Mildred herself knew, pretty Peg had not been in physical danger; she'd simply fallen asleep in her brother's closet. Little ones did such things. But today, Peg, generally a chatterbox, did not even say "Good morning" and seemed withdrawn, even frightened. When the housekeeper smoothed the girl's fair hair, it proved to be damp.

Reluctantly, she watched Eric slip stiffly into place. "How's your head feel, son?" she asked solicitously, knotting her apron at her waist. "I found you that way, y'know. I bandaged your head."

He glanced up at her, nodding. His instant expression of pain brought her a pang. "All right, I guess." He touched his head with one finger. "Okay."

Cautiously, she checked the bandage. "Well, it ain't seepin' through." She smiled awkwardly. "Y'took a lickin' and kept on tickin', right?"

Peg, sipping her glass of milk, sighed like someone aged. Eric said nothing.

"Why'd you do a thing like that, Eric?" asked Mildred. Despite her concern, she was anxious to understand. To know what Lynn had done to him. "Didn't you know people almost always bounce off walls, 'stead of goin' on through?"

He shrugged. He dipped a spoon into his soft-boiled egg, made a face. "I guess I don't know much of anything." He spoke slowly, cautiously moving his jaw. "If I did, maybe I could learn to keep my big mouth shut."

"I wish you'd learn that, boy," Mildred replied, again toying with her apron. Her eyes, beneath the thick brows, were very earnest. "I really do. Peggy, sweet. D'you want some more milk? Or some fruit juice?"

When Peg looked up, the usually vivid blue eyes were clouded. "Could I have a little real cream for my oatmeal?" she asked.

"This mornin', child, whatever you want, you get!"

The housekeeper bustled away into the kitchen, and Peg tugged anxiously at Eric's forearm. "Did you have a bad nightmare last night?"

His eyes were strangely distant, pained. "You could call it that."

Her fingers squeezed his arm. "Was there a werewolf in it?"

Something altered in the boy's expression. He'd considered lying. Adults, he'd heard, sometimes told lies to help people. But that was dumb. "Yes," he nodded. "And I don't think we could both have the same nightmare."

She looked down into her bowl of oatmeal. "Then it really happened."

"No!" Eric exclaimed. He took her wrist, pressed his face close to hers. "Because there's no such thing as a werewolf!"

Peg started to protest. She said, "But we both," and he squeezed her wrist hard.

"Peg, when I got up—before I got you up—I looked around the room. And the window wasn't broken!"

She looked astonished. "Then how?"

"Don't try to figure it out!" He snatched his hand away. "Maybe Lynn *made* us think every bit of it. Grandfather said we'd meet Lynn, and I think we did. In a way." He whispered, ardently, "Let 'em win, Sis. I been gettin' you in trouble but from now on, I'm butting *out!*"

Peg, glancing over her shoulder, saw Mildred was near. "Things can't happen and yet not happen!" she hissed.

191

"It's over," he said into her ear, almost angrily. "Finished! If we keep our noses out of it, everything's gonna be fine—at least, for us. We—"

A scream—a woman's scream so anguished and frightened it seemed to go on forever—came from the second floor. Pounding footsteps rushed up the hallway. A door opened, slammed. Mildred turned whiter than the cream pitcher in her shaking hand.

Then—silence; unnatural, almost forced.

And Grandfather Baldwin, sobbing. "No—oh, no!"

The children were on their feet. Mildred flung out her arms, shoved Eric back into the breakfast nook.

"God knows what's happened in this hell hole," she said, staring in terror, "but that's nowhere for you to be!"

"But Mildred," Peg began, growing whiter by the moment.

"Don't move!" commanded the housekeeper, tearing off her apron and striding toward the kitchen door. "I'll find out if it's fit for children to hear!"

Then the house was quiet except for Mildred Manning's footsteps upon the stairs, and the distant sound of cousin Sue, crying. . . .

When Peg and Eric had awakened that morning, the new, late December day beyond their bedroom windows had appeared much the same dreary gray of endless winter as the day before.

They'd experienced no regrets over past failures, no premonition of future loss. There'd

been no lightning in the sky, no omen, no preparation for the fact that Mama was dead.

When Mildred returned to the kitchen after a
prolonged absence, her seamed face was still
damp with tears, but she had recovered her self-
control.

"I'm afraid I have some bad news, children,"
she said hoarsely, working her hands in her
skirt.

"Sure," Eric replied, trying to toughen himself as he slowly arose once more from his place
behind the table. "What else?"

"Isn't there always?" Peg echoed, looking
world-weary.

Mildred shook her head, too unhappy to be
amused. "Come into your grandfather's library
with me," she said obliquely, immediately leading the way.

Exchanging anxious glances, the children
slowly trudged after her.

The household library had been closed off
and little used since Elizabeth Baldwin Porter
and her husband parted. For convenience, the
Senator continued to keep on its shelves his
own non-reference works; but the large room
had scarcely been entered for ages. Now, as
Eric and Peg filed in, the library smelled musty
—like a used book store which was no longer in
favor.

Instantly they saw Bernard and Sue seated in
heavy leather chairs. It was Sue, they realized
at once, who had screamed and cried. Her arms
rose from her sides like the wings of a pretty
bird which found gravity simply too strong for
her that day. Peg took one cool hand, Eric the
other, and they felt the sick, helpless appre-

193

hension—an alarm tinged with glacial certainty —fill their hearts.

"It's mama, isn't it?" Peg demanded, the suspense unbearable.

"Your mother has been trying to do too much lately," Sue began, her own eyes wide. "She'd felt better, but she simply wasn't strong."

Eric let Sue continue to squeeze his hand but shut his eyes. He didn't need to hear any more; he did not want to hear any more. The past tense in cousin Sue's words told him the facts he wanted less to hear than anything else in his short life span.

Peg broke down immediately, accepting it because she was female and closer to the realities of living and dying alike. She soon moved her tumbled ball of tearful humanity into her brother's arms, nestling her lovely face in the crook of his shoulder for her hardest, deepest crying.

And above her weeping form Eric Porter stared straight ahead, so stoic, so devoid of expression, that the watching Mildred was shocked. For the first time, she felt, she could see the merciless Adam Baldwin in his grandson. She believed that she saw an echo of familial tidiness, of a comprehension so cold it could only probe for facts and slip them into cubicles until there was a proper time to weigh, analyze, and catalogue.

She listened as he asked his questions, tersely, tightly. When did it happen; what was the cause; were arrangements being made; did Grandfather know; was she in pain at the end?

But she didn't quite know what Eric meant when she detected, faintly, the hug he gave his sister and the words he said to her: "We aren't gonna keep our noses out of it." He was still looking at cousin Bernard. "We're gonna keep our promises."

And Mildred didn't know what to make of it all when, just as faintly, Bernard nodded, as soberly and sincerely as any time she'd seen Senator Baldwin do it. "I won't let you down," said the little man, simply.

Eric was still in the family library, alone, when Grandfather came looking for him.

The boy had always felt drawn to the gentility, the feel of permanence which the room gave him. This immense leather chair in which he sat remained one of Eric's few symbols of stability. He liked occasionally remembering the way his father had sat in it, thinking his serious but amiable, often witty thoughts. It was strong and sturdy and ageless, and, besides, Eric liked listening to the air go out of the seat cushion.

One glance told him that his grandfather was severely, probably genuinely shaken. Entering the library, filling the doorway, he seemed a stricken giant, old Jack's foe at the instant before Jack started chopping away the beanstalk. Then Grandfather came toward him, first passing a big hand across his own, bald head, then, with a cough, patting the boy's head.

Limping badly, obviously aging, Baldwin went to the long table and lowered himself into a chair close to it. Gently, he tapped his cane upon the richly carpeted floor but did not peer around. While he certainly was a man who could possess such a room, he also looked badly out of place in it. Here, books were not tools or cold, instructional guides, but friendly companions enjoyed in a loving atmosphere. The fact that this cozy, paneled library once was the special place of Eric's father Raymond hung between grandfather and grandson. Neither of them could speak at first.

Then the words came, unsought, to Eric's lips. "Why did Mama have to die?"

Although the old man did not look at him, the boy saw the questioning expression as the large, lowered head moved sadly from side to side. Detecting little direct challenge, he sighed; to his credit, he did not blame his Creator for it. "It would appear that she suffered a fatal heart attack." Wide shoulders shrugged in helpless woe. "If we had heard her, if we'd been able to attend her, who knows? I fear we did not hear her, not a sound."

"How could you hear her?" Eric leaned toward the old man and the challenge was there. "Either you were up in your study—or whatever it is—or you were doing weirdo things with ole Lynn!"

Wounded eyes rose from beneath shaggy brows. "I was asleep." Wonder existed in the tone. "Simply asleep. I was so very tired last night that I retired immediately after leaving you and Margaret." Then he straightened, seeming deeply ruminative. "Eric, I am cognizant of the fact that you do not approve of Lynn, of me, or what is—happening. I am also aware that you do not care for me. Candidly, I neither care nor blame you."

There was no answer. But if the Senator had expected one, all that he got was a gun-metal cold stare remarkably like his own. The kind of stare a man might direct into a microscope or test tube.

"However, I do care that you accept and believe this," the old man continued. "Please, hear me. I really had nothing to do with your mother's death. In my way, boy, I loved her." There, he paused and cleared his throat. "It is ghastly when the children die before the old. I share that conviction with humankind, if few others. Eric, I was not responsible and, so far as I know, her demise was natural."

"Maybe." Eric's fists knotted. "Maybe that's so. But it wouldn't have happened, she wouldn't have died now, if it wasn't for you and Lynn. You know that too, Grandfather. And I'll never let you forget it—*never.*"

For a time the two pairs of piercing Baldwin eyes were locked. It was not so much a testing gaze as one of understanding, and mutual acceptance of the situation.

The old man stood, finally, leaning his weight upon his cane. "Your mother's remains will be at the funeral home this evening. The casket will be closed; sealed. And the funeral will be tomorrow." Rather impatiently, his large palm raised. "Yes, I know. It is not customary for everything to be finished so quickly." The deep-set, restless eyes roved. "But it was your mother's wish, her final one."

Quite deliberately, the boy looked up at him with eyes on the verge of fresh tears. "Y'know, this is the first time I've ever heard of anyone doin' what *she* wanted." Eric's voice broke. "My mother had to *die* to get her own way just once."

Quietly, nodding, Adam Baldwin closed the

library door behind him.

The housekeeper worked hard to get Eric and Peg ready for the fulfillment of their dreadful duty. She tied the sash on the girl's next-to-prettiest dress, then brushed her golden hair as they exchanged teary glances in the mirror. Peg's best dress was saved for the funeral, the following day.

As for Eric, Mildred had labored energetically to regenerate a pair of respectable shoes, to restore the slight hint of a shine. Clad in a sports jacket and recently outgrown slacks which had been bought for him long ago in Toledo, Eric would do. He suffered the woman's attention to his unruly shock of hair in silence.

Ready at last, meeting Grandfather in the foyer, they also found cousins Bernard and Sue waiting, similarly dressed in their finest. Each hugged the children, wordlessly, in turn. Grandfather shot his cuff, glanced at his expensive watch. "Shall we all go in my car?"

"I thought I might drive," Bernard said mildly. Looking up at the retired senator, he might have been a handsome, precocious child quietly questioning his father. "And we'll be glad to drive the kids, if that's what they prefer."

Immediately the grandchildren drifted to the cousin's side of the foyer. "Very well," Baldwin said simply, opening the door and getting a grip on his cane. "Perhaps you'd like to follow me. I was there earlier and know the way."

Banner & Carter's was an old but well maintained mortuary on the north side of Indianapolis. Filing in, they caught a faint scent of fresh paint; curious despite herself, Peg stared as they moved into an area that reminded her of a theatre lobby. The home did its level best to seem cheerful and utterly failed. There was the outer room with paintings on the walls and a dozen or more comfortable chairs ready for people who sought a break from the steady sadness of the quiet parlors reaching into infinity on either side. Peg saw a turquoise fountain, a steady stream of water pumping from the pale marble hand of a corpse-like cherub, and immediately loathed it. It made her want to go to the bathroom.

Eric, dazed, was almost wholly unaware of the paintings, chairs, fountain, and the tables bearing ashtrays and souvenir matches. He ignored the silent, suited man murmuring to him, ignored the stand supporting a register with lined spaces for people to write their names. With so little warning, few people would be bidding goodbye to Mama. Instead, his anguished eyes sought the place in which they'd put his mother. Grandfather, distinguished in the tailored suit in which he'd accepted the presidential nomination, stopped just inside Parlor D. Eric's questing gaze instantly leaped the length of the somber room and discovered the shining object which awaited them, a single floral arrangement beside it.

It was Bernard who put his arms around Eric, supporting him and preventing an indecorous bolt toward the coffin. Neither child had been inside a mortuary before and, when they moved forward and tentatively caressed the smooth surface of the casket, they said a single word in unison: Mama?

There was no answer. For the longest while, there'd been no answer to their cry.

Bernard, hanging back, surreptitiously watched his wife's uncle. He saw another old man drift toward the Senator with a sympathetic expression, hand outstretched. Baldwin took it, tears glistening in his eyes as he spoke. "I'm glad you're here to handle matters, Fred."

The undertaker's smile was brief, polite. "Well, Senator, that's what I'm here for. But I never thought I'd be of service to your daughter."

"Neither did I, Fred." Adam Baldwin's glance touched the watching Bernard, who closed his eyes as though praying.

"May I speak to you in private, Senator?"

They took two steps away, toward a door, turned their bodies slightly. Bernard watched, breathing so deeply that the fragrance from the flowers was overpowering. Partly covering his face with a small hand, he peeked between the fingers, trying to read their lips.

"I know you didn't request an autopsy, sir," said Fred, the undertaker, his tones discreet and all but inaudible. "Considering who you are, well, I've decided to let it go."

"Let *what* go?" Baldwin's voice was yet so powerful Bernard could hear what he said, despite the rasping whisper.

"Well, I thought of bringing it up but I didn't know if I should." Listening, reading the thin lips, Bernard found his heartbeat accelerating. "I don't doubt it was a vicious coronary that took her. I'm convinced of that." He hesitated. "But it took a while to kill her, Senator. I believe she tried to cry for help. And couldn't."

"Is that all?" The familiar coldness had returned to Baldwin's inflections. Bernard leaned his head closer.

"No, sir, it's not. Senator, it's—her face. The expression on it; the look in her eyes." Now Fred's chin dropped and it required all of Bernard's alertness to perceive the rest of it. "I think poor Mrs. Porter was simply terrified, Senator. She looked—well, she looked like she'd been absolutely scared to death."

Despite himself, Bernard gasped. He had to force himself to turn his whole head and body back to the casket, to his wife and the weeping children.

But not before he'd seen Senator Baldwin reach into his pocket and place something in his old friend's hand. Something that looked, at a glance, very much like money.

Later that night, when Mildred had coaxed Peg and Eric into going to bed, she came downstairs to find Bernard and Sue beckoning her to join them in the living room. Where her employer might be, Mildred didn't know; she wondered if he, too, had retired. The house seemed exceptionally quiet. She couldn't even hear the metallic, machine-like sounds from Lynn's room. Awkward, uncomfortable, she did as she was asked and slipped into a chair near the guests. She saw the look of shock on Sue's pretty face.

"I've just told my wife," began the little man, drumming his fingertips on the arm of the sofa, "what I heard at the funeral home. I think you're a decent person, Mrs. Manning, and you

must know. Elizabeth was frightened to death."
He paused, his gaze searching her features.
"I'm sure you know who, or what, did it."

Mildred didn't reply at first. Eventually, however, she nodded.

"Tonight will be our last night in this lunatic asylum, Mrs. Manning," Bernard said firmly. "Tomorrow we'll be taking Peg and Eric home with us. Where they belong."

Sue clutched his hand. But she continued to look at the other woman. "Which is to say, Mildred," she added, "right after we've visited the authorities. Now, then: will you try to stop us?"

For the first time in ages, Mildred realized that she was smiling. Genuinely. With relief. "I can't help you," she said softly. The smile widened. "But I won't stand in your way. I loved Mrs. Porter dearly."

Sue stood, went to the middle-aged woman, kissed her cheek. "Then it's almost over, at last," she said with relief, and glanced back at her husband.

Bernard didn't answer. He was peering across the room in the direction of the stairs, aware that perspiration was trickling into his collar. There was no way they could have been overheard, not as quietly as they'd spoken.

But distantly, he'd heard the noise of bedsprings squeaking, and a high-pitched voice muttering unfamiliar words with a fervor of fury that sounded utterly mad.

Fifteen

A full three and a half hours had passed since Adam Baldwin arrived home from the Banner & Carter mortuary, and he had the impression now that everyone else in the house was asleep. Under less stressful conditions, he might have been glad. He found it quiet, peaceful and soothing to work when he was the only one awake.

But for the life of him he couldn't remember the last time there hadn't been one other up, regardless of the hour of the night.

That was all right. He felt unbearably tired tonight, too much so to relax, too much so to seek sleeping oblivion, and too much so, certainly, to work. Instead, he'd divested himself of his tailored business suit, then carefully hung it in the closet, ready for poor Elizabeth's funeral the next day. Checking closely, he observed that the elbows of the jacket and one knee of the trousers looked somewhat shiny, close to threadbare. Self-reproachfully, the ex-Senator clucked his tongue. The sacrifices one made! He'd let so damned many things slide, on behalf of Lynn and their crusade, their quest for a safe, logical, well-ordered new world! When this was all over, he told himself, he'd buy a new suit to, well, "celebrate" was an inappropriate, even unfeeling word under the circumstances of his daughter's death.

But it wouldn't be when Lynn finally gave the word that everything was in place.

Donning his favorite mouse-colored dressing gown, Baldwin was aware that his pasty bare ankles protruded like stripped sticks and seemed rather foolish in his old fashioned paper slippers. He smiled in recollection. Before leaving the university experimental lab, years ago, and entering politics, he'd thoughtfully purloined a crammed corrugated box of the silly things, which still felt comfortable on his feet. The slap of the slippers upon the floor of his bedroom or private study gave him an enhanced impression of working as hard at science as he was at international politics. No, *universal* politics—because, if there really were living beings upon other planets, there was no reason he and Lynn could not seize control of them, as well.

Switching on the television set to catch a post-midnight news program, he went to his window and squinted into the darkness. It was streaked by heavily falling snow, the hardest and heaviest snow so far this winter. A man could easily be lost in such a storm. Baldwin sighed, stretched. He couldn't remember having been so completely weary since the days of his campaign for the American presidency. Then, however, he'd been constantly buoyed by a feeling of exuberancy, of standing on the very brink of a success he'd avidly pursued for his entire lifetime. Oh, there'd been plenty of opposition, especially before getting the nomination. But even those members of the party who had regarded him as dangerous, unfit for high office, had fallen into line during the actual campaign. Because their aspirations, too, had been at stake.

And the opposition of the other party, while vitriolic, unfair, and eventually successful in defeating him, had at least come from nominal adults—men whom he could destroy with blackmail or bribes—except for the disconcertingly vast number of them. Considering the awful things they'd said about him—that he had no use for Constitutional principles nor people themselves, that he saw other persons as statistical equations to be molded and manipulated, that he would probably initiate a nuclear war if he were elected—how else could a reasonable man with goals hope to achieve them? A leader *led*, but he led a people worthy of him and that number, Baldwin was fairly certain, did not exceed a tenth of the population. There were too many bodies cluttering the globe as it was; how much better it would be, for them, to die in useful service to a President Baldwin's goals than sucking on the public teat! Why, nobody— not even the self-serving members of his own party—had grasped for a minute how far he'd intended to take America from her silly national and ethnic origins, her time-worn traditions. As to the matter of what people euphemistically called "the Bomb," what kind of candidate for high office would he have been if he'd not been made ready, willing, and able to consider using any means—any means *whatsoever*—to accomplish his vital objectives?

Even then, in any case, he'd been inclined to regard nuclear energy as a chemistry set, as

Building Block A in the arsenal he'd planned to build for his nation against the world—and against the world was precisely where the United States stood, in Adam Baldwin's opinion! He couldn't say much for the majority of American politicians or scientists—the Constitution was outmoded, had to go; the atomic bomb was a joke-store lapel flower gadget compared to what he'd been ready to give his country. But they were head, shoulders, chest and fanny above the quasi-human illiterates peopling the rest of the world. One day, there might be a form of world government, true; but America would run it, right from the top!

Oh, there'd be such grand plans. And it had taken a trip halfway across the world to see what an egocentric dwarf named Verblin had blundered upon, to begin putting them in place. Only a Lynn could have guessed at such an unpredictable means to eventual victory!

Thinking about his youthful charge made the old man's thoughts return to the same unwise and troubling region they'd occupied since learning of his daughter's sudden death. Staring at the television screen, reading about the body count in Laos and the loss of life resulting from the latest Israel-PLO confrontation, he tried to turn his mind in other channels or, at least, to become drowsy enough for bed.

But finally he stood, with a sigh, double-knotted the belt of his dressing gown, left his room and limped down to the second story. There, it was dark with most of the lights in the house off, but he could have found his way with both eyes shut. It took him, however, several seconds before he could conquer the nervousness in his hands and produce the right key.

"Dear heaven," he said lightly, blinking against the brilliant flood of illumination and seeking the properly jovial tone, "don't you ever sleep?"

Lynn's eyes flicked in his direction from the bed. *Others use but one-third capacity of brain. I use more. Brain is Lynn so it is not exhausted as rapidly.* Pages turned in a steady whir.

Baldwin cleared his throat. He kept his distance, tried to look at Lynn only from a slight angle, not head-on. "There was something I wanted to ask you, Lynn." He paused but there was no reply. Lynn would never be a bear for conversation. "Do you remember when I told you about your mother?"

Of course. It was many years ago. I forget nothing.

"I, ah, did not mean your *natural* mother." Suddenly he didn't really want to ask any additional questions but there was no choice if he hoped to rest at all. "I referred to Mama. To my daughter, Elizabeth, who helped rear you."

I remember her too. The expression in the eyes beneath the beautiful lashes was scornful of such a ridiculous question. *Mama is scarcely a subject of ancient history.*

"This is going badly." The Senator spoke the words forming in his mind, instantly realizing he should never be so careless—not in this room. "What I was trying to ask you, Lynn, was if you—" Now Baldwin stopped, flustered. "Lynn. When I came to inform you that Mama had died . . . did you already know?"

Note that I am busy. Pushing back boundaries,

venturing into virgin territories. Progress report: Lynn can now read minds at distances amounting to miles. Good job? You must be proud! My telepathic command is presently at seventy-nine-point-three percent of reading/scanning parameters. Good job?

"That's wonderful improvement, certainly." Baldwin spoke almost roughly. "I must ask you, however, not to be so evasive." He took a step nearer. "You were taught to respond when I ask you a question."

My comprehensive knowledge/skill factor is within accessible range of Quantum Jump 12. I ask again: Are you proud of Lynn?

"Of course I am!" Baldwin stopped within a foot or two of the bed. He made himself move closer, keeping his conscious thought patterns as clear of negative subjective attitudes as possible. Revulsion now would not do. This close to Lynn, he was more susceptible to the entire range of disturbing qualities developed by his charge and, despite all efforts, he'd never fully accustomed himself to conversations that occurred, on Lynn's part, wholly in the mind. Always, it seemed an intrusion; sometimes, a perversion; and there was always the risk of pain at the rare times his pupil experienced passion. But he had to know the truth. "Hear my question, please: Did you know Mama was dead even before I told you?"

All is in control; tiptop shape. Use of biological terms warped by emotion is pointless; meaning is distorted. Lynn smiled coyly. *Today I read two books simultaneously for the second time. Incremental increase in average single-volume consumption period within four-point-one-*

sixteenth of acceptable ratio. You pleased. Proud?

"Damn it, Lynn!" Senator Baldwin's arm shot out; impulsively, the fingers sought to part the material draping the figure. "I *demand* to know!"

Stilettos of scarlet agony probed the pupils of his eyes. The blades extended, darted up into the brain, threatened to bisect it. Covering his pain with his hands, he tried falling forward. He was stopped by mental resistance. As if repaying him for attempting to tumble upon Lynn, the piercing of his brain and eyes swept outward. Cleaving through tissue and nerve-ends in the forehead, it gouged the old man's temples.

The creature that was Lynn remained motionless, except for a miniscule regretful sigh. *Lynn must stop problems before development. I am to bring peace, and order. You are finished with irrational behavior?*

"No, you goddamned brat, I am *not!*" Unable to see more than clouds of red pain, Baldwin made a superhuman effort. He threw up his clutching hands and grappled with the material he knew was hanging around Lynn, like curtains enclosing a stage. "I'll tear it down, I warn you!" he roared. *"Did you kill my daughter?"*

SEE! Lynn urged.

Instantly the old man's body was seized by nothing at all visible, spun in the air as if by robot hands detachedly manipulating something radioactive. Hung sideways, as though reclining on one side in bed, his face was positioned inches from a viewing screen. It came alive; his eyelids snapped open, bringing excruciating pain. When he strove to close them against the torment, he could not. With hot tears streaming down his cheeks, he received the answer to his persistent questioning.

Elizabeth Baldwin Porter was *alive* in the image, trying to rise from her bed. Her expression was one the father knew; he'd seen it often enough: an expression of deep, maternal concern. Her lips whispered two names—"Eric, Peg"—with a catch in her voice. Then, inexplicably, he saw her fall to her knees on the floor. Before her, in shadows near the door, was the handsome, tall man who was her husband.

The man is not present, Lynn declaimed. *Of course. All is product of woman's deepest fear. You know that well, I'm certain.*

Adam Baldwin tried to reply, to swear at the youthful monster. Trying again to close his eyes, he could not; and the tears from them were for a different reason. He'd hated the man on the screen before him, yes; he also realized that Porter was not actually present at all. But when Lynn, too, became an image that tortured his daughter, the old man knew he'd never hated anyone that much.

But what his daughter suffered because she believed she was seeing her worst fears become real was infinitely worse.

He struggled to get one word out—one word, before, in the telepathic tyrant's version of instant replay, he had to watch Elizabeth die. *"Please!"*

Then he was standing next to Lynn's bed again. The screen was dark, his hands were still raised above Lynn, and his terrible pain was gone—utterly gone, as if it had not happened to him. Blinking, bewildered, he had no idea which parts of the experience, if any, had been real. When he realized that he felt neither injured nor emotionally drained, he checked his body with his hands and understood with complete astonishment that he hadn't felt so *well* for twenty years!

The understanding filled him with sick horror. It wasn't only life and death which resided in the control of the incredible being lying in the bed before him; it was *health*, and *illness*—mentally as well as physically.

He had succeeded beyond his wildest dreams, because Lynn could devise or reshape reality at will, and a normal human being could not tell the difference.

I will do what I please because I shall soon contain all knowledge. Lynn is pleased by what is logical, what safeguards the project, what advances it. Those are the fine things you taught Lynn, Father. And all I have learned resubstantiates your primary paternal wisdom. Now, I have more to do this night and you must retire. Raising massive arms, the creature tilted rosy lips to the old man. *I shall keep you alive forever, Father. Because I love you. Kiss-kiss?*

With puckered lips, the old man leaned forward. He was crying again.

For a period of time which he marked in no way, the man who'd almost been President smoked and drank, trying at one and the same time to think everything through, and to think nothing at all.

Lynn had done this job particularly well, this healing-after-pain procedure. It was very in-

211

structive. Because it was impossible now even to feel the result of alcohol. Adam Baldwin rather imagined that he could drink every bottle of bourbon in Indiana and Kentucky without losing his sobriety for a second. Another time, long decades ago when the world was young, the Senator might have been grateful. Rarely a smoker, he'd finished the second pack of the day before going to his charge's room and, since returning to his own bedroom, he'd gone through most of a third—but there was no tendency to cough and his throat felt perfectly clear. "I could probably sing *Pagliacci*," he muttered, aloud, disgusted. Disgusted and worse, much worse.

Perhaps that would be the proper selection, all things considered. Only a clown, a ridiculous joker, would have thought he could go on endlessly controlling the most brilliant mind in the universe.

And going on endlessly, forever, was apparently what he'd be doing. Lynn was more than brilliant, gifted beyond belief, and devoted to their plans. Lynn had achieved the sophistication to play upon the unspoken longings of an old man. "I shall keep you alive forever," Lynn had pledged; and Lynn always kept his promises. Lynn believed in the practicality of truth; Lynn *loved* him.

Reflectively Adam Baldwin smashed his whisky bottle against the wall. Unhesitatingly, he picked up a sharp, brown slice. Without giving it another thought, he drew the sharp edge across the veins in his left wrist.

Not so much as a scratch, a line or crease, resulted.

He glanced disgustedly out his bedroom window. The snow was falling with a cruel heaviness full of intent and malice. He wondered what would happen should Lynn opt against snow. Or, for that matter, nighttime. Or summer; sunshine. When Lynn was ready to begin assuming total control, it would not be a halfway measure. Lynn was not an Alexander, a Napolean, a Stalin, a Hitler.

If Lynn meant to rule the world, he meant to rule everything.

The old man blinked his eyes; knuckled them. Strange. Suddenly he felt so sleepy. It came upon him with a peculiar immediacy and intensity. Quickly, before he might slump forward upon his face, he dropped his malacca cane and flopped upon his mattress. Distantly, he could hear somebody moving around the house, even though it wasn't quite morning yet. Who? He wondered idly. Who was getting up at this hour? The Senator yawned.

In his mind, mental fingers were soothing, relaxing. The old man smiled almost sensually. It was just fine—feeling *good* again; feeling *young*. That, certainly, should be regarded as a compensation; no question about it.

There was another. Lynn would never be able to leave that locked room. And it wasn't all bad, really, now that the old man thought about it— the fact that, after New Year's Eve, he would at least become the *second* most powerful person in the world.

Sixteen

The eyes in the motionless head protruding from the zippered container opened, staring and startled.

First Eric was asleep; then he was awake—with no sensation of having slept at all. There was, as well, no impression that most of the night had passed, since he felt bone-tired and chilly, acutely aware of how tensed his muscles were. Dull early morning sunlight worked apathetically at a bedroom window in his line of vision, surprising him. It had been dark out, when last he looked, and that seemed like no more than minutes ago.

Idly, without a feeling of threat, he wondered what had brought him to consciousness. Quite dimly he remembered hearing noises in the old house, as if others were stirring; but there remained such gray murkiness at the window that it was surely not morning yet. Who could possibly be up and around?

For moments Eric allowed no sign of his wakeful state to show, other than the eyes which rolled from one side to the other, as far as he could make them go. He didn't know why he did it, instead of arising; possibly his mind hadn't finished sleeping, and hoped to lure him back to the quiet world.

But when he tried closing his eyes, they

simply popped open again. It was rather like finding oneself born—possessed of a head full of information and memories, and no clear notion how they had gotten there. The odd sensation was exacerbated by the sleeping bag in which he'd spent the night, since he was lying on one side, that arm pinned, the other one trapped at the wrist in an interior fold of the contrivance. He had the vague idea, just for a moment, of having emerged only in part from his mother's body, then stopping—as if he'd had second thoughts.

And perhaps he should have had, Eric realized; but twelve years ago, not now. Because today, whether his unconscious mind were trying to conceal the drear fact from him or not, it was his mother herself who rested on the edge of infinity—the *outer* edge.

Sighing, Eric managed to wriggle up from the old sleeping bag, unzip it the rest of the way, and squirm to his feet. It didn't occur to him to look at his bed to see who was lying in it. Instead, he padded barefoot to the window where he squinted at a day that was struggling and wriggling the way he had. He saw so much heavy, thick snow on the ground that he thought temporarily of how perfect it would be for building a fort, or engaging in a fierce snowball battle.

But when he again remembered there were other things to do, he turned from the window, reminded of a time when he'd visited cousin Sue in the hospital. The corridors and rooms in the big building had looked impossibly sterile; dead. Today's draping of snow resembled the shrouded form of a patient who had died.

The being in Eric's bed sat up, instantly awake. For her, there was more the impression of urgency—of having to rush. Silently, Peg's gaze met Eric's. Just then, to both of them, there seemed nothing whatever to say.

Then she looked over the side of the bed, and smiled. He'd brought the sleeping bag closer to her, before dropping off. When she looked back at Eric there were tears in her eyes. "I'd rather make a snowman today," she said simply.

"Or go live in Siberia. Or have our tonsils out." Eric nodded, absently scratched himself. He reached unhurriedly for his pants, where he'd tossed them over the back of a chair. "At least it won't be as long as it was last night."

"Why not?"

"Cousin Bernard said that since there was no notice in the papers, there'll be almost nobody there but us. So we just go to the ole home a while and then . . ." He let his voice trail off, unwilling to complete his comment.

"Eric?" She got up, her gaze meeting his. "Why do they call it a 'home?' Nobody lives there."

He shrugged, slipped into his shirt. "Why do they call this place a home?"

Peg grinned. She felt good that Eric was getting all snotty again. Putting on a robe and slippers, she glanced at him as the thought occurred to her. "What's it mean to be cremated?"

"Oh, God," he moaned, buttoning up. Why did she ask him all the tough ones? He'd tried very hard not even to think about what they were going to do to Mama. He answered her question bluntly. "It means bein' burned up."

216

"Oh-h, Mama!" Peg cried, turning pale. "That's awful! I absolutely hate fire!"

"That's because it scares you so bad," he told her, heading for the bedroom door. He paused, his narrow boy's back to her. "Sis, she won't feel it. She's dead, and so she won't feel a thing. Besides, Mildred said she wanted it that way."

"How does anybody know it doesn't hurt?"

His tortured eyes looked back at her. "I dunno, Peg. I just don't know."

They'd gone to bed with every intention of arising early. Of getting the Porter children out of the house, and of telling the authorities everything they knew.

The first portion of their plans was accomplished.

Speaking very little, Bernard and Sue dressed in the semi-darkness of their guest room on the second floor. Because they could not see clearly and did not turn on a light, as well as for other reasons, they bumped into things and made as much noise as if it had been the middle of the afternoon. As Sue applied a pleasant Avon cologne, dabbing it behind her ears and on the backs of her wrists, she suddenly dropped the bottle.

She paid no attention to the crash, the broken pieces, or the strong fragrance rising from the floor. Without so much as looking down at the mess, she slipped into her dress and, as she had done so many other times, turned her back to her husband for the zipping-up.

Bernard did the best he could. He'd always enjoyed that little routine, indeed, most of the little routines linked to a working marriage.

217

This morning, however, his fingers were clumsy things apart from him and, when the zipper stuck, he exerted all his strength and forced it the rest of the way. The material of the frock tore vertically up Sue's pretty back, leaving exposed several inches of skin and a portion of her bra.

"Thanks, darling," she said, turning and kissing Bernard on the tip of the nose. The way she had a thousand times.

"My pleasure, madame," he returned, precisely as he had so often. His palm briefly caressed, then playfully slapped Sue's buttocks.

"Idiotic old lech," she reprimanded him, routinely, and immediately crossed the bedroom floor to where he had put their suitcases when they arrived.

Together, the young couple worked industriously at putting all their clothing into the luggage. They gave no care at all to a separation of the garments, in terms of "Hers" and "His." Instead, smiling vaguely at one another as if they shared a secret, they crammed clothes willy-nilly into the suitcases, literally stuffing in the final few things.

Finished, Bernard sat atop one suitcase, bouncing up and down until it was locked. Following his example, Sue did the same to the other, unmindful of the way the back of her dress gaped open or, when she carried the bag out into the hall, the way the gap widened until the sleeve was halfway down one arm.

"Ready?" Bernard asked.

Sue, one bra-clad breast completely revealed, gave him a private smile. "Ready!" she replied, and each of them giggled.

Passing quickly down the hallway toward the stairs, neither she nor her husband hesitated at the bedroom doors belonging to Peg and Eric Porter. Reaching the door leading to Lynn's quarters, however, there was the slightest of pauses as Bernard lifted his head, eyes and ears suddenly alert.

Then, satisfied, Bernard led the way downstairs, out to the kitchen, and through the door leading to the cellar. Following, Sue slipped in the dark halfway down, fell to one knee, then tumbled the rest of the way.

Well in advance, Bernard did not take notice. Without stopping, he trotted across the cellar, humming faintly to himself, and found what they had sought. Nodding with satisfaction, he returned to the foot of the stairs where he discovered Sue, conscious but collapsed in a heap, her lovely, ripped frock filthy, a gash in one knee copiously bleeding.

Briefly, her face was raised to Bernard's with an expression of bewilderment, of consternation, twisting her features. A perspicacious observer might have seen the baffled question in her eyes, even a stark terror gleaming from some shocked, subterranean depths.

Bernard reached down, locked his fingers in her hair, yanked her to her feet.

Sue smiled at him, if not happily then in a contented fashion that was docile, even bovine. When her husband started up the cellar steps, she limped after him gladly, trailing small red spots from her wounded knee.

Back in the kitchen, she even did her part. Almost immediately she found the small box they required, just inside a cabinet door, near the oven. Bernard, who had waited impatiently while she searched, gave her an adoring look. "You're so pretty this morning," he said.

Wide-eyed, retracing the familiar route, she looked down at her partly-naked breast, the frock that was now halfway torn from her body. The lower part of her left leg was crimson-streaked, her white shoe stained red. Her hair, of course, was a mess and dirt from the cellar steps and floor clung to her petite form from head to toe. "Why, Captain Rhett Butler, sir," she said in practiced, demure tones, "you *do* go on!"

Bernard chuckled, tucked the two-gallon can from the cellar under one arm, put out the other hand to chuck her chin. He winked and raised one corner of his mouth. "There'll be no locked doors in my house, Scarlett!" he declared.

Finished, they left the kitchen. Walking with nearly military erectness and haste, they passed through the old house without seeing the house-keeper, just venturing down the steps. Neither Bernard nor Sue heard her puzzled greeting or stopped until they'd opened the front door, marched out into the deep snow, and paraded around to the side of the house.

There, beneath the offspring's window, they did stop, nearly calf-deep in snow. The neighborhood street wound along in front of the house, a considerable distance down the lane. Here, at one side of the building, there was no one to see them.

The glance up, toward Lynn's bedroom, was made briefly, respectfully, by first the man, then the woman. In each was contained the unspoken question, "Are we doing this right?"

And, while the query had not been put to words, it was answered: Affirmatively.

Relieved, very nearly delighted, Bernard and Sue slid down the slope beside the house and sat, heavily, in the deep snow. Quickly the little man unscrewed the lid of the two-gallon can they'd found in the cellar.

Then he raised the can high in the air and, without pausing, poured its contents partly over his wife's head and partly over his own. A good husband, Bernard did his best to make it come out even.

The can had been full and heavy. Grunting with exertion, he shook out the last few drops, looked at his pert little wife, and smiled conspiratorially. She smiled back with matching pride but blinked when the gasoline got in her eyes. He'd done it exceedingly well; each of them knew that. They were drenched from head to snow-caked hips. It was an ancient annoint-ment, they realized, a ritual of eminence and significance. What a fine, proud thing to be able to do!

Sue laughing lightly, rubbed the slippery stuff into her bare breast, her arms, the wound on her knee. Despite himself, Bernard was slightly aroused. Sue, he saw, was flushed, happy.

"Love ya," he said huskily, extending his arms to hug her, to exchange a kiss.

"Love *you!*" she replied, partly routinely.

—And she opened the box she'd taken from the kitchen cabinet.

What happened next wasn't so easy to do. Gasoline is greasy and it was only good fortune that the box hadn't been soaked. *Someone* must be looking over them, Sue thought with a secret smile. She worked at it with mindless, furious concentration, spilling half the contents of the box into her lap and Bernard's. He watched her efforts with an affectionate but patronizing, husbandly gaze of tolerance.

"There!" she said, at last, their little conspiracy reaching fruition as Sue succeeded finally in striking a single kitchen match.

Hungry, lapping flames instantly consumed them.

Without so much as one agonized sound piercing the stillness of the late December morning, the last two Christmas ornaments in town burned brightly.

Only Mildred, rounding the corner of the house in time to see the rite completed, realized who or what was watching over the incinerated couple. Raising her eyes skyward, in revulsion or perhaps in prayer, she saw at the frosted pane of the offspring's room the shadow of a face as wide as a human chest, and a pair of eyes which belonged, properly, in the face of the first sensate creature to recommend human sacrifice.

Seventeen

By the time Eric and Peg had both washed and dressed in their best for the funeral of Elizabeth Baldwin Porter, there simply wasn't time left for breakfast—certainly not for the ultra-filling kind maternal Mildred served up to folks. The fact, however, disturbed her considerably more than it did the kids, neither of whom desired a morsel of food. But under Mildred's nose, as they stood quietly before the breakfast nook, each was obliged to consume a glass of milk and a slice of toast. "Get on the outside of that," Mildred commanded.

Before they turned at the sound of Grandfather Baldwin's slow, limping step upon the stairs, however, Peg peered curiously up at the housekeeper. "What's the matter this morning, Mildred?" she asked, concerned. Her toast had been scraped, as if the woman had left it in the toaster too long—something unheard of for Mildred. "I mean, other than Mama's funeral?"

"I think that's enough for sure, child," came the reply, less critically than the words suggested. "I worshipped your mother, y'know."

"But you aren't even dressed up," argued Eric, looking hard at her. "Aren't y'going with us?"

"No." A tight-lipped reply, the large head giving a cursory, definite shake. She'd nearly shouted it. "I think I'll be rememberin' my poor Elizabeth in my own fashion, if you don't object —and if the Senator don't." She paused, looking back at the few dishes she had to do and plunging her hands into the hot water. "I don't need to be makin' a fool of myself in public. And frankly, I ain't a hypocrite—and I don't care for his company this morning!"

The children were shocked by her openness about their grandfather.

"Maybe she'll knock old Lynn off while everybody's gone," Eric whispered as they strolled past the dining table toward the living room. He was rewarded at once by a Peg Special. But this time, the amiable giggle was all too brief. "Remember what Daddy used to say? 'She's got fire in her belly and it's burnt a couple of holes in her eyes!' "

Peg shook her head, pushed in front of him. "I don't remember anything Daddy said," she retorted, seeing a figure move back into the living room from the foyer. "You've got all the luck."

"Are you ready, children?" asked Grandfather. He gave them a sweeping glance which, for him, was relatively compassionate, sympathetic. Despite its tentative warmth, or thaw, Eric's curiosity was keyed up by his little sister's observation. He had the impression that their grandfather was rousing himself from some private reflections with difficulty. The old man, Eric felt, was exhausted, edgy, tentative and—it took Eric a moment to recognize the other attribute in the towering giant of a man— strangely fearful. "It isn't going to take long."

"But where are Sue and Bernard?"

demanded Peg, glancing about.

"I was hoping you wouldn't notice they were gone," said Grandfather, looking at them above the ever-present cane on which his white knuckled hands were locked. "Until later."

Eric laughed briefly. "We aren't a couple of infants." He hadn't realized yet that Mama's cousins weren't present.

"It seems they disliked me and the project on which Lynn and I have been assiduously laboring even more than either of you." The ex-Senator looked a last time at them, went into the foyer for his coat. "Which, since they, too, know nothing of its marvelous details, makes it another case of 'good riddance to bad rubbish!' " He fumbled in the closet, his hands trembling slightly. "In common with Mildred, they lack the fortitude for civilized burial services. They've gone back to Toledo and my hands are washed of them."

"They aren't bad rubbish!" Eric flared, snatching his own coat and gazing up at his grandfather. "They're the nicest folks I ever met. You just don't know them."

To the boy's amazement, his Grandfather spun on his heel to shout down at him. "You have my explanation, young Porter. And if you don't like it, be damned with you!" He put on his coat, glowering as he reached for his cane. "I should think attending your own mother's funeral would be enough misery for you without questing so boldly for more trouble!"

Bewildered, Eric and Peg followed after him as he limped across the lane leading to his Cadillac. They looked toward the distant hedge, bordering the lot, at the unused garage which had been built when the previous house was set well back from the street. Eric felt Peg's sympathetic gaze and turned to shrug.

He hadn't questioned Grandfather's word about the disappearance of Mama's cousins. Basically, he'd only defended their right to exist, as worthwhile human beings. The old man was getting so worn out from work and what had happened to Mama that he seemed to be verging upon senility.

Juggling uneasy thoughts as they drove toward Banner & Carter's, Eric gradually realized that he didn't believe Grandfather's explanation. Bernard and Sue had said nothing at all about deciding to go home to Toledo, and there was no way either of the cousins would leave without saying goodbye.

Eric saw that Peg was studying his expression, in the back seat of the aging Cadillac. A glance convinced him that she was asking herself the same questions.

So where had Bernard and Sue gone?

The services at the mortuary were mercifully brief, one of the few true statements made to the children for a long while. Since Mama hadn't belonged to an organized religion, Banner & Carter's had furnished one, in the person of a robust, athletic-looking man of the with-it generation, who drank beer, played football, and kept in touch with his fraternity. With a mane of deep chestnut hair swept back from his pink forehead, the Reverend Robert Eaton was easy for Eric to see in a different light: taking the snap from center in a game of touch, the long hair blowing romantically as he called upon Special Coaches for a completed pass.

When he'd described Mama in certain complimentary terms supplied him by Grandfather, words that emphasized her dedication to advancing humankind through science, the clergyman opened his Bible to a marker and gazed out at the mourners. Other than the immediately family, only a handful of people had come to pay their respects; and they, Eric assumed as he squirmed in his seat, had probably been notified by Mildred.

"Mrs. Porter's devoted friend, nurse, and housekeeper, Mrs. Manning, phoned me this morning with the information that this great lady had a favorite psalm." Now the clergyman was on familiar ground and, when he glanced toward the closed casket, his respectful concern seemed genuine for the first time. "It is Psalm 6, one of the many composed by David, a man who was both very much of this frail, tempest laden world and of the next."

Senator Adam Baldwin gave the minister a scalding, side-long glance which did not make the tears leave his eyes. Tears of ire at presumptuous Mildred; tears caused by the sudden, discomfiting perception that Elizabeth Porter had not seen the interior of a church since her childhood. Even her marriage to that misbegotten Porter was performed by a Justice of the Peace. She had truly believed in the Creator but, because her father, the Senator, had his scientific doubts, she'd kept her faith to herself. Now, Baldwin looked away, to compose himself. He recalled that Mildred's affection for the Psalms rivaled her addiction to numerology. Perhaps this was tolerable.

" 'O Lord,' " Reverend Eaton began in a some-what fulsome baritone, " 'Rebuke me not in thine anger, neither chasten me in thy hot displeasure.' "

The old man again looked up, freshly annoyed.

" 'Have mercy upon me, O Lord, for I am weak.' " continued the clergyman—and now the impudent fellow seemed to be staring directly at the Senator. Accusingly! " 'Return, O Lord, deliver my soul; oh, save me for Thy mercies' sake.' "

The massive hands in Baldwin's lap became vise-like, squeezing fists as his anger mounted. This was not the proper selection for a daughter of a scientist, one who was herself a person of science! Why, it made Elizabeth sound not only weak-willed and helpless, but wrong-headed.

Turning from the man of cloth, the old man's gaze fell upon a man who had entered the funeral parlor, as quiet and unobtrusive as a mouse. Wearing a heavy coat pulled up at the collar, the lower part of his face obscured by it, the stranger reminded Senator Baldwin of somebody. He stared hard, trying to identify the man; but he was scarcely visible as he took a chair at the rear of the parlor.

" 'I am weary with my groanings; all the night make I my bed to swim,' " intoned Reverend Eaton. " 'I water my couch with my tears.' How sad and how alone this lamb of God must have felt," he editorialized, chocolate eyes ranging over the grieving children's pale faces but always returning to the Senator's flushed face. " 'Mine eye is consumed because of grief; it waxeth old because of all mine enemies.' "

All mine enemies? For an instant, the old man nearly spoke up. What had been wrong with the more familiar, less personal 23rd Psalm? And was Mildred trying to tell him something by citing this Psalm?

" 'Depart from me, all ye workers of iniquity; for the Lord hath heard the voice of my weeping.' " Again the minister stopped, alert to almost strangled sounds issuing from the twelve year old son. Eaton hoped passionately that Eric would neither throw up nor pass out. He hadn't heard the boy whisper to his sister: "The Lord heard her, but so did Lynn." And when Eric again faced front, the clergyman finished. " 'The Lord hath heard my supplication; the Lord will receive my prayer.' Amen."

Then the minister, his gaze rising from the holy text, saw what the distinguished, former presidential candidate was doing, and gasped.

Adam Baldwin was on his feet without waiting for permission, gaping openly at the closed and sealed casket with tears of anguish running down his seamed cheeks. Eaton tentatively put out a hand, withdrew it but sustained his readiness to catch the tall, old bird if he fainted. Never before had he seen a father more upset by his child's loss, Eaton believed. The man had become a pitiable wreck. And with his bald old bean tilted back, the neck extended like that of a wrinkled turkey buzzard, the tortured old features reminded the clergyman of a man flinching from a battery of irresistible blows.

Peg could not see her grandfather's expression. "Is that it?" she demanded, aware that the man who looked like a football player had closed his Bible and stepped to one side. She looked up at Baldwin, hoarsely whispering, "Is now when they . . . burn her?"

The old man did not respond. He didn't even seem to hear the child.

By himself, lurching, pawing with the tip of his cane like a man gone blind, the Senator was going to the coffin and resting a wide, trembling palm upon the lid. Nearby, alert, the clergyman remained attentive. Once before he had seen a man embarrass all the proper mourners by ripping open the casket and hurling himself on the body of his wife. It had utterly ruined Eaton's beautiful service, and become the subject of an irate sermon.

Adam Baldwin, however, was restraining himself. Looking across eternity's container to a spot near the ceiling, whether prayerfully or simply to get his thoughts in order, he was speaking aloud. "One of the most essential parts of it all was yours, remains yours, Elizabeth," he said clearly. "You came to see things differently, but I forgive you. And if what we have done proves to be evil, one day, remember always that I share your burden of sin—but I am not solely responsible for it. I shall not let you haunt me!"

As if making sure his point was clear, he looked sharply down at the gleaming surface of the coffin with an expression that was a mixture of outrage and fierce determination. Then he turned, leaned upon his malacca cane, and left his only child to her final, earthly fate.

Shadows slunk through the streets of Central Eastwood. Black on white, like photographic negatives, they crept up craggy fences of snow and tumbled closer to the quiet houses. Outside, the temperature was scalpel-cold; none of the tenants who did not have to leave their houses did so. If the Reverend Robert Eaton had glanced from a window at the nocturnal shadows making chessboard sections in the deep snow, he might have claimed it was the time for families to nestle together, that it was God's way of urging them to discuss their differences, to go bed early, and see the wintry darkness as a sort of cozy comforter.

At the Baldwin house, most of the lights were on; everyone, everything, was awake.

The two children were in Eric Porter's room, still stunned by the suddenness of their mother's death and rapid funeral. Peg was trying not to think about the fire licking at Mama's poor body, burning until her arms and legs fell away. The picture would not leave her mind and, when she tried to tell Eric about it, he refused to talk. His guilty, apprehensive eyes told the girl, however, that his thoughts were not unlike her own.

Mildred Manning, having taken a meal to Lynn, decided to check up on the kids before preparing dinner. Walking up the hallway to Eric's room, she thought of herself as a living receptacle of hideous secrets, all of them brought to the surface of her mind by what had befallen poor Mrs. Porter. Sick at heart, herself grieving, she was miserably confused about the choices facing her—and the growing doubt that any of them might really be an option, at all.

Seeing the expression on Eric's face and Peg's did not cheer her up.

What the boy had to say to her, in his customarily impetuous and direct manner, made matters much worse. "I want to know where Bernard and Sue went!"

The housekeeper, frozen in the doorway with Lynn's tray dangling from one large hand, looked at Peg and saw that she, too, was in a questioning mood. "You know what your grandfather told you," she said slowly. "That they went home to Toledo."

"Bullshit!" Eric snapped.

"You watch your sassy mouth, young man!"

"They wouldn't ever have left us like that, to go to that ugly funeral home without them!" Peg exclaimed, hands on her hips in the center of the floor. "You know that, Mildred—you heard some of the stuff we were talkin' about!"

"And they promised to take us with them whenever they left," Eric persisted. "And to tell the cops what's been happening in this dump!"

"Eric, please stop!" Mildred leaned back, peered nervously around the door frame and down the hallway from which she'd come. "Just stop this nonsense immediately, the both of you!"

Peg jabbed her index finger at the silver tray dangling from the big woman's hand. "What did ole Lynn do, Mildred," she demanded. "Eat them?"

Abruptly the housekeeper stepped all the way into the bedroom. Slamming the door shut, she leaned protectively against it, eyes wide. "For the love of God, kids, don't you remember what happened to you the last time you went wild this way, and started makin' accusations?" Her dark brows were lifted in anxiety almost to her hairline. "You have to stop this, at once!"

"Why?" Eric jumped up, advanced upon her. "Grandfather stopped by Lynn's room and hasn't come out. He can't hear us."

Immediately, Mildred crossed herself. She reached for Eric's hand, tried to hold it and get his attention. "Maybe he can't hear you talking —but Lynn can." She spoke in a loud, persuasive whisper, looking back again as if she expected to see the offspring appear at the door. "And I have to tell you both—I don't think Lynn will allow any more threats, even from you two."

"Lynn's down the hall," Peg argued, her voice a tiny screech. She gestured with her arms to indicate distance. "And what does that mean, 'even from us two?'"

"It means I believe the Senator made Lynn understand that you're only kids, just as Lynn is, basically young. That all of you are—related," She ignored the face Eric made and peered earnestly at them. "But things have changed. Your grandfather is beginning to realize how old he is and that he's human, like everybody. Young 'uns, I flat out don't believe Lynn will put up with any more of your shenanigans. I don't know for sure what would happen. But if you get in the way, I'm plain afraid Lynn may kill you next time."

For some moments the great figure across the room from Senator Baldwin had listened intently, hearing nothing that was being said in the room. There'd been no warning at all, for the old man; he'd heard nothing except the computer paraphernalia surrounding the bed, clucking like hens, and he'd been trying to clarify the philosophical point for Lynn: the moral rationale for not taking human life.

Then the offspring was gone, deep into the ponderous head yet probing with unseen antennae for a conversation Adam Baldwin could not hear. A conversation in another room in the old two story house.

It was a pleasant surprise when Lynn, turning back to him, explained the nature of the distant discourse—but only until the Senator recognized the implications of what Lynn overheard.

"They are simply children, locked in idle chatter," the old man soothed the sprawling offspring. It was, in a way, like looking over at a great Newfoundland or English sheepdog, except that it wasn't allowed to get on the furniture. "Let them be, Lynn. There's no harm they can do us, or the project."

Lynn did not face him. Instead, the creature's gaze was through the smoky window. Baldwin, looking where Lynn was looking, saw little except shadows behind the pane. But that did not mean the offspring could not see much better. They can speak, even communicate in their fashion. *Je suis pret. I am ready. To act.*

"A little compassion, a soupcon of moral mercy," Baldwin pleaded. The room was freezing cold, as always, but he was starting to perspire heavily. "It is the mark of most great men, just as I was telling you before you overheard them."

When the improbable head swiveled on the elephantine neck, it was as if nothing but eyes had formed in a planet of flesh. *Lynn read philosophy books Father brought. No two great men share same convictions.*

234

The scornful note wasn't wasted on the Senator. "They quibble, yes, Lynn, they argue over petty details. But the essence of what they believe tends to be the same! Think about that, child, the fact that hundreds of fine minds from all over the world, from all points of history, agree that human life partakes of the sacred and must be spared except for the greatest causes."

Our cause is great, the other replied. Whether Lynn noticed the sweat, or how he'd wanted to withdraw his comment the moment it was uttered, Baldwin did not know. Lynn's gaze was turned in the direction of the children's bedrooms. *My philosophy is simple. Je maintendrai le droit. Agreed?*

"We shall both maintain the right, Lynn!" The Senator arose, limped forward a few feet. He was careful not to touch the bed, this time, or that which partly concealed it. "They are merely children. *Humanum est errare,* Lynn— to err is human."

You instructed Lynn at earliest age. My role in project isn't precisely human. A flicker of a sharp glance, enough to cause minor pain at this range. *Your Lynn, Father. Fons et origo.* A shrug.

"But *mas vale saber que haber,* child!" Baldwin argued, wondering when his own command of languages would falter. He did not dare show weakness, or intellectual lack.

Wisdom is already mine. A smirk appeared, and became a strangely-youthful, taunting grin. *Now it is time for wealth. For power.* The grin widened; it seemed, now, a grotesque, cruelly teasing smile. *It is what you taught as well, my*

Father. Force majeure—*a greater force!* The smile vanished. The face was grim, assured. *None has a greater force than mine.*

The old man leaned closer, pleading. "Please do not do to them what you did to the cousins. They are only a girl and a boy. Remember what I tried to teach you about justice? Eh? Do you remember that?"

It did not seem, for an instant, that Lynn would reply. Already the creature's unsurpassed concentration was becoming telepathically focused upon the room down the hall. Justice? Lynn's mental communication with Adam Baldwin was surprisingly small, even vague. But again, the sense of malice, of irony, even of inhuman humor, was present. *There is a saying, Father: Jus summum saepe summa est malitia. The extreme of justice often proves to be the extreme of menace.*

"If I begged you, Lynn, fell to my knees and prayed to you," whispered the old man, "would that persuade you not to harm my grandchildren?" There was no reply, although Baldwin waited longer for a response than he ever had before. "Very well." With a sigh that became a tremor, he retreated slowly from the bedside, aware of the discomfort in his bad leg. Apparently Lynn's telepathic nostrums required periodic reinforcement. He stopped, his back to the bedded thing. "Then you will make it nothing more than a warning, Lynn? A message, *in terrorem*—a last warning not to interfere?"

Once more, no reply came. Head bowed, the old man shuffled toward the creature's door, his mind a jumble of conflicting emotions.

Then, with his hand upon the knob, the thought-implant burned into his brain. Like most remarks of Lynn's, when the mood came upon the offspring, it was a foreign phrase and obliged Adam Baldwin to look it up or figure it out: *Jacta alea est*, Lynn said.

The Senator looked back, stared for a moment at the being from another time. Lynn, clearly, was no longer in the room—not in any sense that made sense.

Then he figured out the phrase, embarrassed that he'd forgotten. Especially when the words were so commonplace, so familiar, so terrible.

Jacta alea est. The die is cast.

The Senator shuddered, and escaped from the room in quest of his remaining bourbon.

"I'm scared, Eric. Scared half to death."

He looked over at Peg, who was sitting cross-legged on his bed, her short back flat against the wall and her arms folded. She wasn't trembling much but it was enough for him to know the spooky truth of his situation: at long last, he was on his own.

They'd discussed what Mildred told them, known she would not warn them or frighten them without sound reason, and agreed that it meant a second meeting with the monstrosity down the hall.

And what ole Peg was telling him was that he shouldn't count on her. Not this time. Because the world and the Baldwins in it had taken away all the courage and stubbornness of a child whose age wasn't yet in double figures.

Such facts as those scared Eric more than much that had happened. Problems of the real world—even dreadful things, if they could in any way be called "ordinary"—tended to leave Peg the stronger of the pair and rendered him an emotionally drained, bewildered little boy glad for female support.

Yet in the ongoing surrealism that had become their way of life since returning to the Baldwin house to live, it was Peg who began to squirm and cry, Eric who somehow managed to find the courage and initiative to act.

Since he hadn't sat down for almost an hour, already keyed up even before Mildred cautioned them against candor and made him restlessly angry, he went to Peg, leaned slightly, and kissed her on the forehead. It was close to a paternal gesture. Then he reached down to pull the covers all the way up to his sister's pert chin, and paused, gathering his youthful thoughts.

"I don't think it'll be as bad as last time if you do what I say, Sis," he told her. Somewhere deep in his own thoughts, because the right hemisphere of his mind was activated by the need for inventive measures, a galaxy of brave TV detectives prowled the streets in trench-coats and unmarked sedans. "Really, I think I can handle this okay. But you got to promise to keep your head under the blanket when anything bad happens! All the time, no matter what you hear or what y'think you hear. Got me?"

"I haven't lost my hearing," she said, a lofty echo of the sister he knew.

Eric punched her lightly in the arm and rejoiced in her faint giggle. "I mean, you stay under the covers—no matter what happens!"

"But what good will that do?" she asked him.

"You'll find out." He hesitated as he started to turn from her. "But you should be okay."

"What about you?"

He saw the worry in her small-featured face and made his own expression severely parental. "You must promise me, dammit! Say it!"

Peg blinked several times. She couldn't take her eyes from this already-adored brother who had grown up overnight. "Okay." She felt better then about their nocturnal prospects. She rolled her eyes back, solemnly. "I hereby swear with make-believe blood from your veins and mine that I will obey the rules of the Eric Porter Defense Club, so help me God."

"Great." He gave her a suspicious look and turned from her.

Crossing the bedroom, he looked around and finally found the basically untouched Holy Bible and, several drawers into his dresser, an almost completely untouched cross. Where the latter had come from, he wasn't sure. It had always just been around, like his stuff. Gripping the Bible and the holy ornament in tight fists, Eric went to his closet and settled himself on the floor in front of it.

Here, Sir Eric Porter, the Earl of Robinhood, would remain both awake and alert—one hundred percent ready for combat with the dragons from the north country. He pressed his lips together in a grim line, to keep from yawning.

Somehow, however, Eric's next thought was a realization that he was . . . *waking up*.

His head snapped back, anxious about what he might have allowed to happen by dozing off, and blinked to clear his vision.

It didn't work. Because the room was filled with an oozing kind of red, diffused light. Hazy, crimson, it hung in the air like drifting fingers and slender, swimming arms. His swift glance to the bed found Peg still in it; in fact, he was just in time to see her startled face before her head disappeared, dutifully, beneath the covers.

"Hell," the boy whispered, not swearing. "It looks like Hell."

His bedroom windows were gone. So were his bookshelves, his desk. All that remained were Peg, he, the bed—and the strange red illumination.

And at the moment he spoke the word "Hell," curtains of flame sprang up where his windows had been. Tensing, afraid of total conflagration, he started to rise.

But he realized that this fire was very different from any he'd seen before. Devoid of ameliorating yellows and oranges, the fully-red flames began to break into pieces, and the pieces began to *assume shape*. Forms large, forms small; morsels of living fire like the tips of burning torches in a parade to the monster's castle, giving off a distant, low-pitched chuckle as they moved deeper into the room.

Steeling himself, Eric watched, and prayed he would not be seen in the scarlet mist.

All the fire converged, shot together until a trio of stunted beings took form. Chittering, giggling things, they stood two and a half or possibly three feet in hunched height, the skulls comprising one-third of the mass. Each head was alike, absurdly sloped as if the brainpan had been caved in by a great blow. Hairless, featuring pointed ears and the shocking absence of a human nose, the dwarves possessed mouths which were no more than slits—slits which parted, allowing an asthmatic breathing when they moved, revealing rows of blunted square teeth glowing white as ivory in the diffusion of red luminosity.

Eric yearned to look away but couldn't. They were hideous. They had no brows above the rock-hard, hating orbs which gaped at him now with an appearance of hungry discovery. Despite their limited size, they were clearly adult, old as the recesses of the planet itself are old, and unseen. *Never-born but always-was*, the phrase came to Eric's mind.

And they scuttled toward him, then, in tiny bursts of violent motion. like rolling dust clouds or tumbleweeds with limbs. Pasty hands dragged the floor. The naked legs were partly assisted in locomotion yet so abbreviated that their progress was prolonged, even indefinite. He felt they might move more swiftly, but chose this pace because they'd tasted the fear emanating from him, and found it good.

At that moment, one dwarf put out his hand and its entire shape changed instantly, dropping upon Eric's knee. The boy gasped in disgust, in loathing. Already the other two forms were also altering and attacking—spidery creatures thrice the size of a tarantula, thirty-three times the amount of repugnance and terror. Eric, trying to move, felt immobilized on the floor and experienced the sensation of countless legs climbing on him.

When he felt one of them work its way beneath his pants leg and then dart toward his undershorts, he thrust himself erect, knowing their purpose: each ugly spider-form meant to crawl over his privates, and he knew somehow that if he so much as touched them, there, they would fly into a billion crawly pieces of living black matter, and literally drive him insane.

As the Holy Book in the boy's hand passed his line of vision, Eric remembered his plan of action and, with the effort of will of his lifetime, he sank back upon his haunches and opened the Bible.

Immediately the crawling, tickling threat stopped, vanished. Gasping, Eric shut his eyes, opened them.

And clenched his teeth to keep from crying out. Because the terrifying face before him was *familiar*. It was basically human, the hair a black of deep voids in space, the eyes so mesmeric their gaze seared his soul. Inches from his own face, the gaping mouth showed fangs of bile-yellow, and the vampire dipped toward Eric's naked throat.

This time, he did scream—but the sound rushed back at him, as though striking a barrier. Above him, the great cloak raised toward the ceiling and Eric felt his eyes trapped and held by a tear-shaped crimson medallion lying against the shirt's field of pure white. Almost sensously, caressingly, a clawed hand was seen from the corner of Eric's petrified eyes, ready to tug him forward, to his fate.

"The Bible!" cried Peg's voice; but he did not dare turn. Instead, he thrust the Book before the vampire's maniacal, pale face—and saw it take a backward step! The creature snarled like a crazed hound. With Eric's other hand, he lifted the cross, eagerly, snapped out his arm and pressed the holy artifact directly against the flesh of the Undead.

The effect was that of cauterization. Taking the cross's shape, a hole was burned and torn into the vampire's white skin and, shrieking in pain and mortal terror, the being became a bat! Gulping, repulsed, Eric saw that one wing was broken and it could not rise an adequate height from the floor. Jumping up, Eric stepped down, hard, felt the crunching of bone—and squashed the vampire-bat beneath his foot.

Viscous yellow threads, moist and adhesive, clung to the sole of his shoe.

And the SOUND began.

He had not even noticed how quiet, how still it was, in the bedroom. The vampire's approach had been stealthy, soundless.

But now the world was filled with nerve-rending, ear-battering noise.

There was no time to think, none to rationalize. Barely time enough to cover his ears, pull into himself, try to weather it.

It: every tirade of tympany, every clapping cacophony of thunder breaking and vehicles crashing, was detonated in the small bedroom. The nerve-shattering sound whirled on the threshold of his ears, passed through his protecting palms, pierced his consciousness with the mad and soul-plundering lunacy of all the rock and roll groups in the world.

Eric fell back to his knees, dazed. Uncountable collisions, pyramiding explosions of devastating neutron bombs, inhuman screams and obscene shouts soaring up from Hell itself. I can't take this, Eric thought, almost as if he were sending a thought-wire across an unguessed distance; Much more and I'll die.

Silence. Quietude, as if cued, summoned, ordained.

The abandonment of noise—the kind that pinches one into a corner of the living spirit and reminds the most courageous person that he came from a world unknown and is heading back toward it; informs the stout heart of a human being that he does not, in the final analysis of all, have anything to rely upon but his own undaunted sureness of a God-given right to exist. Stripped, thus, of the brave tools with which the lowliest of beings can find the means for defense, rendered infantile and utterly vulnerable, Eric held his breath for the next attack.

And inhaled it with the knowledge that he had smelled the foulest putrescence either on or within the planet. Because, glancing down, Eric found Things with no name nestling against his calf and hip. Things with the dripping shape of bowel droppings, each sentient stench a gut-wrenching turd from which arose an odor so overpowering that, almost fainting, the boy could barely wriggle two inches away from them. Because they liked him, they wanted him, they yearned to cuddle against his crotch and wrap their turgid brown extremities around his flinching, bare ankles.

Then, with no preparation, each Thing-with-no-name cracked open; and into the reeking air emerged the offspring of turds in a hideous parody of birth . . . prickling plants colored a sickly blending of green and yellow, with puckered red lips that sucked the foul air and made mewling noises, one of which was Eric's name.

The center of the bedroom floor was gone!

Huge, flapping folds like scraps of skin scalpeled back for surgery shuddered in the air around the great gashing wound of apparent Nothingness, causing it to gape hypnotically, and beckon the boy.

The tunnel of Hell, thought Eric; or perhaps, he wondered wildly, the thought had merely been placed there.

But it was genuine, real—he'd gave sworn to that! Fluffy smoke drifted up out of the black hole, palpable on the tongue, a taste of human flesh, charring. Yet as Eric stared, in horrid fascination, all the frightening things he'd seen in his room and those he had not—a mouldering, loafing mummy with gray bandages peeling away; a flying circus of pterodactyl-like birds with the faces of human beings, and vast wings clattering like the passing of a locomotive—were sucked into the gaping hole, the bottomless Pit.

And the acrid smoke was congealing, transmogrifying, coming together in a tower of geysering ash that made the boy think of detonated nuclear weapons he'd seen on television. Now the remnant of sound, supernatural and natural, was also absorbed by the obscenely-gashing hole in the floor like some perverse fallatio, promising such passion forbidden that the great, torn skin-folds would surely close upon a venturing, venturesome youth like the avaricious lips of a monstrous fly-trap.

GO to it!

He thought, just for a moment, it was Peg calling to him; but he knew it was not, without looking; he knew that the thought was cutting through his wits like shrapnel, but whether from the room down the hall or the yawning pit to perdition, Eric could not tell. Revulsed, shaking with fear, wanting to flee anywhere at all but certain the bedroom door would be locked, Eric Porter turned from the Satanic vision and buried his head in his shaking hands.

"Eric, dear," the voice said—not from his mind, he was sure of that—"do help me up . . ."

He screamed at the top of his lungs. The shape-shifting smoke was gone.

—Two, white, human hands were reaching up from the hole, waving to him.

Never knowing why, Eric wheeled toward the Pit, knelt, and very nearly went in. But the arms appeared, then, resting upon the lip of the great hole. Smooth, pale, almost hairless, feminine arms.

Arms that went around his neck, clasped, and pulled.

When he thought he was lost, would plunge into nothingness and fall forever toward another universe of cosmic evil, the head veered above the consuming blackness, and a face turned toward him.

Eric, sounding inane noises, reeled away. Toppled as by the swing of an axe, he fell against the closet door without knowing it, incapable of moving his gaze in any other direction. How he saw her in profile, dazzled: the intelligent expression, the fine features, the flood of chestnut-brown hair tumbling back from a widow's peak, the wide, high forehead, the incredibly sensitive and beautiful eyes.

Mama. Mama wearing a gown Eric recalled with love, one Peg had helped her pick out. Mama, still profiled, lovely, living. Oh, it hurt him to stand by and see her struggle, watch her work so hard to climb from the hole. It disturbed him to see how unladylike she was, forced to throw out one, long leg upon the bedroom floor before she could, finally, shove herself into the world with her terrified, half-maddened son.

Brushing at her gown, straightening, she looked back at him from the visible eye; and in it, Eric saw with an internal rush he'd never known before, there was all the open adoration, acceptance, and love for which he had yearned all his life.

"You two are my own, true children," said Mama, tenderly, turning to look at Eric.

The other side of her face was—depending upon where he looked—disfigured, or nonexistent; unfinished. A mixture of twisted, raw flesh where the eye should be; patches of colorless and paper-like plainness where a nostril went and where the other side of her pretty mouth belonged. The arm on that side was partly rotted away, and, of what remained, Eric discovered with choking revulsion that Mama was missing her thumb and ring finger, and another finger turned to nothing but knuckled, white bone.

It was culminating now, for Eric, within Eric; it started to reach a peak of terror, and while he remained silent, his mind seemed full of mad, gibbering dreads and needs, exaggerated prejudices or dislikes, and severed dreams and favorites. He sensed himself losing control, felt a portion of his mind slowly beginning to turn, to revolve like some dangerous ride at an amusement park. Incapable of motion, he had no choice but to see his maimed and corrupted Mama drawing nearer, limping the way Grandfather limped because of her hideous leg—most of the flesh still clinging, but scarred, shredded and serrated by the mindless flames of her cremation. Closer now, her awful limb displayed wounds like bloody mouths, sticky stuff oozing from them and dripping down toward the still neatly turned ankle.

"I want you with me," she called with the voice of wintry wind howling in a deep woods. "I want both my children with me!"

Mindless, caring only for escape, Eric plunged into the closet, scrabbling madly into the depths among swinging hangers and garments that slipped, and sloshed, as if they, too, might come to life.

Glancing back solely because he had to, Eric did not see Mama for a moment.

And then, horrified, saw that she had changed direction.

Limping badly now, she was headed toward Peg beneath the covers. The ruined hand was raised, multi-daggerish; she dragged the burnt stump of a leg, trailing things on the floor. Clearly, she meant to tug the blankets down, to seize Peg and . . .

"I said that I want my children with me." Her scorched fingertips clutched at the edges of the covers. And then, without turning her body, she looked at Eric, the half-destroyed face revolving sickeningly upon her neck and all pretense of maternal care gone from her violent blue eyes—eyed which showed an unbearable torment which could only be expiated by hauling others with her, to the indescribable depths of agony found in Hell. Incredibly, she smiled at the boy with the good side of her mouth and, with the twisted flesh of the other, managed a ghoulish wink. "I want you with me—in my father's true kingdom!"

"Not Peg!" Eric cried. He darted out from the closet, shaking uncontrollably. "I'll go, but not Peg!"

Flecks of lunacy twinkled like stars in her eyes and spittle drooled from the corners of her corrupted mouth. Her lips, grinning, were the reddest things Eric had seen and, when she held out her arms to him, in longing, he understood why.

Mama had rarely worn lipstick in her life. What inflamed her mouth now was the caked crusting of blood.

His mind collapsed. He wasn't, for a moment, there at all.

But in the midst of his teetering sanity Eric also had blinked, and, in that scant second, he'd needed to refocus. And, in refocussing, he had seen . . .

Nothing at all.

" 'The Lord is my shepherd; I shall not want.' " He couldn't have read the words then, not for anything; he could scarcely see. Yet he did see, clearly, the defiled image of his mother walking toward him. He clutched the Bible, raised it aloft. " 'Yea, though I walk through the valley of the shadow of death, I shall fear no evil.' " He was crying now, sobbing; huge tears rolled down his cheeks, merging with the profusion of terror-created sweat. The familiar words of the Psalm didn't want to come; they felt obstructed, impeded. " 'For thou art with me . . .' "

"Sweet little son," taunted the monstrous Mama.

She was naked now. Between the ruined face and the maimed leg were her high, full, youthful breasts. He gaped, understanding nothing; he looked down at the diamond of chestnut-brown, up again at the Cyclops navel, all but disappearing as she sucked in her breath and her beautiful bosom rose. Her hands, cupped, went to them; she was inches away, no longer disfigured, a Mama before there was an Eric, a Peg, a Lynn.

"And I shall dwell in the house of the Lord *forever!*' " Eric screamed.

Searing light, blinding luminosity pearled by specks of every color in the spectrum, caused Eric unbelievable pain. In a flash like lightning he saw Mama vanish, here one instant and gone the next—but the brilliant light returned, piercing the boy's optical nerves and lodging in the heart of his brain. Running, half-crouched, Eric tried to get away from it, but it wouldn't stop, not even when he closed his eyes. With them squeezed shut, he knew, bouncing off the wall, alternately weeping and keening, the lids could never part again, that they must be cemented forever in his mortal blood.

But the realization came to him that he'd made the creature like Mama leave without touching Peg, without seizing him!

What this was, then, was a child's tantrum!

Lynn was furious because he, Eric Porter, was still sane, still alive, because all Lynn could give him now was the illusion of pain . . . because Lynn had LOST!

Once, aloud, meaning it, Eric laughed.

. . . And found himself sitting in the open closet door of a boy's ordinary bedroom.

The agony of the light, even the pain, were gone. Over there, the dresser, his desk, the bookshelves, all his other great good stuff. The way it had always been.

And Peg, peeping from beneath the covers, aware only of sounds that had disturbed her. "Have you quit runnin' around?" she asked, looking like her old curious self.

"I get it, Lynn!" Eric yelled, jumping to his feet and going on jumping. Amazed and delighted, relieved and roaring, he could not adequately express his feeling of exaltation. "I see how you do it! You can't put anything in anybody's mind that wasn't already there, somewhere! And you can't hold it there if I don't believe it is!" Laughing, throwing shadow punches at will, Eric shouted at his unseen adversary. "You won't ever scare me that way again, you ole stupid bastard—you dumb robot! You ain't gonna . . ."

Eric rose into the air. Gawking, astonished, immobilized, he looked wildly about him—and then, with no further warning, he felt himself being raised to the ceiling—

And plummeted to the floor.

Boy! The word summoned him; he was dragged, moaning with pain, to a seated position. *I have not finished with you, boy. This is only the start!* Eric's body began shaking, and

251

Peg screamed. He was shaken the way a rag-doll can be manhandled, his head snapping dangerously back and forth, all four limbs spasming. *When Lynn is ready . . . you die.* Released, he fell again, rolled, struck his head on his study desk. *When you don't expect it, boy, Lynn will kill you!*

It was, then, over. Bruised, terrified, Eric was assisted to his feet by a gentle Peg. Leaning on her, he made it to the bed, sat on the edge of it.

"Maybe you can kill me and maybe you can't," he said, biting his lip. Quite directly, his gaze was toward the enigmatic room down the hallway. "But this time, Lynn, I won—and you know it! What's more, you'll have to go on knowing it for as long as you live!"

The little sister caught him when he fainted and, smiling proudly at Eric, shook her fist against an otherwise empty room.

Part Four

Out of his blood they fashioned mankind;
Imposed on it the service, let free the gods . . .
It was a work beyond comprehension!
                    —Mesopotamian texts of ancient Sumer

In a city without watchdogs, the fox is the overseer.
                    —Ancient Sumerian proverb

Eighteen

By the time they'd been up the next morning for only a matter of minutes, both Eric and Peg knew any victory the boy might have had over Lynn was a question of luck. The combination of their extreme youth, the loss of their only allies, and the opposition of both Grandfather Baldwin and Lynn was just too much.

Talking quietly in a midmorning walk which Peg insisted her brother take to shake off some of his aches and pains, Eric managed to make something clear to her. Everybody knew that *change* was unavoidable. Even children understood it, every time they outgrew a pair of shoes or a blouse. The sudden death of Mama had underscored their awareness of how life constantly changed, set it in italics and screamed it from a banner headline.

Change alone, even one as personally tragic as theirs, they were prepared to cope with.

But what was happening to them, Eric insisted, taking his time because he was in no hurry to return to the house, was much more difficult than that. Whatever their grandparent was doing, whatever the goals he had established for the mysterious offspring he called Lynn, it was as if the forces of the past had also ganged up on him and on Peg.

"It's like livin' in a haunted house," he explained, struggling to make himself clear. "Not that wonderful world in the future Grandfather keeps yammering about. No matter what he says, or wants us to believe, it isn't neato stuff like in comic books about the years ahead, or in movies like *Alien* or *Blade Runner*. It's more like dead things, crap from the past, was after us—like in *Amityville Horror*, maybe. Terrible old stuff added to change." He shook his head, threw the snowball he'd been working between his gloved hands. "We can't handle it, sis. We really can't."

She shuffled onto their street, chin lowered, as reluctant as Eric to return to the Baldwin house. "You really do think you're so smart," she called back over her shoulder.

Eric grinned, lobbed another, lightly-packed snowball at her thin back. He knew Peg thought so too.

Over the next few days, as both the month of December and the year began to wind down, the children sought normality. Resuming their customary ways, the pair spent a great deal of time in front of the TV in one generally-unused corner of the huge front room. Peg liked what she called "channel flipflop," swiftly clicking from one station to the next, impulsively choosing whatever caught her eye. Since Eric liked the special football fare of the season and preferred checking out *TV Guide* or the Dick Shull column on television in the *News*, there were times when they quarreled.

But there were also times when, distorting the picture of the screen, extraordinary sounds from upstairs ruined the image—turned it, on

256

occasion, into the most wildly-maniacal patterns either of them had ever seen.

Otherwise, as New Year's Eve loomed—not the favorite holiday of pre-teens—the period was uneventful. So much so, in fact, that Eric became occasionally fretful, even fault-finding and querulous. Peg thought if she had to hear "There's Nothin' to Do" one more time, she might go as crazy as Lynn had apparently wanted them to. Sometimes, always after asking Mildred's permission, Peg phoned acquaintances to talk about the holidays and to pretend that they were close friends. Neither child was permitted out of the house enough to have formed intimate friendships, and, when she had no stories to relate about her wondrous Christmas experiences, she tended to hang up quickly and sigh like an old lady.

Less than physically tired, more than emotionally sapped, Peg and Eric could sleep only by fits and starts. Each was always surprised, upon awakening, to realize he or she had not dreamed at all. The nightmares of the creature dwelling on the second floor with them were gone—but gone too were the dizzy, silly, informative dreams of healthy childhood.

There were brief, sporadic comments, oblique as the psychology governing the Baldwin house, ventured by each child. "You look lousy" was a frequent charge of the blonde little girl; and "Don't worry about gettin' more nightmares. I think Lynn just wants me, now," from the skinny boy. He meant, as a rule, to reassure her, cheer her up; he couldn't understand why it bothered her so much that he might begin having hideous nightmares once more.

In the meanwhile, Senator Adam Baldwin's appearances downstairs became fewer and fewer by December thirty-first. That, at least, brought a measure of joy to the children's vacation. Skipping breakfast completely, the old man sometimes ate the later meals in his study on the third floor, or in the offspring's locked room. According to what Mildred said, whenever she'd taken up so many trays of food that she was tired enough to talk, the Senator and Lynn were almost finished. It wouldn't be long until they were "ready to get started"; although what that meant, precisely, was still a puzzle to Eric and his sister.

And enigmas, baffling questions for which there were no accessible answers, continued to proliferate. After Mama's death, little was ever said of her again. But since law demanded that a public notice of all deaths be published—a fact he gleaned, listening to the housekeeper—Eric searched both the Indianapolis *Star* and the *News*.

And, reading what he found, was further astonished.

Because, while he and "Margaret Ann" were listed among the survivors, there was no reference whatever to Lynn, or to the fact that Mama was, or had been, the legal wife of Raymond Porter.

Then, too, it was Peg who went through everything Mama owned before allowing Mildred to take it away for Goodwill or the Salvation Army, and found a scrap of paper tucked in the pages of a Bible—in Mama's handwriting.

Just the existence of a Bible belonging to the

late Elizabeth Baldwin Porter surprised both the girl and the boy; but the uncredited quotation Mama had scrawled left them shuddering: "There was never a time when I did not exist, nor you, nor any of these kings. Nor is there any future in which we shall cease to be . . . I am the sire of the world, and this world's mother and grandsire: I am He who awards to each the fruit of his actions; I have all things clean, I am OM, I am *absolute knowledge.*"

Mama had underlined the final two words. But whether she meant for the quotation to represent her, or the creature she had once attempted to rear, Peg and Eric could not detect.

But they were also unaware, returning home from another walk during mid afternoon of New Year's Eve, that everything they had wanted to know would soon be told and showed to them, as well as other things normal people did not care to learn . . .

Stomping snow from their boots, animated by the brisk, biting weather and by their conversation, the children chattered and chuckled as they passed through the foyer. To Eric's delight, a high school freshman who'd been an acquaintance when both of them attended grade school, had phoned earlier to suggest a miracle—a basketball game between John Marshall High School and Broad Ripple High. After that, the older boy proposed, Eric would spend the night and "talk about all the cute little foxes at Marshall." Ecstatic over the opportunity to get out of the house overnight, Eric froze as they entered the living room.

Both he and Peg saw him at once. Their tall,

powerful grandfather sat in the large easy chair, his good leg sprawled in relief before him and the bad leg so long and so bony that the bent knee seemed to reach the ceiling. His smooth, bald head picked up prisms of light from the dining room at his back, and Eric noticed with a start that the old man looked healthier, more youthful, than he had in some time.

It was Peg who saw the way Grandfather's cane leaned against the chair instead of lying between his legs—a sure sign that he'd been there for quite awhile, waiting.

"Come here immediately, children." His chill gaze trickled over their faces. "Come over to me —*now.*"

"I haven't don't anything!" Eric protested, instantly wary. He glanced down. "Neither has Peg."

"Why, I know that!" exclaimed the retired senator. Abruptly, he laughed and leaned forward, his brows looking darker as a portion of his huge head moved into shadow. "There's nothing to fear. Children, this is a time for celebration!"

They edged forward, carefully; Peg caught a whiff of bourbon on the old man's breath and mixed feminine disapproval with her anxiety. "W-what are we gonna celebrate, Grandfather?"

His arms shot out, snatching her to him. Incredibly, all he had in mind was bestowing a noisy kiss on her forehead. He stretched farther, caught Eric's wrist, beamed upon the two youngsters. "A New Year's Eve which marks the beginning of a new era," he intoned, eyes shining with fervor, "for all mankind . . ."

"You're done?" asked the boy, incredulous. The soft tendrils of hope popped into view. There were times when he'd believed the mysterious "project" would never be completed. "It's over?"

"It's over," Grandfather whispered, "and it's just starting. Lynn announced readiness to indicate Phase I. For my part, children, I wish to express our appreciation for your efforts and to . . . explain."

Little Peg, always able to forgive and ever ready for adult attention, settled at the old man's feet with a contented flourish of skirts. Eric, drawing up a chair, scarcely could control his joy. Not only did it look as if they might be free, again, to live a normal life, but Grandfather was actually going to tell them what had been going on!

"Our entire project has, of course, been under wraps—by necessity." Gathering his thoughts but still jovial, Adam Baldwin settled back in his chair with the air of a paterfamilias telling his grandchildren a simple story. "It wasn't prudent to purchase the many books we required for Lynn's complete education and detailed information since I remain rather well-known. Curiosity, within the corporate structure of the larger bookstore chains, might have proved more damaging than would be the case at a single library. Hence, we enlisted your cooperation."

"Poor Ms. Earhart got curious anyway," Peg said wistfully.

Grandfather paused, thinking. "But your current youthful librarian is more typical of the people today who do not wish to become 'involved.' All she knows is that you have a bright relative, probably crippled, for whom you sweet children run frequent errands. A relative who, she surely presumes, is trying to graduate school by virtue of home study."

"At Sunday School, once," Eric said thoughtfully, "they said that people who have to hide what they do are probably up to no good."

"Are we raising a moral absolutist, then?" Grandfather laughed. "Secrecy is just a bad word for privacy, young Mr. Porter. There was privacy at Los Alamos, indeed, in everything involved with the development of the first atom bomb, wasn't there?"

"Is it a bomb you and Lynn are making?" asked Peg.

"Of course not!" One arm was extended to hug her. "In point of fact, it is my contention—and Lynn agrees—that what we are doing will eliminate the threat of nuclear holocaust forever! What do you say to that?"

"Well, it sounds cool," Eric replied with caution.

"Good, good!" The uncanny eyes gleamed. "And what would you say to a little gift, to put things right for you—a gift that is an example of what your brilliant kinsman can achieve?" Grandfather saw their dubious expressions, and raised a long arm above the chair. "Come Mildred! Bring it in!"

The children stared. Slowly, deliberately, the housekeeper obeyed her cue and, moving past the great organ, came toward them—with something *living* in her arms.

"Soon, my grandchildren," Grandfather said

in low, stately tones, "I shall take you upstairs, down the corridor to the room that has been so puzzling to you, unlock it, and let you express your thanks to Lynn, in person." Nearer to Mildred, he caught a glimpse of the object in her sturdy arms. It wriggled, and he smiled. "There, in Lynn's quarters, you will learn everything." His eyes narrowed. "But allow me to prepare you, somewhat, immediately."

Cursorily, in words as simple and concise as possible, the former senator and scientific prize winner told Eric and Peg Porter of the trip he'd taken to Iraq, "the birthplace of all civilization in a land once called Sumer." Omitting reference to the mad genius who had summoned him there and actually made the discovery, Adam Baldwin discussed Vela X, and how he'd brought the newborn offspring home, "saving its precious existence. My daughter Elizabeth began raising the baby, an infant with the genes of an ancient and uncivilized world Man has forgotten." But alas, "certain physical attributes" of the child "overwhelmed Elizabeth's shrewd scientific judgment."

Eric, fascinated, leaned forward in his chair.

"But before Lynn showed the telepathic skills you have both encountered, your Mama and I tried to learn what had gone wrong with Lynn. I'll explain that, as well, when we go upstairs." The weathered face took on an expression of awe. "Instantly, however, I saw that much had gone amazingly *right* with Lynn, too. For that young genius, blessed by the racial memories of a world which understood virtually nothing about scientific principle, inherited its tendency to see life from the *unconscious mind*

—or more exactly, from the brain's creative right hemisphere." Now the old man's face was flushed with pride. "Immediately, I realized that if I fully utilized that portion of the brain, and combined its unique originality with the objective practicality of the mind's left hemisphere—my offspring would find little beyond reach."

"Lynn didn't know anything about our times —nothin' about our history," Eric said, nodding and trying to understand, "so that's why you figured there was nobody better to *judge* what happens to us?"

"Precisely!" Grandfather was overjoyed. "You follow me admirably. Who else would be more objective about modern man than a being created before our time?" He clapped his hands together. "And with Lynn's freshness of view, all that immense latent ability to devise new realities beyond our wildest dreams, there was a positively incredible hunger for information which I can describe only as God-granted! Why, without much prompting from me, Lynn started consuming data, facts, theories of every possible variety. Devouring books containing entire subjects and disciplines, each and every aspect concerning the whole body of man's organized knowledge—and always I furnished the guidance, pointed the direction, filling in the blanks and gaps as we went; seeing with dazzlingly direct clarity exactly where our civilizations have failed! Perceiving perfectly what must be done now to establish genuine order, logic, and peace in the contemporaneous world which is simultaneously Lynn's prison—and toy!"

"But Grandfather," began Peg, gently, "why did you keep Lynn in one room all the time?"

The old man, stopped short, blinked several times. By the time they had his reply, Eric felt it was obvious that the answer was, at once, truthful and merely a partial explanation. "It was my professional judgment that it was mandatory for Lynn to maintain the crystal-clear *purity*, the detached and uninfluenced viewpoint, of the past. Of ancestors who have been dust for thousands of years, but who were Lynn's brothers, uncles, grandparents." Still flustered, he gestured to Mildred Manning. "Show what our Lynn has wrought for them."

Mildred uncurled her arms, letting the creature jump into Peg's. Eric, at her side, whispered, "A kitten!" But Peg still saw the world from mind-left and, unbelievingly, held up the cat and gaped at it with astonished eyes: "It's my Krazy!" she pronounced.

The boy craned his neck, touched the yellow fur. "It *is*," he gasped, and turned back to the former senator. "Grandfather," he cried, breathlessly, "where did Lynn find him? I mean, it looks . . . just like Krazy!"

"That," he replied, "is because it is." Grandfather saw the tiny creature striking at Eric with his paw, heard the miniature growl it was making deep in its throat. "Do you begin to have a greater appreciation for your relatives?"

"I'll call it Krazy Junior," Peg squealed, delightedly hugging the animal. "I just love . . ."

Suddenly, showing its sharp little fangs, the cat clawed the girl's forearm, twisted free, and landed neatly on all four feet. Swiftly, silently, it sped into the foyer, toward the front door.

And Peg and Eric, simultaneously, felt a wintry breeze that told them they had left the door ajar.

With their coats flapping behind them, the children rushed after the replacement pet, Peg calling its new name in worried, high pitched tones.

Adam Baldwin, chuckling, watched them go and then felt eyes upon him. Accusing eyes. He looked up.

"Lynn did it, right?" Mildred's arms were folded across her ample bosom but her voice was a wisp of wondering awe and revulsion. "Lynn made it, didn't he, Senator? Made a living cat—from the broken-hearted memories of that innocent little girl!"

"The operative words are 'Lynn,' my off-spring's incomparable genius, and 'living,' my dear." The old man stood, with so little difficulty that he remembered his cane only after he was standing and towering above the raw-boned woman. "What do you think we've been doing all this time, Mildred? The little animal is real, genuine; any post-mortem would discover precisely what the coroner expected."

"You're playing *God*," she said, holding her ground even as her dark brows raised in horror. "You—and that *thing!*"

"You're in danger of hyperventilating, my dear Mrs. Manning." Gazing coldly at her, he brushed past, headed for the stairs. His limp was scarcely noticeable. "And behaving ridiculously for one who has been with us from the outset."

"Only to protect my poor husband's reputation!" she exclaimed.

He wheeled, angry but in control. "And that has been achieved, too, has it not?" Senator Baldwin took a breath, steadied his nerves. "You are a prime example of why the world requires Lynn's brilliance, and what the two of us will produce—you and your convenient morality, your untimely emotionalism! Step by step, Mildred, Lynn has absorbed every crucial fact that the functioning of this world since Vela X initiated the inception of what we laughingly call 'civilization.' And Lynn has learned the secrets in the emotional hearts of every person controlling the destiny of this planet— which is *exactly* the full extent of emotion I have allowed Lynn to experience." He hesitated, clapping his cane on the floor. "Lynn finds it *laughable.*"

"But what about your grandchildren?" the housekeeper demanded, moving toward the distinguished giant. Her fury was spent but her maternal anxieties lived on. "Think of what you did to your own daughter, you and that monstrosity—and think of what it will do to Eric and Peg!"

"Think of what it will do *for* them." He gave her a frigid smile. "Together, Lynn and I can give them everything they want from life—a chance to be lieutenants in our scientific army of the future, even majors, colonels, generals!" His frosty eyes bore into hers. "Or, if they wish it, we can give them all there is to fear. It's the choice *everyone* will be making, Mildred, every man or woman alive. And it's the choice *you* will also have to make!"

Nineteen

The snow-shrouded acres of the old Baldwin property, front and back, were stretched before the small girl and boy like a sleeping, white beast. Supine and hushed yet strangely muscled and tensed, it was as if the hump-like clots of snow might be shaken off at any unexpected in-stand—as if the dangerous animal might stand, showing transparent eyes and teeth. Even now, it called to them ventriloquistically, in the faintly derisive voices of uncountable whining, hooting winds; these came howling in from a distance, as ready to materialize as desert mirages, as death-dealing as placid pools of poison forming beneath swaying, oasis trees.

"Krazy Jun-yur, where are you?" Peg's anxious voice echoed as she called forlornly, over and over. It was swallowed swiftly, as though devoured by something they could not see. Now, evening shadows were beginning to crawl, making zebra patterns upon the ridged back of the lumbering land-beast. "Krazy?" she called plaintively.

Eric jammed his knotted fists deeper into his trouser pockets, cold and eager to give up when-ever Peg gave him the word. He stood where darkness was being born and felt digested by it. Shuddering, he saw from beneath his hooded eyes the way additional, fresh snow kept mindlessly coming, coursing downward at a maddening, insane angle against a pale horizon gone recently askew. His shoulders were starting to tremble with the cold. They were leaving behind footprints in a sloping rise which gave every indication that it would fall-through, at any moment.

Peg had come out upon the Baldwin grounds in a clear mood of desperate single-mindedness, pulling Eric along like the sled on an invisible rope. She was busily circling the whole house, oblivious to the depth of wet snow, determined to look for her replacement pet everywhere. He followed, his keen sense of duty sorely tested by the cold and a rising sense of impending danger.

"Can't we give up now?" he asked Peg, panting.

"No!" she snapped, doggedly inching toward the side of the house. "I've been without old Krazy for too long now."

"Hey, *cat!*" Eric shouted, getting disgusted, looking for an out. "Come out, you damn ole dumb thing!"

Peg gave him a shove that was only partly good-humored. "His name is Krazy Junior," she corrected the boy. "Don't you know anything?"

"I know my—hold on!" He stopped, pointing a gloved finger. His eyes were staring. "Hey, that's him!"

Peg, who hadn't spotted the cat yet, caught her brother's arm. "Don't move fast," she pleaded. "You'll scare him away again." She looked around. "Where is he?"

"Up there," Eric replied. He indicated the ledge just beyond a room on the second story.

The yellow creature sat on its haunches as if frozen, looking down with frosty eyes. Something was clutched between its front paws, and twitched.

"Oh, gross," Eric muttered. "It's caught a bird."

Peg squinted up. "And the bird's not dead. Not yet."

"Krazy Junior sure needs training." He shot her a pointed, thoughtful look, colder now than he'd been.

"Yes." She nodded agreement. "And love," she added maternally. "Come down, Krazy Junior. Come down this instant!"

The replacement cat raised the faintly-fluttering bird to its mouth without removing its steady gaze from the human girl. Beside her, Eric made a face. "Never saw a cat that young catch birds before, or eat them."

Something plummeted toward the ground, something tiny. Most of it was wing, and two tiny feet; but Krazy Junior, regarding them, was chewing.

"Maybe that just means he's smart," Peg said beneath her breath, paling.

"Or maybe it means somethin' else." Eric snatched up a handful of snow and, peering back up at the yellow creature, worked the snow between his hands. He looked at his sister from the corner of his eye. "Peg, your new kitten . . . there's no warmth to him."

"He felt warm to me," she replied loyally.

Eric shook his head. "That's not what I mean. He's cold all over, and inside—like this snow. Peg, he ain't real!"

She was just in time to see her brother's thoughtless actions. Aiming like a pitcher with fine control and a respectable fastball, he hurled the completed snowball with all his strength, hoping to knock the kitten from its lofty perch.

What happened next seemed to occur in slow motion. Krazy Junior took three, unhurried, unsurpassingly nimble jumps along the second-story ledge and paused to view the action. Almost simultaneously, the snowball smashed against the window—and both children realized whose room it was. There was a veritable explosion of snow and ice, and when it was over, brother and sister gaped in disbelieving horror at the foot-long, fine crack which Eric's impulsive invention had left in the windowpane.

Distantly, they heard Grandfather Baldwin's angry shout.

Far more clearly, much more alarmingly, they saw an impossibly wide face press in fury against the cracked pane; and they were saved only by the offspring's surprise.

"Run for it!" Eric cried, taking off in the direction of the back of the lot.

But he needn't have bothered. Peg was already running, so fast that she momentarily moved ahead of him.

It was worse than trying to run in sand, wind whipping at their frightened faces as they saw the unused garage take shape near the back of the Baldwin property. Now, even little Krazy Junior was forgotten. For children, it was the worst kind of fear they shared—because they had endangered a vital, adult priority. Without intending to do it, they had infringed upon a magical realm so distinctly not for children that Eric and Peg each accepted, automatically, the feeling common to primitive people who fear they've angered the god in a volcano, and have actually *earned* a punishment for their trespass. The worst kind of punishment any simple folk can be given: An experience of the god-like unknown.

The boy, gasping, reached the garage a step ahead of Peg who leaned against it, breathing fast. While they'd earned high level punishment, they were also duty bound to hide from it if they could. "Shit, there's a new padlock on the door!" Eric growled. "We can't get inside."

Panting more from terror than her run, Peg looked about wildly. "There's got to be a window!"

"Right!" He leaped forward, kicking snow. The first window he came upon was firmly locked. Regardless of his tugging and pulling, it would not raise.

"Try this one!" Peg said, from around the corner of the old garage.

Pounding to her side, he hefted mightily, reddening. "Aw, it's locked too."

She heard his note of despair. "Try it again," she urged.

He did—and with a screech, the window rose several inches.

Together, the two of them worked at it. After half a foot, it stuck. Together, they worked harder; and without warning, it shot upward and they fell against the side of the garage, exhausted and giggling.

A moment later he gave Peg a cupped hand to step in and boosted her into the garage. While he was sweating heavily, night was wearing on and he knew the temperature was plunging toward zero; they *had* to have shelter. Eric rested his waist against the sill of the window, tumbled after Peg, and fell to the garage floor, grunting with pain and satisfaction.

Then, getting his feet beneath him, the boy shoved himself erect and peered into the darkness. "Peg, where are you?"

"Here. You'll get used to the dark in a second." She was whispering, as if others might be somewhere near them. "It's all cobwebby in here."

"Well, what'd you expect?" he asked with a trace of his old superiority. "Nobody uses this place anymore."

"Hey, here's the light switch!" she exulted, her apprehension ebbing.

"Don't bother," Eric said. "It won't . . ."

The garage was flooded with light when she flicked the switch. "It's logical," she said, grinning at him. Her face was smudged with dirt but she appeared happy. "There was that new lock on the door."

"Well," he replied, seeing an automobile against the wall of the old two-car structure, "we can't leave the light on. Grandfather and Lynn ain't blind!"

"That car looks sort of familiar," Peg said, following Eric to its side. "Doesn't it?"

"Yeah, I guess so." He rapped on the hood, then the fender, with a sense of masculine discovery. "If it was Dad's, it'll be ours sometime." Experimentally, he kicked a tire. "Still in good shape, too."

Peg peeked into the nearest car window. It was slightly frosted but Eric, joining her, moped at it with the elbow of his coat. "What's that?" she asked.

Eric ignored her. He was busy playing grown-guy-shopping-at-the-used-car-lot. "Interior is still in super condition."

She tugged his sleeve, pointing. "I wonder what *that* is."

"What?" he asked without much interest. She was pointing toward the backseat.

"Well, a blanket coverin' somethin'," Peg replied. "It looks lumpy. D'you suppose it's something Daddy left for us to find, someday?"

"Heck, I don't even think it's our father's car." Looking disappointed, he tried the rear door, cursed when he found it locked. "It's too late a model; it came out since Daddy went away."

"Well, then," Peg asked, observing his actions with some pique, "whose car is it?"

Again he remained silent. He was looking at a window that had been left open a scant few inches. Moving awkwardly and making a face because of the pain, Eric inserted his arm, wiggled his fingers down, and touched the vertical lock device.

"What are you doing?" she inquired nervously, holding her coat tightly across her thin chest.

"Crap, Margaret," he grumbled, stretching, "you wanted to see what was in the car, didn't you?"

Suddenly the vertical lock released with a small, sharp snap.

Delighted, Eric withdrew his arm and glanced at her with pride. Then, quite simply, he opened the door of the car and reached out for the backseat, slowly pulling the blanket down.

Peg's view was blocked by her brother's back

274

but she felt him tense from head to foot. She also heard him begin making a funny little sound and saw him thrashing out with his arms, as if trying to regain his balance—or to chase something away.

Then he came backing out of the car—fast—and Peg jumped to get out of his path.

She cried loud, startled and then badly frightened. Because Eric was rolling on the floor of the garage, simply to get away from whatever he'd seen.

"Eric!" Her mouth dropped open. Eric, throwing an arm across his eyes, sounding now as if he might be choking, was somersaulting and bouncing to his feet—panting into her face, his eyes round with terror. Peg turned her head.

"Don't look inside!" he warned her.

Peg looked.

For a moment she thought that what she was seeing was something carved from black stone, or the trunk of a tree struck by lightning.

Then she thought she was looking at a creature with a mammoth head and four dead, staring eyes—until she realized that the bodies of cousins Bernard and Sue had been fused together by fire, their heads a single, charred skull. Part of the little man's face was unburnt, amiably expressionless beneath one patch of unharmed black hair. But most of the skin on Sue's petite face was gone so that splotches of white bone exaggerated the general, charcoal motif and, with the solitary unblemished eye staring at her, it was as if Peg looked down at a white dye that had come up "one."

Either her brother or some voice of sanity in her own mind told Peg to retreat, to spin away and run; but she felt hypnotized by the autumn-stick fingers raised in macabre greeting—three sets of blackened stubs, the fourth apparently burned off somewhere and left on the earth to rot. It was impossible to tell where the cousins' clothing left off and the cinder slag flesh began. Immobilized, she stared until one of the arms suddenly, sickeningly dropped to the floorboard of the car, the fingers grazing her calf before two of them—perhaps three—broke off, and rolled to the floor of the garage.

It was the brainless touch upon her leg that freed her, enabled Peg to turn away from the car with her mouth opened in a scream which never sounded. It was trapped, as she and Eric were trapped, smothered by inescapable horror.

But she could move, even before Eric did, and literally threw herself at the garage window. Wincing, scratched, she clambered through it with Eric close behind and tumbled to the night snow lying like ash upon the Baldwin lot. He yanked her to her feet, calling her name from the other side of the galaxy, and the two of them ran and slid across the treacherous, icy earth, going where all children go when they are hopelessly scared out of their wits.

Home . . .

Twenty

With their breaths stolen from them by the winter wind which carved their cheeks and an internal terror fixing their eyes in scarcely-sentient staring, Eric and Peg sped madly around the side of the huge Baldwin house. Propelled by a known horror toward one that remained largely unknown, they were primarily conscious only of the common, human need to tell—to communicate the horrid things they'd witnessed in the old garage, possibly from an unconscious feeling that, by recounting their trial, it would somehow be lessened, even explained away.

And because, being children, they knew full well that by telling, it would all become the responsibility of the adults to Do Something.

The ambivalent housekeeper had watched them through a window as far as she was able, more concerned than she might have confessed. Now, seeing the pair of them return at a frantic dead run, she had the door held wide as they burst into the house, wild-eyed and gasping.

"It was just awful, Mildred!" panted the girl, glancing at her brother but catching at the woman's sleeve. "Dreadful!"

"Terrible, bad—the garage—a car," Eric rattled, nodding his agreement. Automatically, he and his sister followed the housekeeper through the foyer. Head starting to throb, at once half-frozen and dripping perspiration, Eric had the idea that he was speaking unintelligibly but could do nothing about it other than press close behind the grown person, and get it all said. "All *burned*, Mildred—Sue, Bernard, out there—their *faces!*

She turned firmly to them in the living room, palms lifted in an effort to quiet them. She was alternately nodding and shaking her head against this child's yarn they were trying valorously to relate. By now, her own nerves were at the breaking point and, while a part of her mind realized Peg and Eric were telling the truth, she absolutely could not deal with more than one danger at a time.

"I know you're upset but you both must listen to me—now!" She spoke commandingly, louder than they. If they did not shut up, she'd fly into a million tiny scraps. "You made a really awful mistake, hitting Lynn's window with that snowball. Kids, I don't know if even I can protect you now! You might have damaged Lynn!"

"But all that doesn't matter now!" Eric insisted, dazed and freshly frightened but incapable of undervaluing the charred corpses they uncovered. Ignoring the deaths of likeable Bernard and Sue might mean the final loosening of his tortured sanity. "Mildred, everything's changed, a lot worse than crackin' some ole window!" The woman's apparent lack of understanding sobered him, slowed him down so that he could be clear. "Out back—in the garage—our cousins are dead! Killed, maybe!"

"Well, I knew they were dead." Shocked, scantly aware of what she'd said, Mildred stared incredulously at the twelve year old. "They killed themselves just the way my poor husband did, years back. But the Senator informed me he'd had their bodies removed, taken off to a decent funeral parlor!"

"You knew about it?" Peg asked, heartsick.

"I did, yes," Mildred mumbled, folding her large hands in her apron, "but . . ."

"But everything is being handled," called a voice, entering the room.

"Grandfather!" exclaimed Eric, turning and growing pale. "I didn't mean to hit Lynn's window!"

Peg half-ran, half skipped to the old man, whose glance lingered a moment upon Eric's alarmed face, then lowered benignly to his granddaughter. "It's so terrible!" she gasped, looking up into his dignified, somber expression. "Sue and Bernard didn't go back to Toledo—they're out back, burned up!"

Grandfather smiled, patted her blonde head. "That is a shame, isn't it? Don't be afraid, Margaret; I'll dispose of the problem. But thank you for informing me."

Eric stared in growing understanding. Grandfather already knew! He saw the old man raising his hand, gesturing for the children to follow him, and Eric's heart beat rapidly. If Grandfather knew, that must mean . . .

"I promised you a chance to meet Lynn, at last," Adam Baldwin began anew, tightly gripping Peg's hand and wrist. "And Lynn is especially anxious to meet you. Come along!"

His grasp on Peg was like iron. Eric saw her wince, then turn with the old man to trail after him. All confidence in his own wits shattered by the horror in the automobile, which he knew now was his cousins' car, the boy slowly followed them toward the foot of the stairs.

"What really happened to those two?"

Senator Baldwin paused, two steps up, to look over Eric's head at the questioning housekeeper. She was changing, that one, becoming defiant. Unreliable. "You were the one to tell me they had incinerated themselves."

"Yessir, that's correct." Mildred stared up at him with a glimmer of doubt. "But you were the one, Senator, who told me they'd been given a decent Christian interment. And asked me not to tell the kids, because it would frighten them."

"And so, clearly enough," rejoined the old man, "it did!" He made an impatient gesture with a massive hand and she realized, that instant, how the Senator was changing. It wasn't just the darkening eyebrows or fringe of hair appearing at the back of his head—it was his cane, which he no longer carried! His tone of voice held more asperity than austere dignity. "I offered you an explanation that would save precious time. Come along with us, Mildred, if you please! I'm sure you may be of some further use tonight."

Halfway up, still with her hand and wrist grasped by the vise-like hand, Peg caught a glimpse of her cat, Krazy Junior, darting silently up the partly lit hallway. A tail of golden yarn trailed in his wake but he made no effort to go to her; he was wholly independent, now, self-serving, and Eric was right: the replacement pet possessed no living warmth.

Despite his building terror, Eric, third in line as they passed quietly along the familiar corridor, felt his long standing curiosity become rekindled: What was Lynn like? Finally, after months of mystery and bewilderment, he was about to find out!

"Unlock the door, please," the old man ordered the housekeeper, stepping to one side.

Bustling past Eric, Mildred fumbled with the key at the lock. Beyond the house, an angry wind was whipping at the trees on the estate— so far back from the street, and so alien from other residences in the neighborhood, that they might as well be on Neptune. Abruptly, Mildred pushed the door, and a subtle, sinister squeak groaned menacingly in the semi-darkness of the hallway.

Teeth chattering, hearts pounding, Eric and Peg edged forward and were struck, initially, by blinding light spilling from the long-secret room. It was a curiously vicious fluorescence, dissimilar to the bland lighting in the other rooms, bathing everything within Lynn's exquisitely private quarters in such a glare that Eric's good vision could not quickly adapt. Next, he and Peg were conscious of being blasted by a uniquely powerful air conditioning system which gusted arctic air, seeming capable of freezing a feeding mastodon where it stood and holding its meal in undigested stasis forever.

With the air, upon it, there was a gagging odor of stale sweat, so puissant it must have been produced in buckets . . . and the far more disgusting stench of rot, of waste matter dropped repeatedly, with mammoth frequency. Peg, moving nervously beside Eric, had a hand pressed to her nose. He saw her fine brows curve in a plunging frown and the way her eyes watered because all her senses were battered, violently assailed, by stark ugliness.

Across the deep room, in a distance shrouded

by light-shadow, an object stood which might, Eric felt with a shock, have been a bed. It was hard to see clearly, and besides, Grandfather Baldwin had rushed forward to stand before it now, concealing the structure.

And, presumably, the Offspring.

Then, waiting to see clearly, the twelve year old's ears registered again the peculiar sounds that he and Peg had so often heard in the past! Sounds of powered whirring, bone-breaking clicks and snaps; of book pages being turned at an amazingly, impossibly rapid rate; and noises of stentorian breathing—such labored breathing that the being from which it issued surely must quiver and shake the full length of its body.

Having passed over the forbidden threshold at last, Peg did her best to shield her eyes with shaking hands, and squinted into the sourceless illumination. The piercing, frigid quality of Lynn's room wasn't a natural cold, as it had been beyond the old house and around the haunted garage, but a nerve-jangling freeze which made her teeth chatter together and her limbs tremble spastically.

The stink, thought Peg, was so gross it was scary. It came partly from a sweat which began and ended, began and ended and began again, despite the terrifying cold. The faint, lingering sweetness her nostrils reluctantly detected suggested garbage left too long at the curb, rummaged through by avaricious animals. Surely nobody and nothing could stand to eat in such a place—like a dirty operating room, where medicine smells mixed with the reek of blood and death; but then she recalled Mildred's unending visits to the room, and all the trays of food sneakily brought to Lynn.

Beginning to adjust, young Eric's eyes cautiously, haltingly swept the room. He was unable, just yet, to accept more than a segment there, a section here. Too much of Lynn, he knew already, meant madness.

Stacks of books grew in shadowed corners like timorous trees made of paper, like hardcover elms, or maples, stunted in their growth and toppling like so many printed leaves, an abandoned autumn of fallen thought, bypassed and outdated insight.

Eric felt a pang. He thought about the library at Alexandria which he'd read about in school as he saw other books with bent, even missing pages, and with their spines crushed in an unnatural search for . . .

For what? he wondered. For what answers to what screwball questions?

He saw an extravagant, complex recording system against one wall, several cassettes, already taped and bearing today's date: December 31st. Notebooks, too, the pages so filled with a spider's crawl scrawl that they seemed black, marginless; and near the bed-like structure, the computer itself. Stamped IBM 370-135, bearing mass storage devices for swift data retrieval, it was a mutated, intricate thing perched on an island and surrounded by an ocean of precise flow charts, intricate diagrams, miraculously-balanced towers of paper babbling unguessable notations and designs that were at once beautiful and madly menacing. Close to the computer was something labeled a VDU—Video Display Unit. Eric guessed that it took the other beast's regurgitated information and ingested it whole in a simian-like exhibition of fond fealty before flashing a shorthand rainbow of vivid colors to trumpet its brilliant b.m., to inform everyone or, for that matter, no one (if its grunting performance went unwitnessed).

The computer hummed constantly, mindlessly; munching its data, it gave off a contented, oddly effeminate vibration like a neutered but mammoth Krazy, aching to purr but with nothing left to purr about.

For a moment, as Eric turned slightly, he thought he was seeing a series of labels peeled from massive bottles of poison. But his dismay doubled when he grasped the truth.

Stacked and crossed, like an old-fashioned pharmacist's skull-and-crossbones, white remnants of the Offspring's insatiable hunger were picked clean and left dizzyingly neat—as if Mildred Manning could not possibly keep up with her secret charge's fierce appetite, but Lynn had piled the bones from some mad need for perfect order.

Slowly, taking his sister's small hand in his, Eric raised his eyes to the being in the bed. Grandfather Baldwin, his own arms foleded, his own eyes hot with prideful anticipation, could not adequately conceal the oxygen tent which surrounded his incomparable offspring from yesteryear. Smiling, whispering, the old man began to move aside.

"Children," he said at the instant Peg squealed and leaped back, "allow me to introduce . . . Lynn."

Twenty-One

The children stared, from slightly more than a yard away, and would go on seeing the Off-spring for all the days—and the long nights—of their lives. The ugly and awesome sight was, in the strictest sense of the word, unforgettable. It was the kind that is instantly fused to the thin and tender flesh beneath the eyelids, so that it can always be seen again when, at last, one's weary eyes must close.

Peg, starting to sceam, quickly stuffed most of her fist into her mouth, a gesture of automatic and infinite courtesy. Eric first saw the great monstrosity in its entirety, which could never do Lynn justice; but it was sufficient to bring a surge of bitter bile to the boy's mouth and, with Peg, he immediately strove to stop seeing Lynn.

Then there was an imperious, inescapable command within their shrinking minds to Look, and to Perceive . . .

And they saw the most colossal king-sized bed they'd ever seen, its reinforced legs of iron firmly bolted to the floor. Over the bed was suspended the largely transparent tissue of a vast oxygen tent which piped through a life-sustaining umbilicus, to the quasi-embryo partly concealed within its folds, a steady supply of fresh air. Gasps of labored breathing constantly poured from beneath the tent.

Yet the covering neither camouflaged nor modified the apparition within, its broad back supported by the headboard of the bed, its legs sprawled forth, twitching with each intake of oxygen.

The recondite and ambiguous Lynn—utterly naked, seeping sweat from a million dilated pores—looked back at them.

The initial, close impression was of rolling hillocks of obscene fat. Surely there had never been a being so incredibly corpulent, a creature that, in sheer bulk alone, defied the imagination to accept that which the eye detected. Think of a Fat Man in a circus; think of another, and another, perhaps one more: then combine.

But there was more than mind-boggling bulk to be seen, Eric realized, beginning at globular toes and swollen, veined feet like pillows, moving up to calves which were the thickness of the boy's hips, doubled. His gaze swept marvelingly across ponderous tree-stump thighs, awed that taut flesh could contain such grossly inflated immensity.

And his eyes saw the Offspring's privates— two elephantine, distended, hairless testicles of pretty baby-pink, like ripe melons beneath the incongruity of the tiny penis which was now erect and pointed, as it aimed, the sparse and silly tool jutting perhaps three quarters of an inch in a parody of maleness which lacked the humor even of situation comedy.

And Eric's mesmerized gaze, drawn, worked upward, obliged to move literally from side to side in order to take in the fantastic landscape of titanic belly which merged with the bulbous, hilly hips to leave no discernible line of demarcation. Oozing perspiration, the stomach spread to the sides for what seemed the breadth of an entire world, absolutely covering the snowy, white-sheeted bed and dripping over the distant edges. The flourishing, voluminous flesh was scarred by ten-thousand road-map stretch-marks, some seeming capacious as the craters of the moon; while the monstrosity's navel was so sunken, so imbedded in thick fat, that it was merely a miniature star in the universe of Lynn.

And just above the mind-blowing belly, Eric Porter discovered for the first time, the full-blown and improbable beauty of two perfect, high-placed woman's breasts—so ideally proportioned, so sweetly tipped by petite, pink nipples that the exciting bosom might have been photographed for a special and quite costly centerfold.

Reactively, Eric's popping eyes moved again to the swinging bag of huge, hairless gonads and the definitely aroused male penis—back to the puckered nipples cleverly centered in the voluptuous curves of femaleness—and he thought, bewildered: I still don't know what in the world Lynn IS!

"Lynn is androgynous, children," explained Grandfather Baldwin, speaking softly. There was no reason to raise one's voice in a company gripped by total wonderment. "Androgyny is a condition of abnormality in which the primary and secondary, physical attributes of the male as well as the female sexes are present . . . in one person. But why be shocked?" The old man's new tone of reasonableness seemed incongruous, mad, to the spellbound youngsters.

"After all, each infant is androgynous to start with. Indeed, each human being secretes male and female hormones alike: androgens and oestrogens respectively. While a man produces more of the former, a woman more of the latter, none of us is entirely masculine or entirely feminine."

Eric continued gaping at Lynn while Grandfather spoke, like a naive boy at the county fair, examining a carnival of corpulence. The neck, Lordy, the neck was five times the thickness of a big man's throat, a rhinoceros-leg whose flowering amplitude no collar made could ever conceal or cover.

"It's an hermaphrodite," Mildred Manning said, behind them, incapable of preventing the note of revulsion.

"Yes, that's true!" Grandfather declared. "Lynn is an hermaphrodite, of the purest kind. There's always been something wonderfully esoteric and mystical about the state, you know. Among primitives, transvestism is a wistful mimicry of the androgynous. The Turco-Mongol nomads of Siberia are considered powerful beings with a special connection to supernatural forces. They wear woman's garb as do shamans in the Aleutians, Malaya, Patagonia; even the *berdache* of the Crow and Sioux Amerindians, boys who have visions, and are reared as females. And the *xaniths* of Oman, on the Arabian Peninsula, spend their boyhoods as homosexual prostitutes, but often marry and father children!" The Senator's voice grew dreamy. "Why, during the medieval period, a genuine bisexual was referred to an *utriusque capax*, Latin for 'capable of both.' And Lynn, dear children, is capable of almost anything!"

Compelled, Eric regarded the head of the Offspring—a great planet surmounting the universe of Lynn in prodigious extravagance. Saturn-sized, its chins drooped down in dewlaps beyond count, its mouth was a slash or slot —an awful wound, with crimson lips which parted before Eric's wondering gaze to reveal pearly rows of white but blunted teeth—except for the matching, razor-sharp incisors.

"Once it was believed," Grandfather said in muted tones, "that the androgyne symbolizes the complete being each of us might be—wholly detached from others of humankind, truly sufficient unto itself, the ultimate source of sacred power." He raised his voice only minimally but spoke with terrifying clarity. "The kind of power Lynn, alone, possesses."

The nose, Eric saw, was a plopped-on afterthought—a piece of fruity pulp, something kindergarten children might have idly fashioned from clay, and stuck haphazardly between the creature's staring orbs.

But . . . those eyes! Eric marveled, and shuddered. Fringed by beautiful lashes, they consisted of blistering blue pupils rising distendedly from the centers of uremically-yellow whites which protruded from sagging sockets, which overwhelmed the frail encasing skin until it appeared the weighty orbs might just fall out. Yet Eric had never looked into such a simmering blaze of intensely naked knowing. There was such encyclopedic brilliance that he felt shockingly inclined to make a towering, cliff-side drive into those fathomless, cerulean seas, to drown, or batter his frail form against the stony shoals of god-like and altogether forbidden wisdoms.

"What . . . happened?" Peg asked, breaking the contact between the youths of today and long-forgotten yesterday, interrupting the psychic link and, unknowingly, saving her brother from the Offspring. Almost languidly, like the dozing awareness of a beached whale, Lynn's eyes swiveled and trickled thoughtfully over the girl's pale countenance. But Peg was appealing to Grandfather Baldwin. "You told us about finding Lynn, still in its mother, and how it was—fathered—thousands of years ago. But why is Lynn . . . that way—and how come Lynn's so smart?"

"It does require the feminine directness to get down to the meat of the situation!" complimented Adam Baldwin, beaming at her from beside the gigantic bed. "I shall attempt to explain everything in terms you can, ah, have a chance of understanding."

"Don't patronize them, Senator," Mildred murmured, her ample form concealing the computer and VDU. Her eyes sparkled beneath the heavy brows. "The pity of all this, in my opinion, is that you've never known how smart these grandchildren of yours are! If you'd spent all this time teachin' them . . ."

"I believe," Grandfather interjected, "it was Margaret who asked me a question." He folded his long arms, leaned lightly against the bed, years younger in appearance than either child remembered him. "Research scientists have begun learning that life before birth isn't the peaceful existence poets and physicians have pretended it was. Supposedly, the fetus lived in a state of absolute protection, knowing nothing but its warm security in a floating, fluid world devoid of distress. But that simply is not true—and Lynn suffered the longest period of gestation of any living creature in the history of the world."

"What makes life so hard for an unborn baby?" Peg asked, big-eyed.

"Well, the placenta permits many bacteria and viruses to slip through, even the drugs ingested by the mother. It is effected by what she feels and what she hears. Certain of my peers, running recent tests, theorize that the baby recognizes the voice of its mother. But you see, Lynn's mother was not precisely alive. And instead of hearing the reassurances of its mother's voice, Lynn had no choice but to hear the terrified screams of those who witnessed Vela X, the chaos of an entire world ending, the birth of a new one—and then silence, for thousands of years."

"That's sort of sad," Peg said, looking briefly at the monstrosity in the bed. "I guess."

"Consider," Grandfather continued. "All the sleep phases have been recorded in unborn children, indicating they dream. But of what could our Lynn dream? Electroencephalograms of a fetus directly before birth are all but identical to those of a living child—but of what could poor Lynn think? What in the name of heaven, could it have been like, being an entity with life and a thinking brain in a body frozen in time? And what is thought, children, without language, the experience of other living beings, without points of reference, points of fact?"

Eric glanced at Lynn. "You poor," he hesitated, blinking, " . . .guy."

"Innumerable points of ancient wisdom are becoming acceptable more and more by open-minded colleagues of mine." Smiling, the former professor patted a mammoth leg. "In China, even today, a person is one year old at birth. And why not, considering how much of the newborn child is completed? On the other hand, the nervous system, brain, and endocrine system, begun during fetal life, continue developing months after birth. Does that mean it's not being 'born' until it's lived on land for nine or ten months? Science must be more logical, consistent!"

Lynn, looking up, gave its mentor a winking smirk of agreement.

"My remarkable Offspring enabled me to arrive at many major conclusions before my peers," said the old man, emboldened by Lynn's approval. "I learned, prior to delivery, of the special capacities of the unborn, of those uncanny skills which are usually lost after birth. A fetus hears much better than an adult and can respond to frequencies beyond our limited range. That is one reason why I was obliged to keep this house quiet, and peaceful: because Lynn's lengthy gestation permitted the retention of this acute hearing ability, which, coupled with the telepathic gifts, allowed Lynn to hear even the whispered remarks of belligerence, threat, and thoughtless reaction." Baldwin smiled. "The mammoth whale also hears sounds at frequencies from sixteen to one-hundred-and eighty-thousand hertz."

"Grandfather," Eric said in hushed tones,

"what did Lynn think about before he was born?"

"Lynn thought about Lynn." The distinguished old man's brows lifted. "What other choice was there? That is why we cannot, in all fairness, fault Lynn if there are times when a certain egocentric quality is displayed. Yes, quite slowly in prolonged and endless embryo, Lynn learned that which was accessible. How to breathe in the womb and control the functions of the brain."

"I've never got that part," said Mildred, frowning.

"Modern science has learned that breathing seems to be the bridge between involuntary and voluntary functions of the brain." Grandfather spoke impatiently, for the first time. Clearly, Eric saw, he hadn't forgiven Mildred's mild effort at fighting back. "Soon, Lynn learned how to control a variety of functions—hormonal secretions, brain waves, even metabolism. Lynn learned that we alternate between our right and left nostrils, without realizing we do, shifting back and forth every three hours or so."

"Why is that a big deal?" Peg inquired.

"Because it enabled Lynn to control the heart —but my Offspring paid the price in weight gain." He paused, unconsciously stroking Lynn's thigh. "Think about the horror of it, from Lynn's standpoint. If it was even possible to understand that a natural birth had once been scheduled, by nature, Lynn came to realize it would never happen—that all the life ever known would probably be spent in a decaying but suspended mother's body. Would that make you charitable toward those with a real life, children, or would you feel immense injustice, a sense of the worst imprisonment ever experienced and a growing hatred for ordinary men and women?"

Both Eric and Peg looked down, abashed, their understanding and their sympathy growing.

"You see, my dear youngsters, Lynn also learned how to breathe in order to lower blood pressure, and further sustain its circumscribed existence. Doing so altered the fetal diaphragm as air was drawn automatically into the fetal sac." The old man saw their eyes rise to his, tears shining in Peg's lashes. "Gradually, then, this altered Lynn's brain—a brain in which the unborn infant strove constantly to place more and more information, ever influenced by Vela X's cultural demand for self-improvement, for an advanced intellect. Lynn ransacked its own burgeoning body, combed the very cells and tissues of its mummy-like mother, and drew conclusions of sheer, total logic—a logic unimpeded by sentiment, concern for another creature, or anything beyond which it could see or hear. That data was important to Lynn only for bare survival. And I include the survival of sanity, if the word even has meaning for such a fetus. For a living fetus born on the cusp or interface of a raging, illusion-fed world with no knowledge, and the world which the rest of us call, in our innocence and ego, civilization."

"Do you see why I felt I had to help the poor little thing when it—came out?" Mildred asked, taking a single step toward Eric and Peg. "Why, my heart went out to it!" Suddenly she stopped, her expression clouded. "At first."

"I see why Lynn is so brilliant and so different," Peg began, tentatively.

"But why is Lynn like that?" Eric finished for her, coloring. "Why is . . . it . . . an it, and so—so fat?"

Grandfather, seeing the fury in the Offspring's slanted eyes, made soothing sounds. "Regrettably, Eric, Lynn's slowly altering and constantly modifying biology suffered other disorders. A brain-chemical imbalance, exacerbated by years of improvised breathing techniquesk, resulted in the production of certain spatial hormones of an androgynous nature. That imbalance proved to be irreversible." Grandfather looked directly from child to child and they realized, with a passing shock, that Adam Baldwin was crying. "It's all involved with chemicals in the brain. These chemicals are supposed to regulate food breakdown in the human system. In my brilliant and pitiably abused Lynn, struggling to stay alive and sane in constant, confined status, I regret that the neurotransmitters inadequately performed their task, children." The old man shut his eyes, tears seeping beneath the lids. "Cholecystokinin, the CCK, proves to be particularly linked to obesity. And the outcome, for the living child Lynn became, was a condition known as hyperphagia."

"Hyper-*what?*" Eric demanded.

"It means," Grandfather Baldwin said, wiping his eyes with a handkerchief, "pathological overeating."

The boy, feeling genuinely sorry for Lynn, turned his compassionate gaze.

The Offspring's skull was like that of an egg dropped by an Olympian and mythological bird. Massive, dome-like and bald, it was a vast, arid desert which trapped the glaring light and reflected weird images from all over the nightmare room. "I am the sire of the world, and this world's mother and grandsire," Mama's quotation had said—female and male parent alike in the dreadful creature with whom she had empathized, and with whom she'd felt that she failed. Poor Lynn, Eric forced himself to think.

Until he saw the sausage-like fingers closing upon the miniature maleness, and the other white hand alternately cupping the preposterously beautiful breasts, which rose and fell with each hard-drawn breath.

And until he saw Lynn's rosy-red lips turn up at the corners, its long lashes coyly flutter, as it looked from Peg's small body to Eric's, and back again.

Even Grandfather turned, startled, as he heard the sound of desperate breathing increase, the sucking noises It made, and as he saw the scarlet flush of desire mounting the Offspring's leviathan face—effort devoted to an incredible urge to eschew its telepathic gift of communication, and speak.

"The project," cried the old man worriedly, hovering over Lynn, motioning with pleading hands for the creature not to try. "Remember our vital work together, child, our plans. Do not jeopardize them by trying to do those common things any ordinary human being can do!"

"Common, like a housekeeper?" Mildred

Manning asked softly from near the banks of gleaming modern machinery. "Are you going to tell them how you wanted to use your daughter's training in genetics to make it 'unnecessary' for further human beings to be born —except for some dull-brained workers like me?"

"Only for a while!" The old man nervously stroked Lynn's arm, feeling the tension beneath the icy flesh. "Until the population has decreased and people learn how to limit the number of newborns!" He gave Mildred an irritated glance. "There would still be children!"

"Genetically chosen, perfect ones," Mildred corrected him. "The offspring of genius scientists like you; nobody else." Her head turned toward Eric and Peg. "And by 'learning to limit the number,' he means legally prohibiting birth —any that lacks Lynn's selection, and Lynn's authorization!"

Peg risked another look at the Offspring and thought her heart would break. She didn't believe another creature had ever been so abused, misused, or pathetic. She was ready, just then, to forget everything about the being but its need to learn to love.

"Certainly!" The Senator didn't argue with the housekeeper. "The average citizen despises computers and doesn't even trust the government any longer. But Lynn is human, yet reasons like a computer! Lynn is honest, immovable by lobby, beyond bribe!"

"Tell 'em how you intend to take over!" Angry, red-faced, Mildred was going all the way with her years of pent-up and blackmailed servitude, mindless of where her fury would take her. "Never mind, Senator, I will. Kids, your grandfather means for Lynn to create living people from the secret fear and terror of the men and women running the country now—and eventually, all the bigshots in the world! Replacement people, just like Krazy, your cat!" Mildred's fingers clawed, "Soulless substitutes, imitations who answer only to the immortal Senator Adam Baldwin, and that monster in the bed!"

Lynn, gasping, sat up, pointing with an arm like a flipper. "I *want* them!" the Offspring commanded. The voice, a high-pitched whine that curdled the blood and made every face in the room turn in terror and disgust, was produced upon the apex of a rising, laborious intake of air, like fingernails scratching a blackboard. "I want—girl—in bed, s'il vous plait?" The lovely lashes batted. "I want—boy —*to eat!*"

Adam Baldwin blanched, pulled back his caressing hand. "Lynn, for the love of God, you can't!"

"You tell Lynn *no?*" The squealing voice reverberated against the walls. The boardwalk face was crimson, the slanting eyes stretched to stomach-churning heights, afire with youthful indignation. A juggernaut finger rose, pointing, as the lunatic blue eyes disappeared in a terrifying squint of concentrated focus.

Grandfather's tall, powerful body was slammed through the air. Heedless, Lynn sent it flying toward the complex and expensive machinery beside Mildred Manning. She stared, deeply shocked, as the old man collided with the wall and a fountain of blood spewed from his lips and one ear.

Abend! Errata! Computer terms denoting error flashed like laser rays through the minds of the others as Senator Baldwin weakly tried to regain his feet. *Does not interface with project! Does not compute with Offspring's prerogatives! Erase! Erase!*

"My own child," the old man groaned, struggling to one knee and reaching out with a gnarled and trembling hand. "I love you . . ."

Lynn shook its head and frowned.

Gone. Adam Baldwin vanished. Senator Adam Baldwin was *erased*.

Wincing from the pain of the mechanistic chant of destruction burning his mind, his soul, Eric snatched up the old man's cane and, in the same motion, jabbed it through the oxygen tent protecting the being in the bed.

And, for a moment, Eric knew he was dying.

He had to be. The pain left no nerve, no muscle, untouched. The agony given him by the Offspring favored not the eyes or the spine, the stomach or the genitalia, the limbs or the wildly beating heart. Somewhere else in the world, he knew, a little girl was crying and a grown woman was reaching for his hand and arm, dragging him . . .

And in the midst of the cramping, lacerating, gnawing, convulsing pain, Eric Porter saw a burst of awful flame that might have been the last thing seen by his cousins Sue and Bernard.

And, in a single flicker, the image of a great white whale-like thing with its beautiful bosom heaving, sucking for sustenance; mammoth flipper arms flapping; and a pair of long-lashed eyes—tortured, dimming—meeting his. The words came into the boy's pain-bewildered brain like distant wind moaning through a miniature crack in the face of a mountain wall.

Help . . . me . . .

And then, for twelve year old Eric Porter, there was only the mercy of a slithering black curtain.

It was the explosion that brought the boy to consciousness. The explosion caused when the computer equipment struck by his grandfather's psychokinetically propelled form caused a spark that crawled across the floor to welcome the outburst of oxygen.

All that he was to learn later. Hurting, confused, he sat up in the snow on the Baldwin front walkway, conscious of Peg and Mildred holding his hands, looking at the last nightmare.

From fifty yards away, the two story seemed, in the darkness of winter night, an old black-and-white picture to which someone had added the tongues of lapping red fire. But Eric focused upon a single window in a single room; and from it, with the wailing anguish of an electric organ shorted into mindlessly mechanical life, Hell itself seemed to grope into the new year of the living.

Above Eric, Mildred Manning counted only her blessings and, her generous face bathed by the intermittent shadow and light, whispered her prayer for humankind. " 'And the beast was taken, and with him the false prophet that wrought miracles before him,' " she intoned. " 'These both were cast alive into a lake of fire burning with brimstone.' "

"Help me," said a tiny voice beside the stunned and staring boy.

But it was only Peg, his sister, who looked at him with frightened eyes.

The Offspring's miracles were at an end.

* * *

The vision that I saw was wholly awesome! The heavens shrieked, the earth boomed; daylight failed, darkness came. Lightning flashed, a flame shot up. The clouds swelled, it rained death!... And all that had fallen had turned to ashes!

—King Gilgamesh, the only surviving witness
of the might of Vela X

Epilogue

INDIANAPOLIS, IND (AP)—An official spokesman for the Indianapolis Fire Department announced today the completion of a thorough investigation into the "awesome blaze" which took the life of retired Senator Adam Baldwin, formerly a candidate for the Presidency of the United States.

"Apparently the old man had some interest in science, not just politics," said Chief Donald Duncan, explaining that traces of vitamins and chemicals were found in the rubble along with badly burned computer equipment. "We also found remnants of cassette tapes and enough books to begin a new branch library out at 38th and Post. Unfortunately, they were burned beyond any possibility of identification."

Asked if there remained the slightest chance of arson or even a homicide in the guise of arson, Chief Duncan remarked: "Not at all. The other casualty of the blaze was a bedfast relative of Senator Baldwin. An electrical short ignited that person's oxygen tent, just as we theorized in our preliminary reports."

The fire chief was asked whether, in his opinion, an inquest would be held. "Pending the outcome of the autopsies," replied Duncan, "that's hard to say. My own recommendation is to close the books. The old man's place was an out-and-out inferno, to the point that only the medical examiner will be able to determine the gender of the bedfast relative. In my view, it's nothing more than a tragic accident."

Meanwhile, in Washington, D.C., the Vice-President announced that he will ask the Senate for a moment of silence on Tuesday "to honor a great man who, if he had become the Chief Executive, might well have taken his beloved nation in very different directions than those of the past decade." Private services will be held . . .

For nearly a year after the deaths of Grandfather and Lynn, Eric and Peg Porter clung privately to the hope that their father, hearing the news, would return. The fact that he did not only momentarily dismayed Eric, who was older than his sister and had found time to adjust.

"If Daddy did come back," he told her, around Thanksgiving, "I think I'd always believe he was a coward."

"Then you think he's gone for good?" Peg asked.

"I think he's dead," Eric said simply. "That he was Lynn's first victim and died trying to protect us."

The girl had nodded. "Yes, that would make it easier to understand what happened to Mama. If she suspected old Lynn did it, it'd not only make her sicker but turn her against the fat pig." A sigh. "But how will we ever know, for sure?"

"We don't have t'know," he'd shrugged. "Things are pretty good now that Mildred has a place for us all to live. Peg, that part of our lives is over. Forever."

The little girl had agreed until, around Christmas-time, she was astonished to see walking up the block toward her a bedraggled yellow cat. Immediately, she shouted for Eric "to come see," then insisted that the cat was actually Krazy Junior!

"You're crazier'n ever!" declared her brother, hooting with hilarity. "There's no way that cat could have found his way here, miles from Grandfather's house!"

"It happens all the time!" Peg persisted. "You hear about it every week—somebody's loyal pet walkin' halfway across the country to make up

303

with its owner. Besides, it looks like Krazy Junior." She paused, deciding whether to correct herself or not. "Well, it looks like my first Krazy, anyway!"

"Right! Krazy Junior was mean as dirt, but this cat is friendly, like the real one. But we know he's dead—ole Lynn ate him!"

Peg stared at Eric, left with nothing else to say. The facts were puzzling: the newcomer not only looked a great deal like her first cat, he was also likeable, always following her around, coming when she called. Very likely there was no way it could be Krazy Junior, whatever she'd imagined.

But that was yesterday. Today the cat had kittens, four of them.

Three of them were born dead, looking so battered from the experience of birth that Peg could have sworn they'd been slaughtered in the mama cat's womb.

And the fourth, surviving kitten was the strangest thing she'd ever seen—more or less. Because it had piercing blue eyes with long, dreamy lashes.

And it was the fattest, the biggest and grossest kitten Peg had ever seen. It just couldn't get enough to eat!

* * *

To this very day the scholars have no inkling who the Sumerians were, where they came from, and how and why their civilization appeared. . . . Joseph Campbell (The Masks of God) summed it up in this way: 'With stunning abruptness . . . came the whole cultural syndrome that has since constituted the germinal unit of all the high civilizations of the world.'
—Zecharia Sitchen, *The 12th Planet*